"Touch Me, Jamie,"

he murmured. "Tell me what I am. A real man or some Godforsaken shade."

His words were more command than request. Falteringly she ran her palm over his jaw. He was warm and vibrant. Her fingertips glided over his lips. Her heart hammering, Jamie continued her exploration, running her fingers down the cleft in his chin, down the powerful column of his neck.

She paused, and he covered her hand with his own, guiding it to his chest. She placed her other hand beside it and closed her eyes. She could feel his chest rising and falling as quickly as her own. Fighting back a wave of arousal, she caressed his torso, tracing the magnificent contours.

Her head fell back, and his mouth came down upon hers. "Ah, Jamie," he whispered against her lips, "canna ye tell I'm a man?"

Also by Patricia Simpson

The Legacy
Raven in Amber

Available from
HarperPaperbacks

Patricia Simpson

Whisper of Midnight

HarperPaperbacks
A Division of HarperCollins*Publishers*

This is a work of fiction. The characters, incidents, and
dialogues are products of the author's imagination and are not
to be construed as real. Any resemblance to actual events or
persons, living or dead, is entirely coincidental.

HarperPaperbacks   *A Division of* HarperCollins*Publishers*
10 East 53rd Street, New York, N.Y. 10022

Cover illustration by Franco Accornero

First printing: August 1991

Printed in the United States of America

HarperPaperbacks, HarperMonogram, and colophon are
trademarks of HarperCollins*Publishers*

❖ 10 9 8 7 6 5 4 3 2

To
Sharon and Sue
for their friendship and support
and to my mother, June

1

Los Angeles

"WHAT IS IT, JAMIE? One of your damn headaches? Or are you just daydreaming again?"

The sarcastic edge in Brett's voice cut through the stillness of the conference room and startled Jamie. She glanced around. Where had everyone gone? Was the meeting over? Jamie stood at the end of the polished malachite table, vaguely aware that she had shaken hands with Noel Condé, creator of Intimacy perfume, the most sought after scent since Chanel No. 5. Noel Condé rarely allowed anyone to touch his skin, much less shake hands with him. Yet he had taken Jamie's hand, raised her fingers to his lips, and lightly kissed them. Any other young woman would have died to take Jamie's place and would have caught the meaningful gleam in Condé's eyes. But Jamie had not even noticed Condé's unusual attention. She had been too worried about her brother and too nervous about her imminent return to the McAllister House.

"Jamie!" Brett snapped, throwing the storyboards into a leather portfolio. "What's wrong with you?"

"What?" She turned to face her business partner. The slender fingers kissed by Noel Condé splayed across her pale ivory cheek. Her nails were bereft of polish and cut close to her fingertips.

"What's wrong with you?" Brett whispered, trying not to be overheard by anyone passing the conference door. "You just about blew it, standing up there like that, forgetting what you were saying. If old man Condé didn't like you so much, we'd be out on our asses."

"I'm sorry, Brett. I—" Instead of finishing her sentence, Jamie picked up her briefcase. The clasp was not closed but she was too preoccupied to notice. As she grabbed it, the case flopped open and everything spilled out on the floor, including a bottle of her migraine pain relievers. The cloisonné case containing four Valium tablets rolled under the chair. Jamie reached for it, supporting her weight on her other hand. Her palm sank into an inch of plush emerald carpeting.

"God, Jamie! Pull yourself together!" Brett's oxblood loafers appeared near the chair leg at her side. "And hurry up and pick that stuff up before somebody notices!"

Jamie dropped her medicine into the briefcase and stuffed her papers and pens into the upper section. If Brett was so worried about appearances, why wasn't he helping to clean up the mess? He probably didn't want to wrinkle his Armani suit. She knew he hadn't sat down once during the entire presentation for fear of creasing his silk coat. Jamie straightened, lodging her anger and guilt behind a mask of serenity, and met Brett's disgusted gaze.

He shook his head. "You've been a zombie ever since that telephone call this morning."

Jamie turned her back on him. The last thing she wanted to do at that moment was discuss the telephone call. "Let's go, Brett."

"Wait a minute." He caught her elbow. "What was that call all about? Did you get refused by the gallery?"

"No. It wasn't the gallery." She tried to pull her arm away, but Brett held fast.

"Then what was it?"

"It was about my brother."

"Oh, God!" Brett dropped her arm. "What does Mark want this time? Ten thousand dollars? Twenty?"

"See—that's why I didn't want to tell you. You always act like this."

"Your brother is a leech."

"My brother is a genius," Jamie retorted. "And anyway, it isn't about money this time."

"Oh? That's a new twist. What does he want?"

"He's sick." Jamie fought to keep her voice level. "His housekeeper called. He's really sick, Brett. I'm worried about him."

"Have him check into a hospital then. New York's got some great specialists."

Jamie shook her head and looked down at the carpet. "He hates hospitals. He spent half his childhood in hospitals. And besides, he's not in New York. He's up in Washington State working on a project."

"Well, Washington has specialists, too."

Brett took a step toward the door but paused when he realized she was not following him. He looked back, exasperated. "Hon, just what are you trying to say?"

Jamie ran the tip of her tongue over her lips. Her upper lip was full and didn't dip down in the center. Someone had told her once that she had the sexiest mouth he'd ever seen. Then he had come on to her too strong, claiming that she'd asked for it. After that incident, Jamie rarely wore lipstick and selected clothes and hairstyles to downplay her femininity, such as her conservative gray-green suit and severe chignon. "I need to go to him, Brett."

"You can't be serious! Not now!"

"I must."

Brett grabbed her elbow again. "Listen, Jamie. You can't go anywhere. Noel Condé likes you. He likes your work. He likes the campaign. He'll love our ads. They'll be shown all over the world. Intimacy perfume will put us on the map, hon. This is the big break for us."

"I know, Brett, but I just have to go. Just for a few days."

"Jamie, you can't."

"I have to." She shook off his hand and strode around him to the doorway. "I've got tickets to fly out of LAX in an hour. Now will you take me to the airport, or should I call a cab?"

"Call a cab," Brett said. "Some of us have work to do."

Hours later, Jamie drove up the bumpy ramp that connected the ferry *Klickitat* to the Port Townsend, Washington ferry terminal. When she reached the level ground of the terminal parking lot, she switched on the car headlights. Dread washed over her as she drove under the floodlights of the terminal and headed toward Water Street. She hadn't intended to face the McAllister House in the dark. But she had missed the earlier ferry which would have arrived in the late afternoon. Now at nine-thirty at night, the October sky above the bluff was black and forbidding.

Jamie was glad she had just gotten her Valium prescription refilled. She wouldn't be able to face the McAllister House with her nerves raw and exposed. As for sleeping in the house, Jamie didn't know if she was capable of closing her eyes in the old mansion, much less drifting off to sleep.

She drove along the base of the bluff and then climbed the narrow road that led to the upper section of Port Townsend, a neighborhood of stately old Victorian homes built near the turn of the century. The nagging feeling of dread increased as she left the main road and headed down a lane that had no street lights. Perhaps she should get a motel and go up to the house in the morning when everything was light and safe.

"Coward," she mumbled to herself.

She turned the wheel and eased around the corner onto Polk Street. The headlights of her car traced the shrubbery along the unlit street, drawing her attention to the buildings at the end of the block.

There was her destination—the McAllister House— rising above the treetops as if straining on tiptoe to monitor her approach. Slowly, Jamie drove down the street. The trees and the house grew larger and larger until they towered over her. Gravel crunched beneath the tires as she rolled to a stop. Trembling, Jamie turned off the engine and switched off the lights. Then all was still. And very dark.

She pinched the bridge of her nose and leaned her forehead on the cool rim of the steering wheel. Her skull was splitting. Her temples throbbed. God, not a migraine now. Not when she had to face that house.

She stuffed her hand into her purse, found her Valium, and popped the lid off the bottle. She took one of the tiny blue tablets without benefit of water, fortifying herself in advance. Then, still reluctant to go inside, she sat in the car to wait until the drug took effect.

Jamie looked out the passenger window at the mansion. It loomed before her in the darkness, all points and cupolas, three stories of gingerbread and lathe work. The circular window in the attic stared down at her like a big eye, watching her, waiting for her. Though she had not set foot in the house for twenty years, she knew every railing, every windowpane by heart. Twenty years ago she had left the house, but the house had never left her. It was the feature attraction of her nightmares.

The porch light blinked on, startling her from her fearful surveillance. The Valium had not begun to dull her nerves yet, but she couldn't stay in the car now that her arrival had been observed. Jamie opened the car door. A blast of damp air off Puget Sound blew back her dark-blonde hair and pierced through her jacket. Why hadn't she brought something warmer to wear? She had forgotten how cold and dank the Northwest could be in October.

Wrapping her jacket around her spare frame with one hand, Jamie clutched her purse and camera case with the other. Then she walked up the ancient narrow sidewalk to the front steps. An elderly woman opened the door as Jamie stepped onto the porch.

"Mrs. Gipson?" Jamie asked.

"Yes. And you must be Miss Kent."

"Please, call me Jamie." She flashed a quick smile at the housekeeper and then glanced over the woman's shoulder to the main hall. Nothing had changed. The same busy green and gold wallpaper danced along the wainscoting. The same Persian carpets swirled on the hardwood floors. Even her grandmother's furniture, hard uncomfortable pieces of brocade and walnut, squatted in dimly lit alcoves. The familiar trappings should have made her feel at home. But Jamie, sick with apprehension, had to force herself to cross the threshold.

Mrs. Gipson held the door open even wider for her. "Come in, dear. You must be very tired."

"Yes . . ." Jamie's voice trailed off as she sidled into the main hall. The staircase in front of her curved up the far wall and disappeared into the shadows two stories above her. The stairs had always seemed huge and gloomy to Jamie as a child. She had run down them in terror of unseen monsters in the attic for as long as she could remember. Now that she was an adult she'd expected the staircase to appear less imposing. But her age made no difference. The stairs were still huge and the gloom at the top was more black than ever.

Quickly, Jamie diverted her gaze to the kind face of the graying housekeeper. "I hope I didn't wake you, Mrs. Gipson."

"Heavens, no. I was doing a crossword."

"I missed the earlier ferry." Jamie pinched the bridge of her nose again. I'm going to throw up. Another whiff of these musty old things and I'm going to throw up, she thought.

"Are you feeling all right, dear?"

Jamie opened her eyes. "I just have a headache."

"Would you like an aspirin?"

"No thanks. I've got my pills in my—" Jamie said, frowning. "Oh, I need to get my suitcase out of the car." She dropped her purse and camera case onto a nearby settee. "I'll be right back."

When she returned she found Mrs. Gipson in the parlor picking up her magazine and pencil. Jamie stood between her leather suitcase and her flat, black portfolio. "Is Mark up?"

"No. He retires early these days."

"Is he any better since you called?"

"Not much. He looks thinner every day. And his cough is getting worse. If he would just check himself into the hospital—"

"Mark hates hospitals."

"I know. But he's very sick. That's why I finally called you. Maybe you can convince him that he needs help."

"I'll try." Jamie lifted her heavy cases. "Do you have a room I can stay in?"

"The bedroom down the hall from Mark—you know, the one with the bay window? Mark said it was your old room. It's all ready for you. Clean towels are in the bathroom."

"Thank you." Jamie grabbed her purse and camera while Mrs. Gipson followed her to the bottom of the stairs.

"Would you like anything? A snack? Something to drink?"

"No thanks, Mrs. Gipson. I'm going straight to bed. I'll see you in the morning."

Jamie climbed to the second floor. The stairs creaked beneath her feet. She tried to avoid looking at the dark corners and doorways. When she walked past Mark's room, she noticed the door was ajar. Carefully, Jamie put down her bags and slipped into the bedroom, tiptoeing to her brother's bedside. His lamp was still on and Jamie saw that he was awake.

"Hey, big bully," she called out softly.

"Hey, brat," came the reply. "What're you doing here?"

In answer, Jamie flung her arms around her brother. Mark was her only sibling, her only living relative, and she adored him. He had been the only one to take her seriously when she had suffered her period of hysteria as a child. Jamie loved him for trusting her in one of her darkest hours and for giving her a Brownie camera to take pictures of what she had seen. Though the photographs had proved nothing, she had kept the Brownie, exchanging it for an Instamatic and then a Pentax, and finally for the Hasselblad out in the hall. Her brother had been responsible for her interest in photography, an interest that had blossomed into a successful career.

Mark was thinner than she remembered. His shoulder blades and spine stuck out and his head seemed too large for his body. The Albert Einstein T-shirt he wore did little to conceal his sunken chest and bony arms. While Jamie embraced him, she wondered how she could convince him to start taking better care of himself. Sometimes he forgot to eat or sleep when he was immersed in a project. And to be sick on top of it had put his health in double jeopardy.

"What brings you here?" he repeated.

"Just a visit." Jamie sat back with a halfhearted smile. "I thought you might like some company for awhile. So I decided to visit."

"You? Come to this house for a visit? That I don't buy. Not for a nanosecond."

Jamie reached out and brushed lank brown hair off his forehead. "Never could fool you, big brother."

"Did that nosy Mrs. Gipson call you?"

"Mark, Mrs. Gipson is a nice old woman who cares about you."

"She's nosy." He set his computer magazine on the night stand. "Well, did she call?"

"Yes. She thinks you should be in the hospital. Mark, what's wrong with you? It isn't your hemophilia, is it?"

"No." He adjusted a blanket. "It's just a chest cold." Then he brightened. "I'm glad you came, though. You can help me in the lab. Remember that project I told you about a few months ago?"

"When you were still in New York? That hologram project?"

He nodded. "I'm nearly finished with it. I can't wait until you see it in action."

"Mark, I think you'd better take it easy for awhile. You don't look so great."

"Ah, it's nothing. Besides, what I do in the lab isn't strenuous. And now that you're here, you can do all the heavy lifting."

"Thanks a lot!"

Mark laid a bony hand over hers. "Just kidding."

He chuckled and their gazes met. For a moment Jamie looked into his eyes, slanted slightly above his cheekbones like her own. They had both inherited the features of their mother, especially in the eyes. Yet Jamie knew the sharp aggressive green of Mark's eyes was totally dissimilar to the reserved hazel color she saw each morning in the mirror.

As Jamie gazed at Mark, she framed the image of his face with her photographer's eye, noting the play of lamplight along his upper lip and the rim of his ear, the highlights of his hair glinting gold against the shadows of the room beyond his shoulder. He was a study in contrasts of lights and darks, much like a painting by Caravaggio.

"It's good to see you, brat," he murmured and squeezed her hand. "Glad you came."

"So am I," she lied, rising from the bed.

Jamie would have felt much safer sleeping in the same room with Mark. Yet grown women did not sleep in the bedrooms of their brothers. After saying good night to Mark, she dragged her belongings down the hall to the room with the bay window. Jamie strolled to the casement. Far below the bluff she could see the streets of Port Townsend, the tiny headlights of cars winding along Water Street, the blazing windows of the Town Tavern, the Lido Restaurant, and the floodlights of the new ferry terminal at the south end of town.

Across the bay in the black hills, lights were scarce. Stars twinkled above the low mountains. In wonder, Jamie gazed at a sky that contained no artificial lights—no television towers, no satellites, no jets, no helicopters. Then she became aware of the silence, the blessed absence of traffic congestion, sirens, people yelling in the street, and unsolicited music and telephone calls. Nothing but silence.

Suddenly, a moth collided with the glass directly in front of her. The sudden smacking noise startled her. Jamie reared back in surprise, her heart in her throat.

Sighing, she let the drapery fall back. For a moment she had forgotten her fear of the house. For a moment she had escaped the stress of her life in Los Angeles. For a moment she had known peace. But only for a moment. Her headache roared back in full force.

By the time Jamie slipped under the comforter it was midnight. She shivered. Ever since she was a child she had expected something nefarious to happen at midnight. And in this house she knew that anything could happen. Outside the wind gusted over the rooftop and through the gingerbread, whining and moaning, adding the finishing touch to her sense of unease. She bunched up the comforter around her ears, trying to get warm. How long would it take until the sleeping pills kicked in? A few minutes? An hour? Maybe she was too tense. Maybe she'd developed a tolerance. Maybe she should get the prescription changed.

She looked for faces in the texture of the plaster on the ceiling, trying to distract her mind from thinking about ghosts and haunted houses. She dreaded sleep almost as much as being in this house because her dreams frightened her. Her dreams were always vivid and full of terror. Her therapist had told her she experienced the typical dreams of anyone who was particularly intelligent and creative. But Jamie didn't believe her psychoanalyst. No normal human being could spend as much time as she did in a nether world of fright.

That night was no exception. Jamie tossed and turned. Only this time it wasn't a dream about the McAllister House, but of a woman in a blue dress, a long blue dress with an old-fashioned bustle. The woman beckoned to Jamie, motioning for her to follow. Jamie ran and ran but never quite caught up with the woman. Her legs felt as heavy as stumps, her vision was clouded and patchy as if her eyes were partially covered with duct tape.

Jamie followed the woman across the lawn of a house— the McAllister House—down a street full of an incongruous assemblage of horses and carriages and Volkswagen vans. Finally, the woman stopped on the edge of the bluff and looked back at Jamie. The wind blew back her hair. *The woman had no face.* Terrified, but unable to move, Jamie watched the woman point over the bluff. Wind sucked at Jamie's clothing, pulling her to the edge, dragging her so close she knew she would fall. She looked down, her blue gown flapping around her shoes, to the roof of a building a hundred feet below. The wind pulled her closer. *Tree of Heaven,* the woman said. Jamie fought to keep her balance. Her gown tangled around her knees. *Tree of Heaven.* Jamie couldn't save herself. Oh, God, she was falling! Falling down, falling—

Jamie sat up with a start, wet with sweat. She brushed back her damp hair and glanced around, confused at her surroundings. Where was she? She blinked. Then she remembered. She was in the McAllister House. She was trying to get a decent night's sleep in the McAllister House—a contradiction in terms.

With a sigh, Jamie lay back on her pillow and stared at the ceiling. She did not sleep again for hours.

In the morning Jamie made a huge omelet and took a breakfast tray to her brother. She hoped the food might tempt him to eat, perhaps put a bit of meat back on his bones. She sat cross-legged at the foot of his bed, balancing a plate on her left knee.

"Great omelet, sis," Mark commented. But Jamie observed that he mostly moved the bite-sized pieces around and didn't consume more than the orange juice.

As Jamie lifted her fork, the sunlight glanced off her ring, catching her brother's attention. He set his tray aside.

"What's the ring for?" He craned his neck to see the large diamond.

"It's what most people call an engagement ring."

"What do you call it?"

"It's kind of an engagement ring." Jamie gazed at the glittering stone, too large and ornate for her taste. She preferred small simple pieces of jewelry or none at all. "But I haven't really said yes yet."

"Then why are you wearing it?"

"Brett insisted I take it, even though I haven't given him an answer yet. I thought I'd wait until I talked to you."

"Good. Say no."

"I really didn't want to take the ring, not like that. But he just wouldn't take it back."

"Typical Brett."

"No strings attached," Jamie said.

"I'll bet." Mark shook his head. "I'm surprised he didn't ask you to move in with him and skip marriage altogether."

He had, but Jamie didn't want to admit that to her brother. Mark didn't need another reason to hate Brett.

"Christ." Mark lifted her left hand. "Look at the size of it. You could feed the Third World for a year with this. Doesn't he have a brain in his head? Or a conscience?"

Jamie snatched back her hand. "I think he was trying to express his affection."

"Don't be so naive, sis. Brett doesn't do anything for anyone but himself. He wants something from you."

"That's not true!" Jamie scrambled to her feet. "Why must you think the worst? Why can't you accept him?"

"Because he's a phony. Bad media."

"Mark, why don't you speak English for a change!"

"Just trying to be as clear as I can." Mark shrugged. "When I think of Brett, I see that little bomb icon you get when your system crashes on a Macintosh computer."

"I don't know why. Brett's always been nice to me. He's done a lot for me."

"Sure, for now." Mark smoothed the comforter over his chest. "Everything's going his way. He has you right where he wants you—making money for him. Brett Johansen's little photo whore!"

"Whore!" Jamie paled.

"Yeah! You're prostituting your talent making commercials when you should be doing something more meaningful."

"Oh? My commercials pay for your research—or have you forgotten?"

"I haven't forgotten," Mark retorted. "Brett never lets me forget how I waste your money. But don't let my projects be your excuse to stay in Los Angeles. And don't let Brett become your excuse either. I know you, Jamie. You won't be satisfied settling for second best."

"What do you mean, second best?"

"Jamie, you've always excelled. At school. In your work. I keep telling you—you have rare artistic vision. And yet you'll settle for Brett Johansen? It doesn't figure!"

Jamie glared at him in exasperation. Then she slammed down her plate and fork on the night stand and strode to the window. Her appetite had vanished. She drew back the curtain and stared out at the grayness of the morning as the sun slowly burned through the layers of mist and fog.

"Things are changing," she said simply.

"What things?" Mark turned on his side so he could see her better.

"Well—me." Jamie ran her fingers along a fold of the drapery fabric. "I used to be satisfied with my work. It kept me alive, interested. But not anymore. I don't know what it is—I feel this compelling need to do something else."

"To marry Brett?" Mark snorted. "That does sound compelling."

Jamie ignored his remark. "Maybe it's my biological clock ticking away. Maybe it's a pipe dream. But I want to have children, Mark. And Brett can give me children."

"Hell, any man can give you children."

Jamie no longer saw the mist and fog outside. All she was aware of was a burning sensation deep within her, eating away at her, draining her heart. She let the curtain fall.

"I don't expect you to understand, Mark. You've got your projects, your computers, your logic." She faced him. "But I'm lonely. I'm so lonely I'm growing black and hollow inside."

"And marriage to Brett will help?"

Jamie shrugged. "I don't know. I've never found a man to fill the void. So maybe it's a maternal need I'm going through. That's all I can think of. And Brett's steady. We work well together. He's the only one I'd even consider."

"What I can't figure out is why he wants to marry you now. Why all of a sudden?"

Jamie frowned. "Maybe he finally decided he likes me."

"No, nothing that simple." Mark shook his head and held up his hand. "Wait a minute. Let me think. Ah, yes. He asked you to marry him on—let's see—October ninth."

"How did you know?" Jamie gasped.

"Wasn't October eighth the day you found out that the gallery in New York was interested in your work?"

"Yes, but—"

"Well, just take that date and add one day for Brett to do some serious consideration."

Jamie paused. Oddly enough, Brett had proposed to her the day after she received the call from the gallery. She had been so happy that day. She remembered taking Brett's hands and swinging around in delight, a wild departure from her usual reserved behavior.

"That's just coincidence," she said.

"I don't think so. Brett can see you slipping away from him, trying something on your own. That makes him nervous."

"Why should it?"

"Because you're the genius behind JK Productions and Brett knows it."

Jamie moved away from the bed, uncomfortable with the topic of conversation. "I'm only half of JK Productions. Brett's the business part of the team. Without him, I'd be a starving artist living in a garret somewhere." As she talked, she folded Mark's jeans and set them on a chair by the window.

"Brett is nothing without your talent, Jamie. He knows it. Everyone knows it. Everyone except you, that is."

"I wouldn't be where I am without Brett. We need each other. I just wish you could see that, Mark, and accept him." Jamie turned and glared at her brother.

He pointed to his chest with both forefingers. "Me accept him? Hey, I'm not the one who'll have to live with the guy."

"Yes, but he'll be part of the family. And it's important that you like him."

"What's more important is whether you like him, Jamie. In fact, you should even love him. And you don't, do you?"

Did she? Jamie regarded the cold fire of the diamond, so like her fiancé. On the surface Brett was the perfect man—handsome, well-groomed and well dressed. He played tennis, attended charity functions and the opera, and was invited to all the right parties. But underneath Brett's polished facade was a stranger. He never talked about his feelings. Had Brett even mentioned that he loved her? She couldn't remember.

Jamie slowly raised her head. "I suppose I love Brett. In a way."

"In a way? That doesn't sound very convincing."

Jamie glanced away from her brother and stared at the clock on his night stand. "I never felt that bolt out of the blue, that zap, that zing—"

"You sound like Mel Torme. God, I'm hallucinating." Mark fell back theatrically. "My sister has transformed into Mel Torme. Shoot me! Put me out of my misery!"

Jamie dove at her brother, throwing a pillow over his face. They were convulsed with laughter until Mark started to cough. After a minute he gained control over his wheezing and managed to smile weakly. Jamie hovered over him, worried that she had gone too far. Finally, he caught his breath.

"I'm okay," he whispered. "I'm okay."

"You sure?"

"Yeah."

"Mark, you should see a doctor. You might have pneumonia or something. Why don't I call a doctor for you?"

"I don't need a doctor. I just need some rest."

"Are you sure?"

"Yeah."

Jamie lifted the tray of dishes from the night stand. "Can I get you something at least?" she asked, lingering at his bedside.

He shook his head. "I'll take it easy this morning. Then this afternoon we can go to the lab."

Jamie smiled at him and turned away.

"And brat?"

Jamie stopped. "Yes?"

"Don't marry Brett if you don't love him. I'm serious."

Jamie tried to disregard Mark's remarks, but all the way down the stairs she heard his voice in her head. *Don't marry Brett if you don't love him. Don't marry Brett if you don't love him.*

Jamie deposited the tray of dishes in the kitchen sink and walked back to the main hall to go upstairs. Before she ascended, she paused at the foot of the staircase and glanced down the dark hall toward the study. She had done the same thing a thousand times in her nightmares. A chill raced down the back of Jamie's neck and made the hair on her scalp prickle, as if she were wearing a swimming cap stuck full of pins. In her dreams she could never resist walking to the study where she would relive the horror over and over again.

Jamie's hand slid off the newel post. She was not in her

dream now. She was fully awake. It was broad daylight. Nothing could hurt her. And she knew that facing the study was imperative if she were to ever escape her nightmares. She took a step toward the shadowed hallway.

Tree of Heaven.

Jamie glanced over her shoulder. Who had spoken to her? She peered up the stairs. Down the hallway. No one was there. Yet where had the voice come from? It sounded so real! Wary and unnerved, she sidled toward the study door.

2

AS JAMIE MOVED DOWN THE HALL, the doorknob on the door of the study seemed to grow larger and larger. A strain of "Joy to the World" welled up on the fringes of her consciousness, a faint sound from the depths of her memory. Then a child's scream pierced through the music, a cry from the past that sent Jamie reeling. The child screamed and screamed, until Jamie became one with the hysterical ten-year-old girl she had once been. Panic locked Jamie in a familiar trance and swept her into the past, even though she knew she was awake.

"No!" she cried. She careened down the hall, trying to block out the stark fear that still gripped her after twenty years. By the time she threw open the study door, her breath came in heavy pants and she was perspiring even though the house was chilly.

"Leave me be!" she whimpered. "Oh, God, just leave me be!"

After her outburst she hung in the doorway of the study, with her hands covering her ears. She could still hear the Christmas music, overlapping in a monstrous cacophony of harpsichords and chimes, Barbra Streisand and Perry Como all jumbled together. The music alone was enough to drive her crazy. But there were also the candles, hundreds of them, red and white, blazing, sputtering, flickering, throwing bizarre shadows on the walls and ceiling. She would go blind from all the candles.

Jamie squeezed her eyes shut to block out the vision. She was in an empty study, just a plain old study full of musty books and leather upholstery. It wasn't Christmas 1970, it was October 1990. She wasn't a ten-year-old child who had just lost her parents to a drunk on the highway. She was a full-grown woman. *I'm a big girl now. A big girl.*

Gradually, Jamie opened her eyes. The music was only a faint sound, humming softly in the background. She could cope with that. And there were no candles, just wind and sunlight playing in the bare branches of the sycamore tree outside. *I'm a big girl. A big girl.*

She let her hands slide from her ears. Then she forced herself to look to the side where French doors opened to the overgrown garden. That's where she had seen the ghost. That's where the spirit had materialized on Christmas Eve so long ago, a creature of candlelight and a child's wild imagination.

At first she had believed it to be the spirit of her father, come to haunt her. That she should fear her father's ghost was hard to imagine. But she had been only ten years old, and the thought of her dead parent making a visit had terrified her. However, the shape that had flickered and taken form was not her father or her mother, but a man dressed in a strange-looking black suit and old-fashioned necktie with a stickpin.

Jamie's skin erupted in goose pimples as she remembered the way the vision had called her name. She could still see those ashen lips forming her name, that hand raising to reach out to her. "*Ja—mie, Ja—mie!*" She had known with implacable certainty that the vision was Hazard McAllister, the ghost that supposedly haunted the McAllister mansion. Her grandmother had told her all about McAllister, how he had built the mansion and then murdered two people in the study. Her brother had teased her about the ghost, frightening her with declarations that Hazard McAllister was waiting for her in the closet. Hazard McAllister would get her if she went to the bathroom at midnight. Hazard McAllister could seep under her bedroom door, even if it was locked. Jamie, always one to feel drafts and hear noises, believed her brother's stories and spent most nights at her grandmother's house in a state of panic.

The music swelled full force—"Little Town of Bethlehem" and "Jingle Bell Rock," Roy Clark and Tony Bennett. The child was screaming again—no, it was her screaming. The candles, the music, the candles, the music.

Jamie fell backward against the bookshelves. Her grandmother was calling her name, patting her face, urging her to tell her what had happened. She couldn't speak, she couldn't stop screaming.

"Dear, whatever is wrong?"

Jamie jerked to her senses and whirled around. There stood Mrs. Gipson with a towel in her hand.

"I heard you screaming. What happened?"

Jamie licked her lips. What could she tell the housekeeper? That she had seen a ghost when she was ten years old and that she had been emotionally disturbed ever since, mostly because no one had believed her—not her grandmother, not the doctors, not the child psychologists.

Instead of listening to her, they had shot her full of seda-
tives and sent her to countless therapists who tried to
twist her experience into a dysfunctional family-grief
problem.

The therapy sessions made Jamie lose faith in her judgment of what was real and what wasn't. None of the
adults believed her story. She must have been mistaken,
they told her. There were no such things as ghosts. She
was just a hysterical child. Surely she had seen something
else—a reflection perhaps. Jamie had heard the argu-
ments so many times that she'd begun to doubt what she
had seen. And whenever her judgment was questioned
in the ensuing years, she faltered in the face of confrontation, never quite sure of herself.

Even now, she wasn't certain what she had really seen
or heard, what was real and what was a dream. "Sorry,
Mrs. Gipson, I . . ." her voice trailed off as she was caught
up by memories of her disastrous childhood.

After The Incident, she was sent to live with her aunt
in Santa Barbara, California. Mark, gifted and preoccupied with his solar cells and computer components, was
shipped off to a preparatory school in New York.

At first Jamie thought Aunt Evelyn the best aunt a girl
could have. She was a successful lawyer, beautiful, and
unmarried, which Jamie found unusual and admirable.
When she arrived in California she was shown her new
bedroom, decorated in lavender and mint, crammed with
stuffed animals and dolls. Her closet was filled with expensive dresses and slacks, and her dresser was brimming with
lacy underclothes, gorgeous sweaters, and the latest
sportswear. She was even sent to an elite private school
that had an equestrian program, something Jamie had always wanted.

But the glamour soon faded. Jamie soon realized she

was Aunt Evelyn's pampered prisoner. When she asked to have some of her old clothes back—her jeans were much more comfortable than fully lined wool slacks—her Aunt Evelyn said, "Oh, don't be silly, Jamie. Those clothes just won't do." When she tried to tell her aunt that she didn't like playing with Barbie dolls, her Aunt Evelyn said, "Oh, don't be silly, Jamie. All your little friends like Barbie dolls." Soon Jamie quit making requests, because Aunt Evelyn never really listened to her. Aunt Evelyn was a woman who knew her own mind and obviously everyone else's, too.

In retrospect, Jamie realized her aunt had been too busy with her career to devote much time to her lonely little niece. And Aunt Evelyn did not possess an understanding nature. In fact, she was convinced that Jamie's dreams were simply an attention-getting device, and she punished Jamie for running from her bedroom, screaming because of a nightmare. There were times when it would have been embarrassing to have a raving ten-year-old girl show up in the master bedroom.

Would Mrs. Gipson be any more understanding?

Abandoned emotionally, Jamie grew up alone, stifling her wants, her needs, and her fears. She studied hard and did well in school, and spent most of her free time alone, biking around Santa Barbara and taking pictures. She didn't have many friends, not because she was unpopular, but because she worried what the other girls might think if they ever found out she was half crazy.

College was a lonely experience, too. Jamie blossomed when she entered the arts program where she specialized in photography. She loved the time spent immersed in her studies. But all through college she harbored a secret crush on a sculpture professor. The crush kept her from dating boys her own age. It was easier to fantasize about the older man who would never make an advance than to have to contend with the romantic overtures of acquaintances in class. Though young men badgered her through her school years, Jamie held out for her professor, dreaming of the day he would come to her and confess his love. Of course he never did.

So what should she tell Mrs. Gipson? The truth? Hardly!

"I—I saw something—a mouse. It ran right over the carpet and into that bookcase." She pointed to the shelf and couldn't keep her arm from trembling.

Mrs. Gipson shook her head. "Those mice. I've set traps everywhere. They always come in for the winter about this time of year."

"I have a phobia of mice. They scare me to death."

"Me too," Mrs. Gipson patted her arm. "If one ever ran over my shoe I'd have a heart attack."

Hazard McAllister. Jamie pinched the bridge of her nose and reached into her open suitcase to retrieve two volumes on Washington State history and her spiral-bound notebook. She put the books on her desk and then opened the notebook, staring at the name of her nemesis written in her crabbed handwriting. *Hazard McAllister.* The name blurred as a shooting pain seared through her eyes. After her incident in the study, she had taken some pills, but her headache hadn't abated. She sighed.

What had made Hazard McAllister brutally murder his intended bride and his business partner? He had abused Nelle McMurray, gunned her down in cold blood, shot his longtime associate, and then disappeared from the face of the earth, along with a considerable amount of the townspeople's money.

Jamie picked up one of her history books and opened

it to the photograph of McAllister, the only photo she had managed to find. He stared back at her with his flat, colorless eyes. He didn't look that murderous. In fact, he appeared rather stuffy with his pomaded hair, handlebar moustache, and black suit with the wrinkled lapels. But then, appearances could be deceiving.

Jamie sat down at her desk and picked up a pen. She had come up with an idea a few weeks ago for her own therapy. Once and for all she planned to rid herself of Hazard McAllister, not by denying his existence as recommended by the doctors, but by writing his biography. She was certain if she got to know the criminal and really faced him, she could let the experience fade into the past where it belonged. Then at last she would be free to create a normal life for herself with Brett. If children were the answer to her loneliness, she had to deal with her past before she became a parent. She could never be a decent mother until she put her own lonely and terrifying childhood behind her.

Jamie glanced back at the overexposed photograph. What little she had found regarding McAllister was fascinating. He had been born sometime during the mid 1800s in Dunvegan, Scotland, on the Isle of Skye, to a clan still proud but declining financially each generation. With no hope of a decent education or inheritance, Hazard had run away to sea. By his early twenties he was captain of his own schooner, running the San Francisco-Seattle-Alaska route. By his thirties he owned an entire fleet of steamships and was quickly becoming one of the richest men on the West Coast. In 1888 he built the McAllister House on the bluff and asked beautiful Nelle McMurray to share his wealth and happiness.

Then something went wrong with the fairy tale. Something had snapped in Hazard McAllister. In 1889 on

Christmas Eve he blew the brains out of Nelle and his business partner William Bennett and left them in the study downstairs. Was it a love triangle gone bad? No one knew.

At the thought of the study, Jamie's skin crawled. Hazard had come for her, too, on Christmas Eve. She clenched her teeth together, trying not to remember how his colorless face had frightened her. Yet she could not escape him. Hazard looked up at her from the page beneath her fingers. She slammed the book shut. *I'm a big girl now. A big girl, Hazard McAllister. You can't scare me anymore.*

But she couldn't resist looking over her shoulder at the bedroom door and the dark hallway beyond it. Had something moved in the shadows? Cool air seeped through the old glazing of the windowpane near her desk. Jamie hugged her arms.

"Jamie, watch this." Mark turned in his chair before his Macintosh computer and held up a videotape. "On this videocassette is a short clip I took of Mrs. Gipson the other day."

"Sounds interesting." Jamie idly inspected the array of equipment that stuffed the large master bedroom on the second floor. From what she could tell, Mark had hooked up homemade computer components, a videocassette player, a strange-looking camera on a tripod, mirrors, lasers, and prisms, all connected with a jumble of cables and aluminum duct tape.

"Observe," Mark instructed, pushing the cassette into the machine. He rose and adjusted a laser, and then used a remote control to start the tape.

"Where's the TV?" Jamie asked.

"No TV. Look right there." Mark pointed to a spot

central to the lasers just as Mrs. Gipson appeared, cleaning the tops of the dining room chairs with a fluorescent pink feather duster. She looked so lifelike that Jamie gasped in wonder.

"That's a hologram?" she sputtered. "It looks so *real.*"

Mark nodded. He could hardly contain his excitement, and hugged his thin chest with his bony arms as if to keep himself from bursting.

"Aren't holograms supposed to be a weird green color?"

"Not my holograms."

Mrs. Gipson leaned over to pick a penny off the floor. She looked at the date and then shrugged and put it in her apron. Jamie stared, dumbfounded.

"Touch her," Mark said.

Jamie shot him a questioning glance. She suspected another of her brother's pranks. Jamie knew she couldn't touch a hologram. Her hand would pass right through. Even though the image might appear three dimensional, there was no substance to it. Holograms were a trick of crystals and laser beams, and virtually done with mirrors.

"Go ahead. Touch her." He couldn't suppress a grin.

Hesitantly, Jamie reached for Mrs. Gipson. She tapped her on the shoulder and felt *flesh* beneath her fingers. Jamie snatched back her hand as if she had been burned.

"Mark! She's—Mark, I touched her!"

Mark nodded. His eyes blazed. "She's three dimensional. She is displayed in two hundred and fifty-six glorious colors. She has mass. She has a ninety-eight-point-six-degree body temperature. And she takes up a helluva lot of memory."

Jamie could only stare. Her power of speech had disappeared in a flash of awe.

"Mrs. Gipson the Hologram could give you a glass of milk and cookies if she thought about it. She could actually pick up a glass of milk and hand it to you. I haven't worked that bug out yet—how to direct the hologram to perform tasks—but it's coming."

"Mark—I never dreamed—this is unbelievable!"

He clicked the remote and shut off the video player and Mrs. Gipson vanished. Jamie stared at her brother.

"How does he do it, she wonders," Mark remarked, stepping up to the camera on the tripod and smiling at his overwhelmed sister. "God, I love computers! Don't you love computers?"

"Mark—"

"Actually, the secret lies in this camera. This is one special Brownie, sis."

Jamie moved closer to the tripod. "What does it do?"

"This camera records three things—any energy emission no matter how small or how insignificant, how far away from the camera that energy is, and how much heat is being radiated. That was easy. I simply incorporated infrared technology."

"Mark, I knew you were a genius, but this is—" She shook her head, lost for the right word.

"This is radical," he interjected. "As they say in L.A., this is fresh! One-hundred-percent outer limit stuff. Want to try it?"

She gaped at him, dying of curiosity about the camera. "Can I?"

"Soitainly," he imitated Curly of the Three Stooges as he sat down at his computer. Jamie smiled and shook her head. How could a clown create such advanced technology?

"The controls are like a video camcorder. Autofocus and all that. Just a minute, though. I've got to patch the camera directly into the video player."

"Can I record over Mrs. Gipson?"

"Sure. I don't think it was award-winning footage. Let me start all this up first."

Jamie looked through the lens. Drapery and wallpaper wasn't her idea of stimulating subject matter. She needed a subject. Glancing around, her gaze landed on her brother. "Mark, let me film you. Then you can show me how a hologram can interact with the real world."

"Excellent idea, brat! Excellent." Mark scuffled through cables and equipment and positioned himself in front of the camera. "As a hologram I'll hand you this." He pulled a fingernail clipper out of his jeans pocket. "Ready?"

"Ready."

"Oh, click on the video player."

Jamie pushed the remote button and then turned to the camera. She was tense with excitement as she put her eye to the viewfinder. She pressed the record button and looked to the side where the lasers were set. Mark appeared in hologram form, grinning from ear to ear.

"Back up, Mark, so I can get your entire body. I can't get your hand in view where you are now."

"How's this?" Mark shuffled backward.

"A little more." She waved with her hand. "Just a bit more."

Suddenly Mark stumbled, his foot catching in a length of cable, and he crashed to the floor, disappearing from the tape. Without shutting off the camera, Jamie looked up. "Are you all right?"

"Yes, dang cables!"

As he got to his feet the lights flickered and the Macintosh computer honked so loudly that Jamie ran over to it. The monitor whistled and the screen went from blue to black and black to blue again. Mark dashed to her side. "Christ, what did I do? It must be a power surge."

A movement near the lasers caught Jamie's eye and she glanced up. For a moment she couldn't speak, so great was her shock. All she could do was clutch her brother's arm, digging in so hard that her fingernails bit into his skin.

"Damn!" Mark swore. "Let go, Jamie!" He pulled his arm away and lunged for the surge protector on the floor. It bristled with an assortment of power cords. He snapped the red toggle switch to off and the earsplitting whistling wound down as the computer shut off. "Probably blew out the mother board," he muttered in disgust.

"M—M—Mark!" Jamie stammered, trying to grab his arm again as he straightened. Annoyed, Mark followed the motion of her hand as she pointed to the lasers. "It's him!"

Mark stood up. "Jesus," he whispered.

Jamie felt her blood turn cold with terror. She couldn't move. She couldn't run. She was in the dream all over again.

There, surrounded by lasers, was Hazard McAllister in—so to speak—living color.

3

IN TERRIFIED ASTONISHMENT, Jamie stared at the hologram of Hazard McAllister. Seeming equally astonished, Hazard felt the solidity of his chest and then looked at his hands, turning them over and over. He moved one of his feet. Then he looked up. He stared right at her. Jamie wanted to scream, wanted to bolt from the room, but she was riveted in place with unutterable shock.

She knew that face well. She had seen it as a filmy vision and again in the photograph of the book that lay on her desk upstairs. But neither of those representations had prepared her for the sight of Hazard McAllister in three-dimensional living color.

What struck her most was the physical presence of the man. She had never guessed that McAllister was so large. He was well over six feet tall, with broad shoulders and long legs. Energy emanated from him, mainly from his face, but also in the way he stood, as if ready to stride forward. His hair was a wild mane of tawny gold a shade lighter than his handlebar moustache. His fair skin was branded with bronze and vermillion from years spent on the open sea. And his eyes were blazing points of blue, far from the flat eyes she had seen in the photograph.

"Jesus!" Mark repeated in wonder.

Jamie broke from her trance. "Turn it off, Mark! Turn it off, for heaven's sake!"

"It is off! Everything's off!"

Freezing dread poured over Jamie. What did Mark mean, everything was off? How could that be? The hologram was standing there as big as Mike. If the computer was turned off, what was producing the hologram?

Then Hazard McAllister straightened. "By Saint Andrew!" he roared. "I'm alive!" He glanced from Jamie to Mark and clapped his chest again. "I'm bloody breathin' alive!" His baritone voice thrummed with a Scottish burr. He grinned, an uneven grin that pulled to the right, exposing two rows of flawless white teeth.

Before Jamie could make a move, she saw McAllister step away from the lasers that surrounded him, as easily as if he were walking across the littered deck of a ship. Her heart thudded in her chest. This was it. This was the end. Hazard McAllister had found a way to get her at last. Why couldn't she move? And how could he?

Jamie gaped in disbelief as he strode forward.

"Nelle!" McAllister called. " 'Tis you, Nelle!"

Jamie stumbled backward, afraid of what he might do. Why was he calling her Nelle?

"Stay—stay away!" she stammered.

McAllister stopped in his tracks. "Dinna be afraid. Ye know me, love. 'Tis Hazard!" He held out his palms. His hands were long, his fingers slender.

At his gesture, Jamie stepped backward even more. "I'm not your love!" she screeched. "I'm not Nelle!"

He dropped his hands and tilted his head, inspecting

her as if she were lying about her identity. "Who are ye, then?"

Jamie crossed her arms. "I'm Jamie Kent. Ellen Jamie Kent."

Surprise flooded his face. Did he actually recognize her name? Jamie watched in dread fascination as he surveyed her, from the tips of her leather boots to the curls of her fawn-colored hair.

"You're Jamie?" he inquired. "Jamie Kent?"

"Yes." Her name had never sounded so foreign to her as it did when pronounced by this hologram ghost. And it gave her the creeps that a ghost knew her name.

"Jamie Kent!" Hazard exclaimed. "Well, blister me, lass!" Then he grinned at her. His smile possessed such a physical force that Jamie stepped back even farther. "Ye've changed, Jamie girl. Ye've grown up! And into a bonny lass!"

"Who are you?" Mark demanded. "How do you know my sister?"

"I'm Hazard McAllister." He bowed. "The very late Hazard McAllister."

"The ghost." Mark stated in disbelief. "You're the ghost my sister once saw?"

"Aye." McAllister grinned again. He seemed overjoyed with the situation.

Mark glanced at the video player even though he knew it wasn't running. "This has to be some kind of a trick."

"Why?"

"Well—" Mark looked at him askance and then glanced at the equipment again. "I don't know exactly, but ghosts don't just show up every day, know what I mean?"

"Ye dinna believe me? Come now, Mark."

"How do you know our names? Who put you up to this?"

Hazard took a step forward. "Somethin' ye did with your contraption there just pulled me clean out o' th' air. As t' your name—well, I've been watchin' and listenin' t' ye for months now, Mark, ever since ye showed up." His glance fell on Jamie and he bestowed upon her what he probably thought was a warm smile. But his attentions chilled her to the bone. "I know Jamie from a previous engagement. Although ye look a sight different all grown up, lass."

Mark's eyes narrowed. "This has got to be somebody's idea of a joke. Are you a magician? How did you get in the house?"

Hazard chuckled and shook his head. "I've been in this house longer than you've been alive, my boy. And I was just standin' there, watchin' Jamie fiddle wi' tha' device on th' tripod while you were movin' backward, workin' t' land on your rear, when I saw this whirlpool. 'Twas the only way t' describe it. This blue whirlpool comin' at me, pullin' at me. I couldna move. I just let it take me. Somethin' poured over me, I canna say what. Felt like warm butter. And I felt my skin tinglin' and ticklin', and my hair standin' up. And then, saints be, everythin' cleared up, things quit buzzin', and there ye be, and here I stand!"

"Out of thin air! You expect me to believe that?" Mark shook his head in disbelief. "That's some story!"

" 'Tis the truth."

"I believe him," Jamie murmured.

Mark turned to her. "What?"

"I think he's telling the truth. I think he is Hazard McAllister. He looks just like him."

"Aye! 'Tis the truth, sae help me God."

Unconsciously, Jamie reached for her brother's arm as if he could protect her from the imposing figure of McAllister. A wild light gleamed in McAllister's eyes. He was not the stuffy man in the photograph. Not by a long shot.

"I don't believe this!" Mark said.

"Ye dinna believe in spirits?" McAllister took a step toward them. "Did ye never think ye saw somethin' out o' th' corner of your eye, Mark? Felt a cool draft?"

Jamie had felt both things many times in the McAllister House, but kept silent.

Mark shrugged. "Sure. Everybody feels that once in awhile."

" 'Twas most likely a ghost. But ye weren't in th' right frame o' mind to accept it. Not like Jamie."

Jamie straightened. Hazard's gaze returned to her face. "Some people are more receptive than others. Jamie, here, is a rare one. She felt me on more than one occasion, didna ye, lass?"

Mutely, Jamie nodded. She was talking to a ghost. How could she stand here and talk to a ghost? Had she completely lost her mind?

"And then ye saw me tha' Christmas Eve. I didna mean t' scare ye. Ye were weepin' and I wanted t' know wha' 'twas breakin' your heart so. Poor wee lassie. They dragged you away before I could explain mysel'."

"Please—" Jamie implored. "Please, leave me alone."

"So," Mark put in, finally beginning to lose his doubts. "You've been here all these years, floating around, waiting to scare people?"

"Floatin' 'round, aye. I seem t' be trapped here."

"And now you're a hologram," Mark replied. "Or you want me to think you're a hologram."

"Whatever a hologram may be."

Mark reached out for McAllister, but Jamie pulled him back. "Don't go near him!" she said.

"I'm just curious—"

"He's a murderer!"

"Murderer!" boomed McAllister. "The devil ye say!"

"Yes, murderer." Jamie pulled her brother farther away from the hologram, trying to drag him toward the door.

"Hold on, lass." McAllister lunged for her to keep her from leaving.

Horrified, Jamie screamed, and Mark flung himself in the hologram's path. "Hey!" Mark shouted. He pushed McAllister's chest, but his gesture was futile and rather ridiculous. Mark was hardly a threat to McAllister. "Keep your hands off my sister!"

McAllister checked himself, though a glint of anger turned his eyes to ice. "Ye gave me life, man, but dinna make me angry."

"Don't touch her!" Mark choked. The effort sapped him of his last reserve of energy. He hunched over, coughing.

McAllister glared at Mark. "She called me a murderer. I want t' know why."

Mark couldn't stop coughing. His face grew crimson.

"Mark!" Jamie cried.

"My in—" he dropped to his knees. "Get my inhaler—"

"Where?" she screamed.

"Bed—"

Jamie tore out of the room and across the hall, fumbling through the magazines and papers scattered on Mark's comforter. Her hands felt the cold metal of his inhalant dispenser and she grabbed it, running back to the lab as quickly as her shaky legs would carry her. By the time she arrived, Mark was on the floor, supported by McAllister.

Kneeling, Jamie put the inhaler to Mark's mouth. His eyes were closed as he gasped for air.

"Breathe!" she commanded.

Weakly he responded. His chest rose slightly.

"Breathe, Mark!"

After a few moments he inhaled deeper and deeper until he caught his breath. His face had lost all color and he seemed to be unaware that he lay in the arms of the hologram he had created. His eyes fluttered open and then closed again. The coughing fit had drained all his strength.

"Oh, Mark!" Jamie exclaimed, brushing the hair off his forehead. He felt feverish. In her anguish she looked at McAllister and for an instant forgot her fear of him. "He's so sick."

"He should be abed."

"Could you—could you carry him there?"

"Aye."

Jamie slipped the inhaler from Mark's lips and rose to her feet. "This way," she motioned for McAllister to follow. The hologram easily lifted Mark's wasted body and gently cradled him in his arms. He strode out of the lab and down the hall to Mark's bedroom. Jamie scrambled to clear the debris from the bed and then flung back the covers.

Carefully, McAllister lay Mark upon the mattress, making certain to support his head as he lowered it to the pillow. He straightened Mark's legs and then took off his shoes. Jamie hovered on the other side of the bed, watching in amazement as the murderous Hazard McAllister saw to the simple comforts of her brother.

Hazard stood up to his full height. "Has he a doctor?"

"He doesn't want to see one."

"He needs a doctor."

Jamie blinked. She was discussing medical problems with Hazard McAllister. It was beyond comprehension. Before she could answer, Mark raised his hand.

"Don't let—" he mouthed the words barely above a whisper. Jamie bent closer. Mark swallowed. "Don't let anyone—"

"Don't let anyone what?" Jamie urged.

Mark opened his eyes and peered earnestly at his sister's face. "Know."

"About him?" Jamie asked, referring to McAllister. Mark nodded slightly and closed his eyes. His hand dropped to the comforter.

Jamie glanced at McAllister. Of course she wouldn't let anyone know. She had spent twenty years keeping the truth about McAllister to herself so that people wouldn't think she was crazy.

"Get a doctor," McAllister remarked. "I'll stay with your brother."

Jamie hesitated. Could she trust him? What if he killed Mark when she was gone, to get him out of the way? Would she be next? Why did she ever give Mrs. Gipson the afternoon off?

"I won't hurt him, lass."

Unable to think of an alternative plan, Jamie headed for the door. "I'm just going across the hall to the lab," she warned. "I'll be able to see whether you're lying or not."

"Sae it's lyin' now, is it?" he retorted, his eyes flashing. "A lyin' murderer I am, is it? Have ye anythin' else t' add t' my crimes?"

"Just don't touch my brother. And don't move!" Jamie skittered to the door. "I'll be right back."

Hazard's voice followed her. "After th' doctor comes, Jamie girl, we need t' talk."

She paused at the doorway and looked over her shoulder at him. He stood bathed in the afternoon sunlight streaming through the window behind him. The outlines of his body diffused into shimmering gold and floating dust motes. Jamie thought if she stared long enough she would be able to see right through him.

Hazard studied her as well. What did he see? Did he see her as Nelle McMurray? Jamie fled from the room.

By the time the doctor left, the sun had set, pulling all the light out of the huge old house. Jamie switched on the lamps after she let the doctor out and closed the door. Then she looked up the stairwell to the second floor, wondering what she should do. McAllister had graciously offered to keep out of sight while the physician was at the house. Apparently, he was just as eager as she was to keep his presence a secret, which was hardly a surprise considering he was a criminal who had never been brought to justice. All the time the doctor had ministered to Mark, Jamie had kept one eye on the doctor and one eye on Hazard McAllister across the hall. Now that the doctor was gone, however, what would she do with McAllister?

Jamie ran up the stairs, worrying about keeping McAllister a secret from Mrs. Gipson. The housekeeper was due back at the house any moment. And Mrs. Gipson was not the type of woman who would let the appearance of a stranger slip by her.

Somehow Hazard McAllister would have to be contained. How else would they all be safe from him? There weren't any weapons in the house. Without one, Jamie wouldn't be capable of overpowering such a big man. She was just over five and a half feet tall, hardly a match for the hologram.

When she gained the second level, she proceeded quietly, uncertain in which room McAllister was located. She looked in on Mark, who slept peacefully. The doctor had given him some antibiotics for his pneumonia and urged him to call if his condition got any worse. McAllister was not in the room with Mark.

Across the hall the lights were on in the lab. Jamie stole over the carpet runner and peeked through the doorway. Hazard stood in front of the computer with his back to the door. He had heard her step, however, and glanced over his shoulder. "Ach, look here, Jamie. The machine's a Macintosh. A bonny Scot brought me back, wouldn't ye know!"

Jamie slammed the door on his speech and turned the key Mark had left in the lock. She heard McAllister's footsteps as he ran forward.

"Let me out, lass!" he shouted, pounding on the other side of the door.

"Not on your life!"

"Lassie, let me out!"

Jamie hung back, with the key to her lips. McAllister was furious. What would he do to her if he got out? Jamie's head began to throb. What could she do? She couldn't trust McAllister, yet she couldn't call the police. Damn it, Mark. Why did he have to collapse now? What was she supposed to do until Mark was well enough to send McAllister back to wherever he came from?

A door slammed downstairs. Mrs. Gipson was back. Jamie stepped closer to the lab door. "Quiet, McAllister! Someone's here."

His pounding ceased and Jamie walked down the stairs to greet Mrs. Gipson as if nothing of any note had transpired while she was gone. That evening she planned to keep Mrs. Gipson as far away as possible from the front of the house, just in case McAllister decided not to cooperate.

Later that night Brett called. Jamie curled up on the parlor sofa to talk to him. At first the sound of his voice was a welcome note of sanity in a totally insane day. She applauded herself for disguising her distraught condition. Brett didn't notice that anything was wrong. She surveyed the ring he had given her as he briefly asked about her trip and her brother. She answered in monosyllables, finding it difficult to concentrate on his small talk. Then he launched into a harangue about how busy they were at the studio and that she should come back in a day or two.

"Brett, I can't come back, not immediately."

"Why not?" His voice buzzed on the other end.

"Mark is sick. He collapsed today."

"Listen, Jamie, I know you love your brother, but for God's sake put him in a hospital or get a nurse. You're not a health professional. You're a photographer. The best there is. And if you don't get your sweet cheeks back here and film that perfume series, we're going to lose the account."

As he spoke Jamie twirled the engagement ring until the diamond setting was underneath her finger. The ring looked much better that way, just a plain gold band. Brett's voice blurred in her ear. She had been pressured by Brett for as long as she had worked with him. Every job was an exercise in pressure, every shooting done under a deadline. His words and threats had little effect. She was weary of deadlines. Tonight, deadlines didn't seem important, not when her brother was half dead upstairs, and something really dead was up there locked in the lab.

"Jamie, are you listening to me?"

"I'm sorry, Brett. You'll have to postpone the shooting. I just can't come back right now."

"Jamie! Hon! Don't do this to me! Not after what I went through to get this client."

"Have Laurie do the shoot. She's good."

"They want you, Jamie. You."

Jamie massaged her temples. "I can't. That's final, Brett."

"You're letting me down, Jamie, I've got to tell you. You're letting yourself down. Opportunities like this don't happen every day."

"Brett, I've got to go. I'm tired. I've got a raging head-ache."

"Sure. See you." His voice was terse as he hung up.

Slowly, Jamie put down the receiver. Why couldn't Brett be more understanding? How could he think that a commercial could be more important than her brother?

Going into the kitchen, Jamie lined up the pills on the kitchen counter near the sink. One white Percodan for her headache, a blue Valium to ease her nerves, and a red and yellow Dalmane to force her eyes to close, no matter what horrors she imagined. Not only was her conscience bothering her about her work, she was worried about Mark and scared to death of Hazard McAllister. With a trio of such topics, she could spend the entire night wide awake in a cold sweat. If she didn't get enough sleep she would lose her edge and become dull and careless, easy prey for a murderous Scotsman. She must not allow herself to get overtired.

Jamie gulped down the pills and then trudged up to Mark's room. She was not about to leave her sick brother alone during the night, not with McAllister around. Jamie pulled the comforter off her bed and dragged it to the recliner in Mark's room. After locking the door from the inside, she stretched out in the chair and settled down for the night. She stared at the ceiling, waiting for the medication to take effect. Why had Hazard McAllister called her Nelle? Did she look like Nelle McMurray, Hazard's intended bride? Jamie shivered. Hazard had killed Nelle. Would he kill her, too?

Somehow, Jamie fell asleep and spent the night without dreaming. Then, close to dawn she awoke at the sound of a gunshot.

4

JAMIE SAT UP, disoriented and confused. Why was she sleeping in her brother's room? And what was that noise she had heard? Squinting her bleary eyes, she tumbled out of the recliner, swaying groggily for a second and feeling lightheaded from the sleeping tablet she had taken earlier. She grabbed her robe and dragged it over her flannel nightshirt as she stumbled out of Mark's room. The noise had sounded like a gunshot. Had the shot come from the lab? She could hear the sounds of a struggle in the room. Jamie paused to force her fuzzy thoughts into a semblance of logic. Suppose Hazard were tricking her. He could be throwing furniture around the room just to make her think someone was in there with him.

She stood in the hallway muddling over what to do when she heard a strange voice shriek, "Get away from me!" That was not the voice of Hazard McAllister, but the ravings of someone who was scared out of his wits.

Jamie rushed back to her room and got the key to the lab. Someone fell against the wall near the door just as she put the key in the lock. Startled, Jamie jumped. Then she heard the unmistakable voice of McAllister bellow. "Ye coward!" She heard fist meet flesh. Whom could he be fighting?

With a trembling hand, Jamie turned the key and opened the door. There stood McAllister holding a strange man at bay. The stranger had a gun in his hand, but from the look on his horrified face, he had discovered his gun had no effect on the hologram. At Jamie's entrance, he glanced her way. His face was ashen with fright. Blood ran from his nose and his left eye was already swelling shut.

"Get him away from me!" he implored as Hazard wrenched the gun from his hand.

McAllister glowered at him and then turned to Jamie. His glittering eyes didn't soften. "Here's what a murderer looks like, Jamie. This man tried t' kill me!"

"Keep him away from me!" the stranger exclaimed. He was a short middle-aged man in a black jacket and slacks. Something about his attire—perhaps the shine of his shoes and the cut of his clothes—struck Jamie as being out of place on a common thief. The stranger reminded her of an undercover cop on a typical television police series. Yet this man was not grappling with a typical television criminal. He was fighting a ghost.

"Get him away!" the stranger cried. "He's crazy!"

"The coward willna fight like a man."

"You're no man!" the stranger cried. "What are you?"

"The Spirit of Christmas Past, ye bugger."

Jamie didn't know what to do. When McAllister took a step closer to the stranger, the frightened man bolted, shoving Jamie aside in his fright. He raced out the door and down the hall with McAllister in hot pursuit. Jamie heard them thunder down the stairs, and she followed.

She saw the stranger fling open the door as McAllister leapt from the last step. Jamie flew down the staircase, holding her robe in one hand, and skidded onto the porch. McAllister sprinted into the darkness, trying to catch the intruder. All she could see in the gloom was his golden hair.

"What in the world is going on?" Mrs. Gipson screeched, bustling into the main hall. Her robe was untied and she wore pink sponge curlers in her hair.

"Someone tried to break into the house."

"Oh, dear! I'll call the police."

"No!" Jamie jerked around. Then she caught herself. She shouldn't raise Mrs. Gipson's suspicions. Jamie brought her voice under control and managed a weak reassuring smile. "It won't be necessary, Mrs. Gipson. Nothing was taken. I think whoever broke in was after my brother's lab equipment."

At that moment, Hazard ran up the walk, his hair wild, his jacket off, and his shirt ripped open. Mrs. Gipson gasped.

"Who's this?"

"Ah—" Jamie grimaced. Hazard had put her in an impossible predicament. He had been seen by Mrs. Gipson, who would spread the news like wildfire if she knew that Hazard McAllister had been resurrected from the spirit world. What could she tell Mrs. Gipson in place of the truth? How could she explain the presence of this tall, unusually dressed man? She must invent something immediately, some kind of cover for the hologram, so that Mrs. Gipson wouldn't suspect anything. Luckily, Hazard's disarray somewhat disguised his outdated clothes and hair. It was dark, Mrs. Gipson was half-asleep. Maybe she could be fooled.

"This is—this is er—Mr. McDougall, a friend of mine,"

she stuttered. "And Mark's. He showed up this afternoon when you were gone. Kind of surprised both of us."

McAllister grinned at her and strode into the light of the porch. "Lost the bugger," he commented. "Sorry, Jamie girl."

"Ooh," Mrs. Gipson exclaimed, smiling. "What a lovely accent!"

"Hastings McDougall," he replied, bestowing a warm smile on her. "An honor t' make your acquaintance, ma'am."

Mrs. Gipson giggled and extended her hand. "Edna Gipson. You can call me Edna, Mr. McDougall."

He shook her hand. Amazed, Jamie watched Hazard slip effortlessly into the identity she had created. He hadn't hesitated for a moment. Being a criminal, he was probably accustomed to quick thinking and deception. Jamie knew she would have to be doubly wary of him.

Mrs. Gipson tied the belt of her robe. "How about a cup of tea, you two? I could use one after all this excitement."

"Oh, I don't think—" Jamie began, but Hazard interrupted her.

"A fine idea, Edna. Let's go in. I'm freezin'."

Jamie glared at him and he winked in return as they followed Mrs. Gipson into the house. How would she get Hazard back to the lab where he could be kept out of trouble? And now that Mrs. Gipson knew about him, what excuse could be used to keep him locked up? Jamie was still worrying about the mechanics of the situation when Mrs. Gipson brought their cups to the table. McAllister raised his mug.

"Here's to the land o' the bens, the glens, an' the fens!"

"Oh, Mr. McDougall," Mrs. Gipson tittered. "The way you talk!"

Jamie shot him a stormy glance.

After tea, McAllister announced that he was going back to the lab to make certain nothing was amiss. Jamie stood up immediately, intending to follow him and not let him out of her sight until she could decide what to do with him.

"I'll go with you."

"Suit yourself."

Jamie turned to Mrs. Gipson. "Why don't you go back to bed, Mrs. Gipson? It's only six-thirty."

"What? After all this excitement? I couldn't sleep a wink!" She carried the teacups to the sink. "I'll make us a nice breakfast."

"You don't have to, Mrs. Gipson."

"I want to. How do you like your eggs, Mr. McDougall?"

"Fried, if you please." Hazard watched in fascination as she squeezed green dishwashing liquid from a plastic container into the sink. He caught himself staring and smiled.

Jamie eyed him warily. Hazard's roguish lopsided smile had a winning effect on Mrs. Gipson. Jamie, however, would not be so easily fooled. Hazard was a criminal, a murderer, and no amount of charm could make her forget his crimes.

At the stairs Hazard insisted that she go first. Afraid that he might try something while her back was turned, Jamie protested. McAllister put his hands on his hips. His ripped shirt opened wide. Before Jamie could avert her eyes she caught a glimpse of his well-defined chest and a bit of his shoulder.

"Listen here, lass. Ye locked me in th' room upstairs. I'll no' have more o' that. There's naught t' be scared of, and that's the end t' it."

"The devil you say," she retorted, using his own phrase. She saw a shadow pass through his eyes. As soon as she had uttered the words, she regretted them. She shouldn't goad him or make him angry. There was no telling what he might do.

"If I wanted t' harm ye," he growled, "I could ha' done sae already. You're but a wee slip of a woman."

"You expect me to trust you?" she asked incredulously. "You're a ghost. You're not even real. And you have killed two people. Maybe more for all I know."

"There ye go again, callin' me a murderer. I'm no murderer. I killed a man once in a duel, but tha' was a fight, fair an' square."

"Then you are forgetting about poor Nelle McMurray? Did your memory slip in a hundred years?"

"Nelle? Murdered?" His voice cracked.

"And your partner. What was his name, William—"

"Bill Bennet?" he exclaimed. His hand grasped the bannister. "I didna kill him. Why would I kill him? Bill was one o' my best friends." He stared at her. "An' Nelle! My God, I loved her!"

"Well, somebody killed them. And stole a lot of money, too. Since you never showed up for the funerals or for anything else, everyone assumed you did it."

Hazard seemed genuinely shocked. He ran a hand through his hair. Jamie paused, and for an instant she believed he was truly puzzled. Then she chided herself for being naive. She was not astute at reading people correctly. Why should she be any better at reading spirits correctly? Hazard was probably lying, trying to trick her into believing he was not a criminal.

"Jamie," McAllister began, "Ye must—"

He was interrupted by the harsh ring of the telephone. At the sound he whirled around.

"It's the phone," she explained as she hurried into the parlor. He slowly followed her into the room and stood in the doorway as she picked up the receiver.

"Hi, hon, it's Brett," came the voice on the other end of the line, although Jamie had difficulty hearing because of the noise in the background. Brett must be calling from a pay phone. Why would he be out of bed this early?

"Brett?" Jamie shot a glance at McAllister. She wished Hazard would give her some privacy, but he remained in the doorway watching her. His surveillance made her nervous. "What are you doing calling at this hour?"

"We're at LAX, Jamie, on our way there."

"Who's at LAX?" Jamie sunk to the sofa.

"Tiffany, Dan, and Jack, and that guy from the agency—"

"Bob Fittro? The writer?"

"Yeah. I just wanted to call and let you know. Listen, I gotta go. They're boarding already."

"Wait a minute, Brett!" Jamie clutched the receiver close to her ear. "What's going on?"

"We're coming up there to do the filming, hon. I thought of it last night. Pure genius, isn't it!"

"Brett—"

"Bye, Jamie. Gotta go. See you this afternoon."

"Brett—you can't come here!"

The dial tone buzzed in her ear for a second before Jamie realized Brett had already hung up. Slowly, she replaced the receiver, sitting in dazed shock and wondering what else could happen to complicate the situation. She glared at Hazard, the source of her misery.

"Who's Brett?" he asked, strolling toward her.

"He's my—" Jamie broke off and looked down at her left hand where the engagement ring should have been. She had forgotten to put it on while preparing for bed the night before. Feeling a twinge of guilt that she had forgotten Brett's ring, she rose. McAllister did not step backward to allow her much space, and she felt as if he were confining her to the sofa until she answered his question. She wished he would just leave her alone.

"Brett's my business partner," she said. "We own a photography studio in Los Angeles, California."

She wrapped her robe more tightly around her nightshirt, suddenly feeling awkward about wearing her nightclothes in the presence of McAllister.

"You own a photography studio?"

"Yes. I'm considered a fair photographer where I come from."

She could see disbelief and amusement twinkling in his eyes. Rankled, she added, "And I make a very good living at it!"

"I didna say otherwise."

"I can see that look in your eye, Mr. McAllister." Jamie brushed past him. "Men in your time didn't think much of women, did they? Well, you've got some surprises in store for you, Mr. McAllister, because in this day and age women aren't content to go around barefoot and pregnant."

"Just barefoot then, eh?" Hazard let his gaze drop to her naked feet. Jamie had forgotten she had run out of Mark's room without putting on her slippers. She blushed as his gaze ran over her feet, up her slender figure, and came to rest on her face. He smiled. "And a neat little pair o' feet, too. I like a woman wi' small feet."

"Mr. McAllister, I don't really care what kind of feet

you like. I just want you to go away. I want you to go back where you came from."

"Ach, lass, dinna say that." Hazard sank to the overstuffed chair next to the couch. "Ye dinna know what it was like for me there. An' ye canna know what it feels like t' be a man again." He leaned forward, resting his forearms on his thighs. " 'Twas a miracle just now, runnin' outside for th' first time in—" He looked up at her. "What's th' year, anyway?"

"1990."

"Saint Andrew! 'Tis been a century!" He stared at the wall, lost in his thoughts for a moment. Jamie surveyed him out of the corner of her eye, never quite turning her back on him.

"A hundred years, lass. I've been a prisoner o' this house for a hundred years. And ye want me t' return t' my cell? 'Tis inhuman!"

"Mr. McAllister, you are inhuman. You are not a man. You may feel like a man and touch and see things like a man, but you are a product of a computer and some highly technical scientific programming. That is all."

He sighed. "Well, no matter what I am, Jamie, ye canna make me go back. I dinna want to. I'll fight ye tooth an' nail. Besides, I dinna know how t' go back, even if I wanted to."

"I thought as much." Jamie frowned. "And your presence here in the house is going to make it very difficult for me when Brett and the crew show up."

"Why is your partner comin' here, anyway?"

"Because he thinks we have to shoot a commercial series this week or the world will collapse."

"What is a commercial?"

"It's a—" Jamie paused and glanced at Hazard. How could she explain a commercial to someone who had never seen a television. And why should she have to explain anything to a ghost, much less answer any of his questions. "It's an advertisement of sorts," she ended lamely.

"Ye dinna want this Brett t' come, do ye?"

"No. The more people who see you, the more complicated this all becomes!"

"Complicated?" McAllister sat down. The tight legs of his turn-of-the-century trousers showed the outlines of his muscular calves. "Why?"

"Why do you think?" Jamie paced to the window. Hazard turned in his chair to watch her. "What if someone finds out who you really are?"

"Why should they? I'm Hastings McDougall. And by th' way, Jamie girl, how did ye ever come up wi' such a name? Th' McDougalls, ach!"

"It was just a name I pulled out of the hat. What do you expect?" She crossed her arms. "You know, to protect your identity, I'll have to make up all sorts of stories about you." She glared at him and he raised his eyebrows, dark brown eyebrows that were as expressive as his lopsided grin. "And I just don't feel up to it."

"Ye've done a fine job so far."

"Just because the story worked with Mrs. Gipson doesn't mean it'll work with Brett and the others."

"I dinna see why not."

"You don't see why not? Look at you!" Jamie turned and gestured toward his tall lean figure. "Your clothes look like something out of a silent movie, your sideburns and moustache belong in a barbershop quartet, and you don't know the first thing about cellular telephones or televisions. How long do you think you'll be able to fool the others?"

"Ye can get me some clothes, Jamie. Ye can show me how t' shave and comb my hair. And I'll learn th' rest."

"In one day? Hazard, they will be here this afternoon."

"This afternoon? I thought you said your partner was in California."

"He is. But he's flying up here on an airplane."

"Flyin', ye say."

Jamie nodded smugly, hoping he would see the futility of his intentions to become a modern man. "Flyin'," she retorted, mimicking him again.

McAllister rose. "Well, we shall have t' gallop then, instead of canter, eh, Jamie girl?"

Jamie sighed. "Wouldn't it be easier if you just stayed up on the third floor where no one ever goes?"

"Ah, you'd make me a prisoner again, would ye?"

"It would be easier."

"And who'll fix the window in the lab where th' intruder broke in? And who'll protect ye, lass, th' next time?"

"I don't need you to protect me."

"Well, I want t', Jamie." His eyes softened as he gazed at her. "I owe ye tha' much, after scarin' ye so."

The vision of the ghost which had beckoned to her on Christmas Eve appeared before Jamie's eyes. But this time the visage of the ghost was overlaid by the vibrant face of the man standing before her. She was surprised when the memory did not clutch her with abject fear as it usually did. In fact, she felt a strange pang of sadness, knowing how drastically this man's appearance had changed once death had snatched away his charm and animation.

Hazard's voice lowered. "And Jamie lass, ye look so much like Nelle, 'tis—"

"Jamie! Hastings!" Mrs. Gipson bustled past the doorway. When she caught a glimpse of Jamie standing by the window in the parlor, she turned. "Oh, there you are! Breakfast is ready, you two."

"Thanks, Edna. We're comin'." Hazard motioned for Jamie to lead the way. She stopped a few paces from him and looked at his face.

"I don't trust you, Mr. McAllister. But at this point, I don't know what else to do."

"It's into th' nineties then?"

"Yes!" She whisked past him, exasperated. "I must be crazy!"

5

"**T**HIS IS A DISPOSABLE RAZOR." Jamie held up the plastic implement and Hazard surveyed it in the mirror while he stood behind her in the small bathroom. A towel was draped around his bare shoulders and his hair was wet, ready to be cut. He had just finished trimming off most of his moustache with a pair of scissors. Jamie met his glance in the mirror and he smiled. His smile made her so nervous that she quickly reached for the can of shaving cream. She sprayed some out on her palm.

"This is shaving cream. It's medicated." She handed the can to him and picked up a towel with which to wipe her hands.

Hazard paused when he saw she was about to wipe her fingers. "Nay, Jamie. Dinna waste what ye have. Here, put it on my cheek." He tilted his head.

The last thing Jamie wanted to do was lay her hands upon Hazard McAllister. But it would seem rude if she declined. In her nervousness she forgot that she was not dealing with a real man. Awkwardly, Jamie spread the white foam along his jawline. She felt a blush spread over her face.

He watched her with a twinkle in his eye as if he enjoyed her embarrassment. "I haven't felt th' touch of a woman for a hundred years," he remarked. "Ye've soft hands, Jamie."

Flustered, she moved away to allow him access to the sink and mirror. She should have left the room, but she didn't. Instead, she made a pretense of folding a towel more neatly and hanging it on the rack. When she looked at him again, he was spraying more shaving cream on his palm. Then his glance darted back to her as he spread the cream over his moustache and the rest of his jaw with deft masculine strokes. "Cat got your tongue?" he asked.

Jamie shook her head and stared back at him. She couldn't help it. Hazard was a handsome male specimen, the most exceptionally built man she had ever seen. His shoulders were mounds of well-developed muscle and his forearms flicked with strong tendons and sinew. His powerful chest narrowed to a trim waist at his belt line. A build like his was attainable only by spending many hours at an athletic club. She wondered what he had done in his past life to develop such a physique. Jamie wished she had her camera to capture his perfection on film.

He put the shaving cream on the edge of the sink in front of him and looked at her in the glass. "When a lass looks at a man th' way you're doin', Jamie, th' man might get th' wrong impression."

Jamie blushed again. "I—I was just—" She crossed her arms and cursed herself for gawking at him. "Mr. McAllister, I am a photographer. When I look at things, I'm visualizing them as a photograph. It's purely professional interest."

"Ah, professional." His eyes crinkled at the corners as

he chuckled and picked up the razor. "Professional, in regard to ladies, had a different connotation in my day."

Jamie stood behind him feeling utterly foolish, and hoped he wouldn't say anything more about her behavior.

"Now show me, Jamie, how t' trim my whiskers."

Thankful that the subject had changed, Jamie stepped closer and lightly traced a line in front of his ear, showing where he should shave.

"That high?" he protested. "I'll feel bare."

"If you want to be a man of the nineties—" she began.

"That I do." He sighed. "Well, here goes." He scraped the razor along his skin, rinsing it in the sink while Jamie watched him. She had never seen a man shave before, not even Brett. McAllister stretched the skin of his neckline tight by tilting his head and made all sorts of contortions as he shaved around his mouth and nose, cutting off his handlebar moustache. Jamie watched him in fascination and marveled at the intimacy of the moment.

Hazard lifted the towel and wiped the remaining bits of foam from his face. When he looked up, Jamie stared anew. Without a moustache, he looked vastly different, so unlike the man in the photograph that her jaw dropped. With his moustache and sideburns, Hazard had reminded her of a country-western singer or a truck driver from Montana. Without them, his face took on a totally different appearance. He was much younger and much more handsome than Jamie had realized.

"Have I cut mysel'?" he questioned, seeing her reaction. "Am I bleedin'?"

"No, you just look so different." She didn't think it prudent to add that he looked disarmingly attractive.

"I'm headin' for the nineties." He laughed and glanced back at his reflection. "I've had hair on my lip since I was a lad. Don't even look like mysel'."

"Wait until I cut your hair." She picked up the scissors. "Ready, Mr. McAllister?" She posed the shears above his head.

"Aye, lass. Do your damage." He strode out of the bathroom and settled in the straight-backed chair Jamie had dragged to the middle of the floor.

Gingerly, so as not to touch his skin, Jamie arranged the towel around his neck to prevent his clipped hair from falling onto his trousers. Jamie lifted a shock of his hair. From what she had seen in his photograph, she remembered that the front section of his hair was worn long and combed back, parted in the middle and held down by a generous application of hair tonic. She snipped off a good three inches and let it fall on the towel. At first she felt self-conscious about standing so close to him and touching him, but soon the job preoccupied her. She snipped her way around his head, taking care not to nip his ears. By the time she finished, his hair was already half dry. She was surprised at how soft it felt, like the hair of a child, spun gold glinting in her fingers. Jamie combed it back, parting it on the left side. She smiled at the waves that would not be tamed, and guessed that McAllister's hair was a bit like his nature—somewhat unruly.

Nearly a half-hour passed before she was done. Her heart pounded in her ears as she finished and asked what he thought of her handiwork. Nervously, she combed a portion above his left ear again and then stood back. McAllister rose up, ran his hand over his hair, tilted his head to one side and then the other, and stared at his reflection.

"Saint Andrew, 'tis short!"

Jamie nodded. "Not too short, I hope."

"Well, at least I willna have t' plaster it down. Never could make it stay."

Jamie held her breath as he surveyed her work again. He was probably not much older than her brother, who was just thirty-five. With his clean new look and his sunny face, there was no denying that Hazard McAllister was an extremely attractive man.

He broke into a smile and removed the towel from his shoulders. "It looks fine, lass. I like it."

Jamie cleaned up the hair on the floor while he brushed himself off and put on his ripped shirt.

"Now all you need are some clothes."

"Aye. No time for a tailor, is there?"

Jamie shook her head. "I'll go to a store downtown and buy you some."

"I can't have you buyin' clothes for me."

"What do you expect to wear? Those?" She pointed to his ripped shirt and wrinkled trousers.

Hazard looked down at himself. "Well, nay. But no woman's ever bought for me before."

"This will be a first for the both of us then. I've never bought clothes for a ghost before, either."

"I'm no ghost, Jamie. I don't know what I am exactly, but I'm sure no ghost."

"Well, you're certainly not a man of flesh and blood."

He was silent while he looked at her. His jaw flinched. Jamie felt a stab of guilt. Had her words offended him? She folded the towel and placed the scissors on it, trying to keep her hands busy while her mind raced. Why should she be concerned with his feelings? He was the creature responsible for all the misery she'd endured, the creature that made her life a mess. Besides, he wasn't really a man. He wasn't even human! And she wasn't about to feel sorry for him.

"Can you give me your shirt size, your inseam length, and waist measurement?"

"I'll not have ye payin'."

"Mr. McAllister—" Jamie sighed, although she felt much safer arguing with him than she did gawking at his altered appearance. Her attraction toward him disconcerted her. "I'm doing this more for my benefit than for yours. If you don't look right, someone is bound to question your identity. Now I intend to buy you some clothes. You can either tell me your size and what colors you prefer, or I will just have to guess."

He narrowed his eyes. "You're a stubborn lass, aren't ye?"

"Me? Stubborn?" Jamie had never thought of herself as stubborn. The peculiar situation into which she had been thrown had forced her to be far more firm than she would have been otherwise. If Brett had accused her of being stubborn, she would have taken offense. Coming from Hazard McAllister, however, the words seemed more like a compliment than a criticism. Jamie shrugged, not betraying the odd pleasure she felt at his words. "Well, maybe a little."

Jamie left the room and put the towel in the laundry. She reserved the scissors and slipped them into the pocket of her cardigan. Why hadn't she thought of the scissors sooner? A small weapon was better than none at all. Even though she knew a gun had been useless against Hazard, she felt a bit more secure with the sharp little scissors in her pocket. Plunged into the right place, they might do more damage than a bullet. Jamie took comfort in the thought, while at the same time she wondered if she need fear Hazard McAllister. So far he had done nothing but smile at her. She slid her hand into the pocket and fingered the scissors. Better to be safe than sorry.

Before she left for town, she checked on Mark. Her brother had slept for most of the morning. She gave him his medicine, tucked the covers around him, and then left the house.

Two hours later Jamie returned, lugging three large sacks. She was thankful that Mrs. Gipson was preparing the guest bedrooms and was too busy to ask where Jamie had been.

She found Hazard in the lab. He had boarded up every window, and was just pounding in the last nail when Jamie walked into the room.

"Thought I'd secure the place," he explained. " 'Twill be harder for a thief t' gain entrance now."

Jamie glanced around the lab. "Do you think he'll come back?"

"He didna get what he came for last night. I heard him tryin' t' get in and jumped him when he climbed through th' window."

"I bet he wanted Mark's camera."

McAllister walked across the room to her, the hammer in his big right fist. Jamie glanced at the tool and wondered if it would become a weapon. A few blows to the skull with that hammer and she could be another McAllister victim. She had forgotten her fear of him again, and chided herself for letting down her guard.

"I—I—I got your clothes. You should try them on before Brett and the crew get here."

"All right." He put the hammer on the computer table. "Where should I change?"

"You don't have a room, do you?"

"Nay. There's a bed and chest on th' third floor. I'll claim it before your friend Brett comes. It's quiet up there."

"Here then." Jamie hoisted the bags into his arms. "I'll get some bed linen for you from Mrs. Gipson."

He took the bags and she hurried downstairs, feeling pressed for time.

A few minutes later she puffed to the top floor, a level never used by her grandmother. Hazard had chosen a room in the tower at the end of the dark hallway. The door was ajar. Jamie paused at the top of the stairs and felt a bolt of fear at the sight of the door.

She clutched the sheets and blankets closer. Two days of insanity had turned her world upside down. Instead of being scared to death of a ghost, she had gone shopping for him. It seemed absurd. But she hadn't had much choice in the matter. Jamie stumbled forward, not sure what to be afraid of anymore. She shuffled the rest of the way to the room and knocked softly.

"Come in, Jamie," Hazard's rich voice called. Jamie opened the door all the way. There stood Hazard, dressed in a pair of dark-blue corduroy slacks, a blue and green shirt, and a slate-blue wool sweater that complemented his eyes, just as she had hoped when selecting the sweater. He looked absolutely gorgeous. Jamie couldn't help but grin at him.

Hazard fumbled with the topmost button of his shirt.

"An' what are ye grinnin' at?" he inquired.

"You!" She put the linens on the bed and strode up to him. "Don't button that," she instructed. Before she thought twice, she reached up and pulled the ends of his collar forward, straightening them at the neckline of the sweater. McAllister gazed down at her. Suddenly she felt self-conscious about her forward behavior. It wasn't like her to fuss over strange men. And it wasn't like her to want to touch a man's chest the way she had almost slid her palms across McAllister's sweater.

"You—you usually don't button the top one unless you wear a tie or something," she stuttered, her glance fluttering back to his face. He was still looking at her with a warm expression in his eyes and a slow smile on his lips. He was much too close for comfort. Jamie backed away.

"I like what ye got for me," he said. "Ye've good taste."

"Thanks." She hugged her arms, not certain what to do with her hands.

"They feel comfortable, too. Th' collars aren't starched, are they?"

"I don't think so. We don't use starch much these days."

"That's what I call progress." He winked at her. She smiled and turned to the bed before his charm could affect her further.

While Hazard put away his new clothes, Jamie made the bed and turned down the comforter. She fluffed the pillows and arranged them against the headboard. When she was finished she turned around to find McAllister watching her. Quickly, he averted his gaze and bent down to pick up the bag of plastic wrap and price tags that lay on the floor. For an uncomfortable moment Jamie stood near the bed, wondering what Hazard had been thinking.

Then down on the street below she heard car doors slamming and the sound of voices. Hazard strode to the circular window and surveyed the activity below him.

"They're here," he remarked. His eyes met Jamie's.

She stepped away from the bed and raised a finger. "I just want to tell you one thing, Mr. McAllister. Don't try anything. Don't even think about it. Brett has a black belt in karate."

"An' what's a black belt in karate?"

"It means he's an expert in a type of martial arts." Jamie put her hand on the doorknob. "It means he could throw you on the floor so fast you wouldn't have time to react."

"Sounds terrifyin'," Hazard drawled.

"Laugh. Go ahead," she retorted. "But he could kill you with his bare hands."

Hazard gazed out the window, measuring each man as he stepped out of the van. "Well, I willna want t' cross your partner Brett then, will I?" He obviously bore little regard for her threat.

Jamie slammed the door, but the image of his grinning face hung in her thoughts.

Jamie hurried down the stairs as Mrs. Gipson opened the door for the guests. In poured the crew, carrying suitcases, cameras, lights, recording equipment, costumes, and makeup kits. Tiffany Denae, the star of the commercials, brought up the rear in her silver fox coat. She wasn't carrying anything but a cigarette. Jamie watched Tiffany pause on the threshold and glance at the main hall.

"My, isn't this charming!" she exclaimed, taking a drag on her cigarette. "Brett, darling, this is just charming, isn't it?"

"Genuine Old World charm," Brett replied as he took off his sunglasses. "Jamie!" He held out his arms for her and kissed her cheek. She was glad to see him, thankful for his protection from Hazard. Brett's breath smelled faintly of gin. He had never liked to fly, and always drank a cocktail or two to settle his nerves.

After the kiss, Brett draped his left arm around her shoulders. For some reason, Brett didn't seem as tall to her as he had before. He stood beside her, his hand hanging over the top of her shoulder in something short of an embrace. She noticed the signet ring he wore on his little finger and was reminded of her engagement ring still sitting on the shelf in her bathroom. Hoping Brett hadn't noticed her bare hand, she shoved it into the pocket of her jeans.

Brett's expensive cologne swirled up and filled the air. "How you doing, hon?"

"Fine. How was your trip?" Jamie nodded to the man who had written the copy for the commercials they were going to shoot. "Hi, Bob."

"Hi, Jamie. Nice old house."

"Thanks."

Brett took off his driving gloves. "The trip was great. We got to see that volcano on the way up. What's the name of it?"

"Mount St. Helens."

"Yeah, that's it." He looked around the entryway. "Well, where shall we put everything?"

"How about the drawing room?" Jamie motioned with her hand. "It's the first door on the left. I think it will hold all the stuff."

"Super." Brett directed the rest of the crew as they unloaded the equipment in the drawing room. Tiffany oozed out of her fur coat and gave it to Mrs. Gipson. The housekeeper ran an appreciative hand over the fur.

"Is it real?" she asked in awe.

Tiffany scorched her with a stare of scorn. "Of course it's real. I wouldn't be caught dead with anything else."

"Tiffany, this is Mrs. Gipson, our housekeeper."

"Hi." Tiffany had beautiful blue eyes, but they were cold and cutting, fixed with an eternal bored expression. She turned her head and her tangle of red hair, caught up in a rebellious side ponytail, flopped against her neck. "Where's the ladies' room, Jamie?"

"Under the stairs to the right."

"Great. My contacts are killing me. Getting up at the crack of dawn and putting those things in after two hours of sleep is just murder on the eyes. I could just kill that Brett if he's made me ruin my eyes. Do they look all red?"

"No." Jamie shook her head. "They look fine."

"They're burning like hell." Tiffany grimaced and minced past them, sleek and seductive in her black leggings and short ruffled skirt. As she turned the corner she left in her wake a mixture of hairspray, vanilla perfume, and cigarette smoke. When a woman smelled like that, how could men find her so irresistible?

Beyond the stairs, the crew slammed doors, shouted instructions at each other, and turned on some rap music loud enough to punctuate every room on the main floor. Mrs. Gipson turned to Jamie with a shocked expression.

"Mrs. Gipson," Jamie said, placing a hand on her shoulder. "Live through this week and you'll be getting a bonus."

6

AFTER DINNER, Brett, Jamie, and Tiffany retired to the parlor where one of the men had built a fire. Brett turned on the stereo equipment stacked near the window, and Jamie sat down to the music of the Miami Sound Machine. Tiffany strolled around the room looking at the antiques Jamie's grandmother had collected, from ancient reading glasses to beautiful beaded purses. Smoke from Tiffany's cigarette rose while she fingered one item after another. Jamie watched her out of the corner of her eye, hoping she would not drop ashes on anything.

More than once during dinner, Jamie had wondered where Hazard McAllister was and what he was doing. She hadn't expected him to remain so scarce. Worry hovered in the back of her thoughts as Brett chatted about plans for filming in the morning.

Brett put his arm around her shoulder and pulled her into his chest. "You look great, hon," he said. "The cold north winds seem to do you good."

"I guess it's not having to contend with the traffic and all those people."

"Yeah, but what do they do for fun in Port Townsend? It's like totally dead up here."

"But it's cute," Tiffany put in, looking at him. "Don't you think it's darling, Brett?"

"There are a few places to go here," Jamie put in. "In fact, there's a jazz club at the foot of the bluff."

"Is there?" Tiffany stood up and took a drag on her cigarette. "Why don't we go check it out?"

"You can if you like, but I want to stay near Mark."

Tiffany minced to the couch and leaned over, displaying the tops of her rounded breasts for Brett's benefit. "How about it, Brett? Why don't we check out the club? Do a little dancing? Maybe Bob and Dan will want to come along."

Brett put down his coffee cup. Jamie surveyed his blond hair cut in the latest style with a small slave tail at his neck. His bangs were spiked and stood up crisp and rigid in the front. He had always seemed fashionable in Los Angeles, with his stylish hair and his silk shirts and baggy rayon pants. But against the backdrop of the old house Brett's modish appearance seemed out of place, almost absurd. Jamie chided herself for being too critical. She had always disliked faddish clothes and favored jeans and sweaters over designer dresses. She was hardly qualified to critique someone else's taste in clothing.

"Come on, Brett," Tiffany begged.

"Well, I don't know—"

"Why not?" Jamie put in. "I don't mind."

"Are you sure, hon?" Brett asked. "I don't want to leave you here all alone."

"Oh, I won't be alone," she answered before thinking

twice. "Mrs. Gipson is here. Besides," she stifled a yawn. "I've had a long day."

"You never were much of a night owl," Tiffany commented as if Jamie had uttered sacrilege.

Brett rose. "Well, if you're certain—"

"I am. I'm going to get my cameras ready for tomorrow and then hit the sack."

She leaned over and pecked Brett on the cheek while Tiffany reached for his hand.

"Come on, darling. Let's do the bright lights."

Jamie watched them go. The entire crew jumped into the van and sped away toward the road on the edge of the bluff. Jamie walked upstairs to Mark's room. The peace and quiet was a welcome change. She had never felt comfortable with the group that had just left, especially Tiffany Denae. Tiffany made an art form of being sensually feminine, which left Jamie feeling inadequate, almost androgynous.

Jamie walked to Mark's bed and gazed down at him. He was sleeping but seemed to be aware that she stood near him. After a moment his eyelids fluttered open.

"Hi, big bully," she greeted.

"Hi," he croaked in return.

"How are you feeling?"

"Well, I won't be playing racquetball tonight, if that's what you had in mind."

Jamie sat down on the mattress. "Can I get you something?"

"That water glass."

Jamie gave him the glass and watched him drink. His forearm was so thin, his elbow so bony that she looked away in dismay. As she turned her head, she caught sight of McAllister. His head nearly reached the top of the doorway.

"Is that you, McAllister?" Mark asked.

"Aye." Hazard strode across the room to the foot of Mark's bed. "How are ye feelin'?"

"Like a truck loaded with nuclear waste just dumped on me."

Hazard, not making sense of his remark, shot a questioning glance at Jamie. She shook her head. "Don't ask," she said.

Mark struggled to sit up. Jamie helped by stuffing pillows behind his back while her brother surveyed the hologram with interest. "What did you do to yourself?" he asked, noting Hazard's changed appearance.

"I've taken on a new identity. 'Twas Jamie's idea, so I wouldn't raise anybody's suspicions."

"Jesus!" Mark swore. "You look great."

"I'm a man of the nineties now. Hastings McDougall, friend o' the family." Hazard gave a mock bow.

Mark laughed, which brought on his cough. Jamie watched him in concern and gave him the water glass again.

"Mark, maybe you're overdoing it."

"Nah." Mark pushed away her hand. "This is fascinating. Is your moustache growing back?"

Hazard ran a hand along his upper lip. "Not yet."

"What about other body functions?"

"I've drunk some tea. Oh, and I ate a bit o' breakfast."

"Has food caused any problems?"

"Didna notice any."

"I've been lying here thinking all day about how you were created. I just can't figure it out. You're a hologram, but much more than a hologram." Mark ran his tongue across his cracked lips. "The only theory I have is that your spirit is made up of some sort of energy field and that it got picked up by the camera and translated by the computer into something tangible."

"Tha' sounds plausible," Hazard said.

"Can you feel hunger? Pain? Can you feel objects?"

Hazard nodded. "I dinna find anything different. I feel just like a real man." He stressed the last word and glared at Jamie. She gave him a sheepish grin. "The only exception 'twas last night when an intruder shot me. The bullet passed through me, clean through me. I dinna think I have any blood."

"An intruder?"

"We think he was after the camera," Jamie explained. "He broke through the window in the lab."

"I've boarded up all the windows, so he won't be comin' in tha' way again."

"Good. We've got to keep this under wraps. I'm not ready to unveil this project yet. Too many people with the wrong ideas could get hold of the technology and abuse it."

"If you tell Jamie here not t' lock me up, I might be able to prevent another robbery. Maybe even catch th' thief this time."

Mark glanced at Jamie. "You locked him up?"

"What else could I do? He's a criminal."

Jamie took a shower and changed into her robe and nightshirt before she remembered her intentions to get ready for the shoot in the morning. She walked downstairs, rubbing her mop of dark blonde hair with a towel, and then checked her equipment in the drawing room. After she finished, she walked past the darkened parlor and noticed a shadowed shape sitting near the window.

"Hazard?" she asked softly, a tremble in her voice.

The figure turned. "Aye, lass." His voice was gruff and for a moment Jamie hesitated.

"Well, come in, then!" Hazard barked.

Jamie walked into the room and eyed Hazard warily. "Where were you all afternoon, Mr. McAllister? You made yourself so scarce I was worried."

"I'm a grown man, Jamie."

"You shouldn't just leave without telling me. What if something happened to you?"

He laughed curtly. "Anythin' tha' was supposed t' happen t' me, lass, has already happened."

"But Mark doesn't want you to—"

"Silence!" he roared. Hazard jumped to his feet so quickly that Jamie stumbled backward, afraid for her life. She scrambled behind the couch, ready to bolt for the hallway at the first sign of trouble.

Hazard glowered at her. "That's enough bloody questions."

For the first time Jamie noticed his eyes. Hazard wasn't angry. He was disturbed but not angry. His eyes smoldered with troubled lights, not rage. Jamie put a hand on the back of the couch.

"Hazard, what's wrong?"

For a long moment he studied her face as if to decide whether or not to divulge his problems. Then he flopped back down in his chair and let out a sigh. "Ye want t' know where I went then."

Jamie took a step closer. "Yes."

"I went t' th' graveyard."

"Why?"

"T' see for myself." His big shoulders sagged, and Jamie felt a surge of compassion sweep through her, tightening her chest.

"I didna believe ye, Jamie, when ye told me Nelle was murdered."

Jamie came from around the couch so she could see his face better. His profile was strong, his nose sharp, his prominent jaw clearly visible in the fading light. "You didn't believe me?" she asked. "Why would I lie about a thing like that?"

"Saints know, lass, saints know."

"So you saw her grave."

"Aye. She was but twenty-five. Twenty-five! And if ye mention again tha' I did her in, sae help me I'll lay ye low, Jamie, no matter how much ye look like her!"

"I was only repeating what the history books say about you."

His eyes narrowed. "An' wha' *do* they say about Hazard McAllister?"

"That you killed two people on Christmas Eve in this very house, right in your own study. Then you absconded with money belonging to the railroad project and were never seen again."

"And what else do they say?"

"Why, nothing else. Is there more?"

"More, ye ask? As if my whole life were nothin'? So, history finds me a murderin' scoundrel, eh? They canna find anythin' better t' say about an immigrant Scotsman tryin' t' better himsel'." He shook his head, his tone bitter. "Ah, nothin' changes, Jamie. Nothin' a'tall. A Scotsman takin' th' blame again for somethin' he never had a hand in."

"Well, you did disappear. It did seem suspicious."

The scorn in Hazard's eyes filled Jamie with hot shame. "Do I look like a murderer?" he demanded, rising to his feet. "Do you think I'm a killer, Jamie?" He held his hands away from his sides. "Look at me now."

Jamie looked, her cheeks burning. "Well, it's hard to say—you've got quite a temper."

"Any man with a bit o' passion has a temper. It's th' cold fish ye must worry about. Th' cold fish tha' can kill and blame his crime on some other poor soul."

"Then who did it?"

Hazard let his arms drop. "I dinna know! I wish t' God I did! I'd like t' kill the bastard that murdered Nelle! But I'm just a bit late for that, aren't I?" He scowled. "And you, Jamie girl. You stand there pale as a sheet. Ye dinna trust me even a wee bit, do ye lass?"

"It's hard to decide what to believe without proof of some kind."

"But your heart, lass. What does your heart tell ye?"

"My heart? I don't take things on faith, Mr. McAllister."

"But ye must not mistrust me altogether. Otherwise ye would not be here. You'd be hiding behind tha' Brett Johansen, shakin' in your shoes."

He stepped toward the parlor window. For a minute he stood in silence, as if dealing with his grief and anger alone. Then he slid his hands into his pockets and sighed.

" 'Tis still a beautiful sight," he murmured. "Though 'tis but a ghost town now." Jamie came up behind the chair in which he'd been sitting. Deep down she wasn't frightened of Hazard McAllister, but she could not give a logical reason for her fearlessness. Even more surprising, she was not at all anxious to end their conversation. Jamie followed his line of sight.

Far below the bluff the lights of the city twinkled. Beyond them were the lights of the ferry coming in to dock, and away in the distance points of light flickered on Whidbey Island. Bucking the tide off Point Wilson at the end of the peninsula two large ships sailed silently out to the open sea.

"Like lights pulled on a velvet ribbon," Hazard commented. Jamie looked at the tankers in surprise. She had never thought of them as subjects of poetry. She didn't say anything, but felt no pressure to make conversation. Instead, she leaned against the back of the sofa behind her and crossed her arms, content to gaze at the glittering nightscape.

"The night has a thousand eyes," Hazard went on. "The night has a thousand eyes. And the day but one. Yet the light o' the bright world dies, wi' the dyin' sun."

Jamie closed her eyes and listened to the deep tones of his voice. Oddly enough, his voice had a soothing effect.

"The mind has a thousand eyes, and the heart but one. Yet the light of a whole life dies when love is done." His voice trailed off as he sat down in the chair.

"That was beautiful," Jamie remarked softly. "Did you make it up?"

"No. 'Twas Bourdillon, a French poet whose works I once admired. Some poets ye can never forget."

Jamie shifted against the couch. "Do you mind if I ask something personal?"

"Fire away, lass."

"What was it like, being a ghost?"

"Well—" Hazard rubbed his chin. " 'Twas like a dream. I could hear things, but in a muted sort o' way. And I could see things, but in a filmy sort o' way. I had no physical power t' do anything. And I would drift in and out o' the dream, always comin' back t' this house and never goin' anywhere else. It was a confusin' and lonely place. And I didna want t' be there." He looked down and paused. " 'Tis a relief, Jamie, to be back in this world, back wi' people again. I'm sae grateful t' Mark."

Jamie hung her head, listening to words she could have uttered concerning her own life in Los Angeles. She had always felt adrift, without a true friend or confidant with whom to share her troubles. Her talent as a photographer had plunged her into a fast-paced life that was as filmy and unclear as Hazard's dream. She had never felt comfortable around the agents and actors she had to work with or with the indulgent, materialistic lifestyle that was part of the successful L.A. attitude. At first she had thought she was uncomfortable because life in L.A. was so foreign to her, but as the years flew by, she felt more desperately adrift, more out of place than ever before.

Hazard's words struck a chord deep inside Jamie. She knew just what he was saying. Confusion and loneliness were her daily companions. She swallowed and blinked quickly to avoid spilling tears.

"Sorry, I dinna mean t' ramble," he said.

Jamie gave him a tremulous smile. "It's all right. I think I know what you mean."

He fell silent as if remembering his past century of confinement in the spirit world. Or perhaps he simply gazed at the night beyond the window. She wasn't certain.

"If you don't mind my asking," Jamie said at length, "how—how did you die?"

" 'Tis an interesting question." Hazard rose to his feet and slipped his hands in the pockets of his slacks. "Would ye believe I canna recall th' incident?"

"You don't know how you died?"

"Nay. Ye know how ye forget things—bad things tha' happen to ye?"

"I wouldn't think you could forget your own death."

"Well, I dinna know what laid me low, that's for certain." He picked up the remote control to the stereo and flipped it over in his hands.

"What's this, lass?"

"A remote control." She explained its use and Hazard pointed it at the stereo. He pushed buttons until the radio came on, blaring.

"Turn it down!" Jamie cried, laughing at the horrified expression on his face. "Hit volume."

Hazard clicked and pointed, but couldn't affect the music. Jamie jumped to her feet and guided the remote in his hand toward the receiver. Though she knew he possessed a human body temperature, she was still surprised by the warmth of his skin.

"Press it, Hazard!" she urged.

He obeyed and the music quieted.

"Press the button marked tuner until you get to one-oh-seven-point-nine," she continued.

He complied. The music changed from an earsplitting rock-and-roll riff to a soft guitar instrumental. Hazard smiled his lopsided grin. "Do ye think I cracked th' plaster on th' ceilin'?"

Chuckling, Jamie glanced up. "I wouldn't be surprised."

Jamie couldn't sleep. She heard the van return and the muted laughter of the crew coming into the house. Someone turned on music in the parlor directly below her room, and the driving beat of the bass drum kept her awake. Wishing she had ear plugs, Jamie tumbled out of bed. If she couldn't sleep, maybe Mark couldn't either and needed someone to talk to. She pulled on her robe and pattered down the hall. Carefully, she opened his door and peeked around it to see if he was asleep. His light was off. She could hear him snoring quietly. Jamie pulled the door shut, latched it, and nearly cried out when she saw McAllister standing at the doorway of the lab.

"Don't scare me like that!" she whispered.

He held up his hands. "I didna mean to. I heard ye walkin' in the hall and wondered who was roamin' about."

"I can't sleep," she explained, tying the belt of her robe. "All that noise downstairs—"

"You should move. In fact, Jamie, I was thinkin' about th' location of your room. Look here." Hazard motioned for her to follow him into her bedroom. He walked to the window and drew back the curtain. "Someone could easily get up on th' roof and come in this way. See how th' roof o' th' porch comes close t' your window?"

Jamie padded across the room and joined him at the window. He was correct.

"I never even thought about it. But I don't want to move all my things, not tonight," she said. "Couldn't you do something to the window?"

Hazard surveyed the window sash. "We could put a small board on th' side o' th' top pane there, so th' window can't be raised."

"That sounds reasonable."

"I'll get somethin' from th' lab. Your brother has all sorts o' odds and ends in there."

Hazard strode out of the bedroom while Jamie brushed the tangles out of her hair. She was still brushing when McAllister appeared with a one-by-two piece of wood. It fit snugly, as if he had made it to order. Jamie stood in the bathroom doorway with the hairbrush in her hand.

"What an eye, eh?" McAllister commented. " 'Twas just a guess."

"It's just the right fit."

Hazard closed the curtains. "You'll be a wee bit safer now."

"Thanks." She expected him to leave, but he paused when his gaze fell on the photograph at her bedside table. In a silver frame was a snapshot of her and Brett dressed for the Clio Awards. Hazard picked up the frame and inspected the photo.

"This is you?" he asked.

Jamie nodded. She had never liked that picture of herself in which she was dressed in black satin and long diamond earrings. She didn't look bad, just not her usual conservative self. She kept the photograph mainly because it was the best candid shot of Brett that she possessed.

"We're getting ready to go to an awards ceremony," she put in.

"Ye look fetchin'." He glanced at her from across the bed and smiled.

"I can be attractive when I work at it."

"I think ye look attractive now."

Jamie blushed. She hadn't expected flattery from a hologram. "What—in this old robe?"

"Ye look vulnerable. Soft."

For a moment Jamie gazed at him, unnerved. Hazard had a way with words and a voice to make the words magical. She had never heard such a seductive phrase stated so simply. What unnerved her most, however, was the fact that his words sounded genuine. And yet, whom was he actually seeing—Nelle McMurray or her?

Before she could utter a syllable, Brett rapped on her half-open door. "Knock knock, Miss Kent. Room service."

Jamie snapped from her trance and turned to the door. There stood her fiancé in his hand-painted silk robe. In his hands he held a tray with a bottle of wine and two glasses. He grinned a tipsy grin at her, trying to charm her with a boyish smile.

"I—I didn't call for room service," she replied, laying a hand on the doorknob. Brett couldn't see Hazard McAllister from his position. She wanted to keep it that way, and planned to block Brett's advance into the room.

"Aw, have some wine, Jamie." He raised the bottle with one hand and nearly lost his hold on the tray with the other. Jamie caught the goblets before they fell to the floor. "I got this 'specially for you. It's your favorite fumé blanc."

Jamie glanced at the label and shook her head. "Not tonight, Brett. You've had enough by the looks of things."

Brett frowned and lowered the bottle. His hair smelled of cigarette smoke. "You're no fun, Jamie," he said in a surly tone of voice. "No fun at all. Why don't you loosen up sometime and have some fun?"

He stepped into the room, much to Jamie's alarm. What if Brett should see McAllister? How would she explain the presence of a stranger in her bedroom? She moved to the wall next to the door, hoping Brett would face her and keep his back to McAllister.

Brett put the tray on a chair near the dresser and then turned to Jamie. She glared at him warily, knowing well the gleam in his eye. "Now, don't get all nervous, Jamie," he began and sidled up to her. He put both palms on the wall beside her head and trapped her. His breath was sharp with the smell of gin. "I just want a kiss. Haven't got a decent kiss since I got here."

"Brett—"

He bent to her mouth but she turned her head aside. He paused and then rubbed against her. "Jamie, I'm horny as hell."

"Brett—" She pushed away from him, offended by his

behavior. Did Brett expect her to jump into bed with him? She wasn't interested, especially not when he was drunk. In the back of her mind Jamie could hear the voice of Aunt Evelyn saying, "Don't be silly, Jamie. All your little friends like Barbie dolls." Or in this case Ken dolls, Jamie thought wryly. But she had never been able to let herself succumb to Brett's advances. Something had always held her back. She had often worried about her lack of response to Brett, and hoped it was merely her sense of chastity and not a psychological hang-up about men. "What do you expect me to do?"

"What any red-blooded American girl would do." He lowered his head and nuzzled the top of her shoulder. Jamie looked up to see Hazard watching from the other side of the room. She stiffened.

"Jamie!" Brett kissed her neck but his kisses had no effect on her. "Jamie, I want you. I've wanted you for months now! Let's go to bed." He fondled her left breast. "The time is right."

She pulled away from his lips. "Brett, no!" In a jerky movement, she ducked under his arm and broke free of his body, but he caught her arm before she could dart away.

He glared at her. "Dammit, Jamie, I've been patient. And you just string me along." His eyes were bleary with drunken anger. "Like some goddamn puppet."

"Brett!" she cried as he roughly pulled her against him.

"I've had it with your excuses, Jamie!" He forced down the shoulder of her robe and nightshirt to expose her ivory shoulders and the tops of her breasts. Frightened and angry, Jamie struggled against him.

"Brett!"

"It's time, Jamie." He kissed her while she tried to dodge his mouth.

"The lassie told ye no," a voice declared from across the room.

Brett jerked to attention. "What in hell—" he blurted, turning toward the sound of the strange voice with the even stranger accent.

Deliberately, McAllister put Jamie's photograph back down on the night stand without taking his eyes off Brett. "Leave the lass alone," he commanded.

Brett dropped his hands from Jamie's shoulders and she fell backward, still holding the wine glasses. Hazard strode around the end of the bed and stopped a few feet from Brett and Jamie.

"Who in hell are you?" Brett demanded.

Jamie looked from one man to the other, feeling ashamed of Brett's behavior, but also highly aware that two males were confronting each other because of her. It was a primal sensation, one she had never experienced. She felt strangely aroused by the way Hazard had come to her defense, and slightly frightened for Brett.

"The name's Hastings McDougall."

"What in hell are you doing in Jamie's room?"

"I could ask th' same o' you."

Brett's gaze shot from Hazard's tawny hair to his feet planted firmly on the ground. Then he turned to Jamie. "Hon, who is this clown?"

Jamie watched in horror as Hazard's eyes flared with anger. She was well aware that Hazard had a quick temper and a set of fists to back it up. Hazard grabbed a handful of silk robe and nearly wrenched Brett off his feet.

"Careful, now, with your bloody insults." His blue eyes were dark and threatening.

Brett looked up at the stormy face of the hologram and tried to wriggle free. But he couldn't break away from

Hazard's grip. Hazard tightened his hold and Brett choked.

"Jamie told ye no. An' she meant it."

"Come on, man." Brett gave a nervous laugh. "Chill out. You know how women are. They say no, but they mean yes."

"The devil ye say!" Hazard threw him across the room. Brett landed on his rear and slid into the dresser, knocking his head against a drawer pull. He clapped a hand to his skull.

"Goddammit!" he swore, wincing. Hazard lunged for him.

"McDougall, don't!" Jamie cried. "He's drunk. He didn't mean it!"

Hazard yanked Brett to his feet. "Hie out o' here," he ordered. "Before I break your blisterin' head wide open!" Hazard released him with a disgusted shove and Brett stumbled backward, holding his head.

"Ye can thank Jamie that I didna thrash ye."

Jamie stood in the middle of the room, uncertain whether she should comfort Brett or stand beside Hazard, so she remained where she was, holding the two wine glasses, like a bad imitation of Hellenic sculpture.

Brett glowered at her. "I'll want an explanation of all this," he said.

"Ye deserve none," Hazard interjected.

Brett shot a malicious glance at the tall blond man standing next to Jamie and then he wobbled his way into the hall.

Jamie watched him leave. She was in a daze and couldn't move. Not until Hazard touched her arm did she come to her senses.

"Are you all right, Jamie girl?"

"I think so." She gave him a shallow smile. "Thanks."

Hazard crossed his arms. "I can put sticks in the windows, but I canna nail boards across your door."

"I'll be okay. Brett was just a little drunk, that's all."

Hazard surveyed her as if to judge for himself whether or not she was truly all right, and then he strode to the door. He turned at the threshold.

"Black belt in karate, eh?"

Jamie shrugged sheepishly.

7

"ALL RIGHT, take one! Action!"

Jamie watched through her camera as she filmed the first take of the commercial series. Brett stood near her elbow, cranky and hungover from his indulgence the night before. He claimed that he had not intended to force himself on Jamie, and that she and her Scottish friend had misinterpreted his actions. Jamie didn't believe him but decided not to argue. She had enough on her mind without adding more drama to her personal affairs.

All night she had tossed and turned, unable to sleep. Brett's amorous advance had really shocked her. She had never dreamed he might someday ignore her request to leave her alone. Granted, he had been drunk, but drunkenness did not give him permission to rape her. If Hazard had not been in the room, Brett would have taken her against her will.

At the thought of Hazard, Jamie flushed. She had been deeply affected by the way he had come to her defense. No one had ever fought her personal battles for her before. In fact no one had ever given her much support at all. She also couldn't forget what Hazard had said to her before Brett had interrupted them. He had told her she was attractive. Soft. Vulnerable. Jamie shook her head in an effort to rid her thoughts of the sound of his voice. Hazard McAllister could roll a few syllables off his Scottish tongue and turn the most common words into poetry. He must have been quite the ladies' man in his day.

Jamie checked her light meter for the tenth time, trying to distract herself from thinking about McAllister. But his words hung in her thoughts. "Ye look vulnerable. Soft. I think you're attractive now."

What did it matter how Hazard perceived her? He had no business saying such things to her. What did he think he would gain from such flattery? Jamie frowned. Then she heard the sound of a female voice chattering in the hall, and she looked up from her camera. Tiffany had finally arrived to start the day's work.

Bob Fittro directed the actors from the sidelines. Rick Covington, a male actor from Seattle, had ferried over that morning. Jamie had used Rick in previous ads and he had always done a good job. She anticipated an easy and productive film session. In the commercial Rick portrayed a sea captain coming home to his wife-mistress after a long voyage.

"Burst through the door," Fittro said.

Rick opened the door, caught his foot on the rug and stumbled. Everyone chuckled and Rick sheepishly returned to the porch.

"Cut!"

"Take two. Action."

Once again Rick opened the door and rushed into the house. He was wearing a dark-blue jacket, captain's hat, and tall black boots. He looked dapper—not a hair out of place, not a button unfastened, not a scuff on the sheen of his boots. Up to the stairs he strode where he met Tiffany. She came floating down from the first landing, all silk and bows, her red hair flowing behind her.

"Now fall into his arms," Fittro directed. "Drape yourself over him, Tiffany. That's right."

Tiffany tried to drape, but frowned and shook her head. "Cut," she said. "I didn't drape drapey enough."

Bob Fittro and Jamie exchanged knowing glances. They knew the prima donna antics of Tiffany Denae. Even though she did commercial work, she took her acting quite seriously and fancied herself a great dramatist.

"Take three."

The morning wore on with countless takes. Something wasn't clicking, something wasn't right. Even Brett, who tended to rush through shoots, wasn't satisfied. Jamie watched Rick Covington embrace Tiffany. He was too wooden, almost awkward, and Tiffany was too tall for him. Jamie tried to avoid the height problem by concentrating on close-ups, but even then the lack of chemistry was apparent.

Jamie zoomed back and her camera took in the entire main hall. She was surprised to discover Hazard McAllister had come down to watch the film session. He leaned against the doorjamb of the parlor and observed the proceedings with a twinkle in his eye. He was dressed in a thick, cabled fisherman's sweater and a pair of jeans. The sweater accentuated his wide shoulders while the jeans displayed the trim line of his hips and legs. Jamie zoomed in on his face and studied him for an instant. He was a handsome man, ruggedly good-looking, with sharp planes for cheekbones, ruddy coloring, and a cleft in his chin.

As she zoomed back from viewing Hazard, she heard Tiffany drawl out, "Well now—" in the most seductive tone Jamie had ever heard. Jamie glanced up from the camera, wondering what Tiffany had seen. She should have known that the redhead had caught her first glimpse of Hazard McAllister.

"Just who might you be?" Tiffany inquired, leaning over the stair railing. Hazard pulled away from the doorway when he realized the actress was addressing him. Tiffany chuckled in her low, throaty voice. Perhaps it was her voice men could not resist. "Yes, you, Mr. America."

Out of the corner of her eye, Jamie saw Brett take a big gulp of his Bloody Mary.

"Th' name's McDougall, lass."

"Ah!" Tiffany tilted her head. "Listen to that Irish accent."

Hazard glared at her. " 'Tis Scottish, I'll have ye know."

"Scottish, Irish, whatever." Tiffany smiled and rippled her spine seductively while Jamie watched in disgust. "Why don't you come over here and have a screen test?"

"We're wasting time, Tiffany," Brett interjected. "And time is money."

Tiffany grimaced at Brett and then turned back to Hazard. "I'll bet a man like you knows all about Intimacy."

Hazard stared at her, slightly confused by her embarrassing topic of conversation with a stranger. "Come again?" he choked.

Tiffany oozed down the stairs, enjoying the perplexed expression she had produced on his face. She dragged her fingertips along the bannister as she might drag her polished nails down a man's naked chest.

"Don't you know what Intimacy is, Mr. McDougall?" she taunted. One of the crew members smothered a guffaw and Hazard shot a glance his way, realizing he was being made the brunt of a joke.

Tiffany giggled and sidled up to Hazard, picking up a

bottle of perfume from the small table near the bottom of the stairs.

"See?" she laughed, spritzing some of the liquid onto his neck. "It's a perfume."

"Ach!" Hazard wiped his jaw, annoyed at having been branded with the cloying scent. "Intimacy never smelled like tha' t' me."

Bob Fittro sputtered with laughter at Hazard's reply.

Tiffany, surprised that Hazard had made such a quick comeback, lowered the bottle. Obviously, she had assumed the handsome Scotsman was all brawn and good looks like most of her other costars. That he had a brain was a pleasant departure from the norm. Her blue eyes, made a startling turquoise by tinted contacts, flashed sparks at him.

Jamie observed Tiffany's antics with increasing disgust tinged with jealousy, the latter reaction coming as a shock to her. Why should she be jealous of Hazard McAllister? Who cared if Tiffany made his blood—or whatever flowed in his veins—race with desire. It wasn't any of her concern.

Yet she was secretly gratified that Hazard's response to Tiffany was not the usual response the woman got from a man. Hazard's eyes didn't linger on her lithe figure, her ample breasts, or her petulant mouth. In fact, Hazard's eyes didn't linger on her at all, even when she lay her hand upon his arm and said something to him that no one else could hear.

Jamie had seen enough. She shut off her camera with a snap. "All right. That's it, everybody. Break time. Smells like coffee in the kitchen."

"God, I could use a cup," Brett muttered. "Got some of your headache tablets, Jamie?"

"They're on the windowsill above the kitchen sink."

Brett pried Tiffany away from Hazard and dragged her into the kitchen, reminding her of the work to be done. Flirting with house guests would have to wait until after the shoot. Rick Covington followed them, complaining about his lines.

Bob Fittro put down his script and took off his glasses while Jamie stuffed her hands in the rear pockets of her jeans. Bob strolled across the room to her.

"What do you think?" she asked.

Bob shook his head. "It just isn't happening. I have this vision you know, of a romantic figure sweeping a damsel off her feet. I don't know what it is—Rick's good for stills, but he's just not pulling this one off."

"I agree. He's a mannequin."

"He's too short for Tiffany."

"I noticed that, too." Jamie looked over Bob's shoulder as Hazard approached the camera.

"Good mornin', Jamie," he greeted.

"Hi." She glanced at his face, still grappling with the strange tide of jealousy that had swept through her a moment ago. Struggling to gain her composure, Jamie introduced Bob to Hazard.

Bob replaced his glasses on his nose. "I liked the way you handled Tiffany," he remarked. "She can be such a bitch sometimes. You into film?"

Hazard chuckled. "Not in th' least."

"He's Mark's friend," Jamie put in.

"Ah, a computer buff."

"Nay, 'tis a seaman I am."

"You don't say!" Fittro gave him a measured glance over the top of his glasses. "You're a big guy, too. And I like that accent. Sounds so authentic."

" 'Tis authentic," Hazard replied, frowning. "I'm a Highlander born an' bred."

"Tell me, Mr. McDougall. As a sailing man, what do you think of the scene we're trying to film here?"

Jamie shook her head, certain that Hazard didn't know a thing about the morning's activities. But Hazard wasn't the least reluctant to make a reply.

"Well, I'll tell ye one thing, Mr. Fittro. If I were a lass, I wouldna run into th' arms o' tha' man."

"Oh?" Bob chewed the wing of his glasses. "Why not?"

"He's no' the kind o' man t' interest a woman. He's a mollycoddle."

"A mollycoddle?"

"Aye. Too tame. Too scrubbed. Women like a man with a bit o' mystery, a bit o' danger. Somethin' tha' scares them a wee bit."

Jamie felt a chill race down the back of her arms.

"They like a man tha' can control them, no' by force mind ye, but by sheer male energy."

Fittro nodded, captivated.

"And, I canna remember a seaman tha' buttoned his coat all th' way. A seaman's a free spirit, an active man who needs room t' move 'round. And one more thing, th' redhead doesna like him."

"How can you tell?" Jamie asked.

Hazard gazed down at her and smiled. "You can see if a lass favors a lad by th' way she looks at him."

"Oh?" Jamie's voice went hoarse. Did Hazard think she favored him because of the way she had taken his measure while he shaved? Had he noticed her observing him through the camera? She would have to quit staring at him so openly; she didn't want to give him the wrong impression. Although she found him handsome, she knew the attraction must end at simple physical appreciation.

Bob looked at Jamie and raised his eyebrows. "Are you thinking what I'm thinking?" he asked.

Jamie thought she knew what he was hinting at, but couldn't believe it. Hazard in a commercial? It wasn't possible.

That afternoon the film session continued. Rick Covington had been sent on his way, with a promise of a call if they needed him again. Brett had agreed to try McAllister in the commercial if only to make a fool of him. Brett stood on the sidelines drinking another Bloody Mary and gloating. Jamie was worried. If there was a sure way to humiliate a man, it was while filming, when he was onstage for everyone to ridicule and criticize. She had voiced her reluctance to use Hazard, but the rest of the crew thought the idea was great and overruled her.

"Take one. Action!"

Hazard burst through the door. He wore the same dark jacket over his cabled sweater, only none of the buttons were fastened. The cap was jauntily tilted on his head, and he carried a duffel bag over his shoulder. As he broke through the door, he swung down the bag and looked up at Tiffany. Their eyes met and locked for an instant and then he strode to the stairs just as she hit the last step. Into his arms she leapt, and he embraced her, swinging her around in joy and kissing her neck and then her lips as he held her aloft. Their mouths pressed together fervently, as if they truly hadn't seen each other for a long time. Tiffany's hair fell in ripples to his broad shoulders. Right at the last moment a shaft of sunlight poured through the window by the door and set their heads aglow. It was a perfect cinematic moment.

"Cut!" Brett called.

Jamie's gaze was riveted to the scene on the stairs. She couldn't stop staring at Hazard as he kissed Tiffany. She gaped at the way his mouth covered Tiffany's and the way his hands caught her around her ribs with his thumbs under her breasts, and the way Tiffany's white hands spread out at the base of Hazard's neck. Jamie could almost imagine her own hands there, her own lips pressed into his.

"Cut!" Brett called again.

Tiffany leaned into McAllister and twined her hands in his hair, knocking his hat to the floor, kissing him in earnest. Slowly, Hazard lowered her to the step and pulled away from her mouth.

"Cut, dammit!" Brett yelled.

The entire crew, including Jamie, was mesmerized by the scene. Hazard was a natural in front of the camera, undeniably natural, and something magical had just occurred between the two actors. Jamie was sure a single take was all that would be required.

"Do we need to do another take?" Bob inquired.

"God, yes!" Tiffany smoothed the bodice of her gown and put a hand to her hair. She breathed heavily, obviously aroused by Hazard's kiss. "I think we're going to have to put in some overtime on this one." She eyed Hazard. He gave her a smile but did not return her sultry stare.

"What do you think, Jamie?" Brett asked.

Jamie had to get control of herself. The scene had set her heart racing. Her tongue was dry. Her knees were shaky. She could not believe how the kiss had affected her. "Definitely a wrap," she finally replied. "That's it. Good job, you two."

"And McDougall can do a voice-over," Fittro put in. "With that accent, it'll be the icing on the cake. I'll rewrite the script and he can cut it tomorrow."

While Hazard took off the coat, Brett scowled. He had missed his opportunity to ridicule McDougall.

"I'll transfer this to tape right away," Jamie added. She was anxious to see the footage again. If it was half as good as she thought it was, it would be another award winner.

"Well, I'm ready for dinner," Tiffany remarked. "That kiss whetted my appetite."

"For raw steak?" Fittro drawled.

Tiffany smirked at him. "How about it, everyone? Shall we try that little restaurant on the water?"

Brett turned to Jamie. "Don't tell me—you have to stay with Mark, right?"

"Actually, I'd like to do some editing on tape. I'm anxious to see how it comes out."

"All work and no play—" Tiffany wagged a finger at her. "Makes Jill a dull girl."

"She's always been like that," Brett replied. "Go change, Tiff." He gave Tiffany a slap on the rump. "We'll wait for you."

He looked over his shoulder to see if his gesture had any effect on Jamie, but she wasn't the least bit jealous. She noticed his frown and glanced away, struck with the sudden realization that she didn't care what Brett did to Tiffany, or to any other woman for that matter. She knew she should care and blamed her reserved nature for her lack of interest, altogether forgetting how jealous she had been of Hazard.

"How about you, McDougall?" Bob Fittro asked, folding his glasses and putting them in the pocket of his shirt. "Care to join us?"

"What's th' hour?" Hazard replied.

Brett turned his wrist. "Four."

Hazard nodded. "I've got some business in town, if ye would be sae kind t' give me a lift."

Jamie shot him a glance full of alarm.

"Nay, dinna worry, Jamie," he commented. "I'll not be gone long."

Brett observed their conversation as his brows drew together. Jamie strove to keep her voice level to conceal her panic while she grabbed at a reason to make Hazard stay. McAllister was going out? What business had he in town? What if something should happen to him? What if someone should recognize him?

Jamie must not have done an adequate job of concealing her concern because Brett stepped forward and took her by the shoulders. "Jamie, look at you. You're getting all worked up about nothing. When are you going to get it through your head? This house can't hurt you. There are no such things as ghosts."

"But—" Jamie's eyes were wide with alarm.

Brett shook his head. "You've got to face it sometime, Jamie."

"Brett, I'm not—" She broke off, unable to explain the reason for her agitation.

He addressed her in a tone of voice as if speaking to a child. "Listen, hon. Mark is here and Mrs. Gipson is here. You won't be alone."

"There was an intruder the other night," Hazard put in. "That's what th' lass is fearin'. No' ghosts. She's no' afraid o' ghosts."

"The hell she isn't!" Brett snorted in derision. "Jamie's spent half her life running from what she thought was a ghost in this very house."

"Ye dinna say."

"She's obsessed with this McAllister ghost. And I think she needs to deal with it. Right here. Right now."

"Brett, you don't know what you're talking about!" Jamie retorted, her cheeks flushed.

"You're not going to exorcise a ghost by writing a biography of him. The only way is to face this house on your own, until you realize that no ghost exists, other than the one in your imagination."

"You think I should stay the entire night alone with a single candle, just like in the movies?" she replied. Her voice was chilled. "That's your idea of therapy, Mr. Hollywood?"

Brett glared at her. "Nothing else has worked."

At Brett's harsh words, Hazard encircled Jamie's shoulder with his arm and tucked her gently against his torso. His protective gesture had a peculiar warming effect on Jamie. Her resentment of Brett's remarks melted in an instant. For the first time in her life she felt the support of someone who believed her absolutely, someone who shared a secret with her. The combined feeling of support and camaraderie sent a bolt of heat straight to her heart.

With it, the huge festering hole of self-doubt that had burned in Jamie since childhood shrank two sizes. Hazard's hand drew all the poison from the wound, freeing her of an ache that had paralyzed her for years. She couldn't speak, she couldn't move. She could only stand beneath his hand, thunderstruck by the sensation of his embrace and his presence, praying he would not step away from her.

"Dinna trouble yourself, Brett," Hazard said, his voice rumbling against Jamie's ribs. "Jamie's not afraid o' ghosts."

"Not afraid?" Brett sneered, put off by the familiarity between the Scotsman and his fiancé. "And how would you know, McDougall. Are you some kind of a shrink?"

"I'm a friend o' th' family, Brett. A very old friend o' th' family."

8

JAMIE SPENT ANOTHER FITFUL NIGHT worrying about Hazard. He hadn't returned by the time she retired. But she could do nothing. She couldn't alert the authorities with a request to find a missing one-hundred-year-old ghost in the form of a hologram. So she had to wait.

She found Hazard in Mark's room early the next morning deep in a discussion about computers. Obviously, Mark had been teaching Hazard the rudiments of the new technology. Hazard flipped through a printout, quoting figures and making predictions. He seemed to have picked up a fair amount of knowledge and was holding his own in a discussion that had entirely lost Jamie. She sat in the chair near Mark's bed and tried to coax him to eat some toast and honey while the men talked.

Mrs. Gipson bustled into the bedroom with a stack of envelopes for Mark.

"No mail for me?" Jamie asked.

"No, dear." Mrs. Gipson reached for the drapery cord and drew open the curtains. Shafts of morning sunlight streamed into Mark's room. "Are you waiting for something in particular?"

"Just a letter from New York. From the Taft Gallery."

"Is that the place you want to have a show?" Mark asked, absently flipping through the envelopes in his lap. He threw a piece of junk mail aside and Hazard picked it up, thoughtfully inspecting the colored photographs of rototillers and riding lawn mowers.

Jamie nodded. "It's my first attempt to break into the world of noncommercial photography." She glanced at Mrs. Gipson. "It's my dream to get away from L.A. and that whole rat race and do something that has more meaning."

"Well, I'll keep an eye peeled for anything from New York," Mrs. Gipson replied with a smile. "Can I get you anything, Mark, while I'm here?"

"No thanks, Mrs. Gipson." He looked up from a letter he had opened and gave her a brief smile.

Hazard gazed at Jamie as Mrs. Gipson left the room. "What kind o' noncommercial photographs do ye take, Jamie?"

"Black and whites. Mostly portraits. My theme is Real People." She chuckled softly. "I guess it's because I deal with so many unreal people in my line of work."

"If you do a show, we'll have to fly back and see it," Mark commented. "Have a big party. Do the town."

"Actually, Mark, you could see most of the show now. I brought my portfolio with me. I wanted to see what you thought of it."

"Great." He stacked the envelopes on his night stand. "Give us a preview."

"You mean now?"

"Sure. Want to see it, McAllister?"

"Aye." Hazard nodded. " 'Twould be illuminatin' t' discover what Jamie considers to be real. Have at it, lassie."

Jamie retrieved her portfolio from her bedroom down the hall and struggled back into Mark's room with the heavy leather case. She unzipped the sides while a nervous thrill tightened around her chest. What if they didn't like her work? What if they were merely polite in their remarks and not touched by the images she had captured? Jamie always felt the dread peculiar to artists, no matter how many times she presented her work.

One by one she stacked her matted photographs against the wall by the door, all fifteen of them. Mark seemed interested, even entertained. Jamie's gaze traveled to the face of Hazard McAllister and hung there, feeding on the appreciative gleam in his eyes.

He liked what he saw, she was sure of it. For a long while he said nothing and continued to study her work. He even stepped forward and picked up one or two for closer inspection. Then he stroked his chin and regarded her.

"Ye pull no punches, lass."

"I only record what I see," she replied.

"Ye see sae much. 'Tis incredible."

Jamie flushed with pleasure at his remarks.

"Look a' this smoke curlin' up by th' man's face. 'Tis like a wraith, an entity unto itself."

"His hopes and dreams," Jamie put in.

"Aye, his hopes and his dreams," Hazard nodded, understanding the deeper meaning. Then he picked up a photograph of a vendor at a fruit market holding a crate in the late afternoon. Shadows from another crate slashed across the woman's face and chest.

"An' this one." Hazard held the matte at arm's length. "This one is unusual, like th' woman's crated up herself."

"You see that? Good!" Jamie looked around his shoulder, keenly aware of the difference in height between them. "That old woman has been at that market for so long, she has become one of the fruit herself."

"She does look like a withered old apple," Mark observed.

"An' this one." Hazard pointed to a shot taken of a fisherman standing by a lake with mist blanketing the surface of the water. "Tell us about this one, lass."

Jamie followed Hazard down the line of her photographs, and gave a brief explanation or a piece of background information about each one. Hazard was fascinated with her work, genuinely interested, and she watched his expressive face for his reactions. She was surprised that Hazard's opinion mattered more to her than Mark's. Yet she realized that Hazard, with his heart of a poet, felt and heard what her work had to say more clearly than her own brother.

That evening, Jamie walked through the parlor doorway to the cozy grouping of couch and chairs ringed around the hearth. No one else was in the room. Jamie plopped down on the couch, grateful for the warmth of the fire that radiated over her chilled body, and grateful that the couch was twenty feet from the drafty windows behind her. For a moment she listened to sheets of rain pounding on the windows across the room. The storm had interrupted their shoot on the beach and had sent all of them running for the nearest hot shower and change of clothes.

Jamie glanced at her watch. What was taking Brett so long? She had expected him to come downstairs by now. He had convinced her to go out for dinner with him so they could talk. If he didn't show up soon they would miss their reservation at the Lido. Actually, missing the reservation might not be entirely unfortunate; Jamie dreaded the thought of plunging into the downpour and suffering wet feet throughout dinner. And she wasn't looking forward to spending time with Brett, the way he'd been behaving lately.

Jamie stared at the fire. She hadn't slept soundly since she had arrived in Port Townsend, and what little sleep she had snatched had been interrupted. Now, those lost hours and the weariness from being out in the chilly wind all day crept up on her unaware. Before she knew it, she drifted into a numbing sleep, her arms wrapped around her torso.

Jamie awoke at the sound of someone talking on the phone behind the couch. She lay still, half napping, trying not to listen, but hearing most of the one-sided conversation. She recognized the voice as Tiffany's, even though she could not see her. Tiffany must have picked up the phone at the end of the couch and walked across the room to the set of windows overlooking the water.

Tiffany was upset about something. Her voice was strident, punctuated with swear words and exasperated sighs.

"What do you mean, you can't—" she exclaimed in a suppressed shriek. "Just wire it up here!" She paused as the person on the other end made a reply.

"Why not?" Jamie heard Tiffany's spiked heels rap on the floor as she paced in front of the window. Jamie didn't know what to do. She could lie there and listen to every word, or get up and leave the parlor. Either way, Tiffany would be embarrassed once she discovered she had an audience.

"Listen, you know I'm good for it. I've got this job and that other one with Rich when I get back. Hell, yes. And Brett has promised me that other—"

More heel taps and then a pause. "Dammit, just send it up. What do you think I'm living on up here? Seaweed?

"Oh, I don't know. Two or three days." She sighed and lit a cigarette. Jamie could smell the pungent odor of her lighter and tobacco. "Yeah, yeah. What was I supposed to do? Brett calls me at midnight. We get on a plane at the crack of dawn. Like I can be really prepared with notice like that."

Jamie watched white rounds of smoke waft toward the high ceiling as Tiffany exhaled. "Goddammit, don't give me your smartass remarks. I'd be a fool to do that. He's my ticket to—

"Yeah, what about him?"

Jamie was certain the topic of conversation was Brett. Tiffany had said Brett was her ticket. Her ticket to what? Jamie heard Tiffany inhale and then more smoke puffed skyward. The cigarette smoke was strong, thick, and choking, nearly as heavy as Tiffany's perfume. Jamie gagged. She knew she should get up and leave before she had a coughing fit. Yet, she was reluctant to show herself, especially after hearing Tiffany's remarks about Brett.

"Well, that's not what he told me. That's a lie, and you know it. He promised that part to me!" She stalked over to the table near the couch. "Just send the money now, goddamn it!" Tiffany clanged down the receiver and flung the phone onto the table with so much force that the receiver dumped out of its cradle. She leaned over to pick it up and caught sight of Jamie lying on the couch.

Surprised, Tiffany straightened, momentarily lost for words. Then she recovered and smirked her crooked smile as if daring Jamie to say anything about the telephone conversation. Jamie made no comment. What could she say? Sorry I eavesdropped. Sorry I witnessed you being a bitch again. Or, why don't you tell me exactly what Brett has promised you? Is this a little deal just between you two, something he doesn't want me to know about?

Jamie's silence evidently made Tiffany nervous. She took a short, agitated drag on her cigarette. "Spying?" she said.

"I was sleeping."

"Sure. Sure you were." Tiffany mangled her cigarette butt into the ashtray by the phone. Jamie stood up to avoid the smoldering stench.

"Listen, Tiffany, if you need an advance—"

Tiffany squelched the offer with a look of disdain. "I'll get my money. Don't trouble yourself."

Jamie felt as if she had been slapped. She didn't know what to say, and wondered if she should just walk out of the room. That would be clumsy, however. To leave without remark would seem cowardly, as if she were giving in to Tiffany's stronger character. Yet she could hardly fight back. She was a stranger to harsh words and vindictive behavior and was ill-equipped to do battle with Tiffany. Both of them knew it. Tiffany continued to smirk at Jamie and the hard silence between them stretched awkwardly.

Seconds later, the front door burst open and Mrs. Gipson bustled into the house, holding a dripping umbrella and a plastic bag over one arm. An immense sense of relief washed over Jamie. She broke from Tiffany's glare and turned to the parlor doorway.

"My!" Mrs. Gipson exclaimed, catching sight of the two younger women in the parlor. "It's awful out there."

Tiffany watched Mrs. Gipson struggle out of her heavy wool coat.

"The storm made us pack up and run," Jamie remarked. "We were out on the flats near the ferry terminal, and the rain appeared out of nowhere. We all got drenched."

"It does that a lot. Comes over the bluff without warning." Mrs. Gipson hung up her coat and glanced at Jamie. "Have you gone out to dinner already?"

"No, I'm waiting for Brett."

"How about you, dear?" she asked Tiffany. "Can I make you something?"

"No, thanks." Tiffany shook her head. "I'm hoping that Hastings will come down in a few mintues. I intend to show him the town tonight."

Jamie's head jerked around in alarm, and she felt an immediate flush. Her reactions regarding Hazard came much too swiftly, much too strongly. Jamie clenched her fists together, trying to regain her composure as a sharp pang of jealousy burned through her. All day she had had to endure the sight of Tiffany throwing herself at Hazard. Tiffany knew a thousand little ploys, from having Hazard help her with the sand in her shoe to feigning fright at the appearance of a dog on the beach or a sea gull dripping too close to her head. She could hang on Hazard's arm for minutes on end, gushing at him and laying her head against his shoulder. Her insincere performances made Jamie want to gag.

Worst of all were the moments during the commercials when Tiffany and Hazard kissed. The kisses went on forever, or so it seemed to Jamie. She didn't want to believe that Hazard actually liked to kiss Tiffany. How could he find pleasure in kissing a foul-mouthed woman whose breath smelled like menthol cigarettes? Yet his kisses seemed convincing if not downright passionate, and Jamie couldn't tell if he were just doing a good job of acting, or if he were actually enjoying himself.

She wanted to scream at him, "Don't fall for that, Hazard! She's a snake, she's a witch!" But she could only stand by, helplessly fuming behind the camera while the film rolled, praying that his experiences on the waterfront of Seattle, San Francisco, and other ports had educated him in the ways of women like Tiffany Denae.

Jamie realized for the first time in her life why women lost control and got into cat fights. Right now she wanted to reach over and yank Tiffany's brassy ponytail. She wanted to yell at her that she could have any other man, but not Hazard.

But Jamie didn't even take a step in Tiffany's direction. It was not in Jamie's nature to confront people. So she just stood near the couch, choking back her jealousy and frustration until it felt like a white-hot ball burning in the pit of her stomach.

"You and McDougall are going out?" Jamie croaked.

Tiffany nodded.

"Oh, that's nice," Mrs. Gipson replied. "Mr. McDougall hasn't been out much since he's been here. It hasn't been a very interesting visit for him, I wouldn't think."

"I know," Tiffany purred, propping herself against the back of the couch. She swung her free leg back and forth. "It's a crying shame, isn't it."

Mrs. Gipson glanced askance at Tiffany's swinging leg and then stepped closer to Jamie. "I don't want to alarm you or anything, Jamie, but when I was downtown I stopped in to see Maggie Nilsen. She does my hair, you know. Well, she mentioned something kind of interesting."

"Oh?" Jamie wondered what a Port Townsend hairdresser had to say that could possibly interest her. "What's that?"

"Mrs. Fisher—you know, she works at the café on the corner across from the ferry terminal—well she told my hairdresser about three strange men that came in the café today. And they were asking all sorts of questions about the McAllister House and Mr. McDougall."

"Oh?" Jamie asked, her brows drawing together in alarm.

"They were dressed like loggers—plaid shirts, jeans, and cork boots. But they were too clean. Mrs. Fisher knows a working man when she sees one. These men had new clothes on. Everything was spotless. Even their fingernails. She thinks they're bank robbers or some kind of drug dealers."

Jamie thought back to the intruder Hazard had chased out of the house. He had seemed odd to Jamie, too, as if he were more than a petty thief. Was the intruder somehow related to the strange men in the café? Could they be trying to get the hologram project? Whatever Jamie suspected, she couldn't disclose her troubled thoughts to Mrs. Gipson or Tiffany. She couldn't let anyone know about Mark's project or the hologram it had produced.

She forced a grin, feeling as phony as Tiffany. "Drug dealers? That sounds crazy, Mrs. Gipson. Besides, what would they want with this house?"

Mrs. Gipson fingered the pin at her throat, tilting her head toward the stairs, and raised her eyebrows as if to convey a silent message to Jamie. Jamie paused. Had nosy Mrs. Gipson discovered controlled substances in the house? Did she suspect drug use? Did she think the strange men in the café were dealers selling to someone in the McAllister House? Obviously, Mrs. Gipson had figured as much and was satisfied with her own conclusion. Jamie chose to let it stand. It was a convenient explanation for the presence of the men.

Jamie also decided to make light of the situation, hoping to lessen the concern of Mrs. Gipson. She touched the housekeeper's arm. "Maybe they're spies, Mrs. Gipson."

"Spies?" Tiffany drawled. "Oh—friends of yours, Jamie? Perhaps a long-lost boyfriend?"

"Long-lost boyfriend?" Brett strode into the parlor. He came toward them, rolling up the sleeves of his oversize jacket. "I'd better be the only boyfriend around here."

Jamie read a double meaning in Brett's words, even though his remark was said in jest. Had Brett sensed her growing attraction for Hazard? Was she as transparent as she felt?

Mrs. Gipson watched Brett walk past her. The censorious look she plastered on his back made it plain that Brett was the drug user in question. "Good evening, Mr. Johansen," Mrs. Gipson said.

"Hi, Mrs. Gipson, how are you doing?" Brett turned to Jamie before Mrs. Gipson could make a reply. "Ready, hon?" he asked.

Jamie nodded.

"Don't you look smashing," Tiffany commented, standing up. She let her gaze wander down Brett's silk shirt, string tie, and pleated pants.

"Thanks, Tiff."

"Where are you two headed?"

"The Lido." Brett smiled as Tiffany took hold of his string tie and tugged at it, forcing him to step closer.

Her lower lip thrust out until it almost touched his as she pouted, "Without me?"

"Sorry, Tiffany. I know I'm breaking your heart." He reached for her shoulders but she stepped backward, releasing his tie before he could touch her, as if toying with his reactions.

"That's all right, Brett. I'm going to drag Hastings McDougall out tonight anyway. Maybe we'll see you at the Back Alley and do some dancing."

"Great." Brett adjusted his tie. "I don't know about

McDougall, though. He's doing something up in the lab right now. He seemed pretty involved with it."

"Oh?" Tiffany glanced at the stairs. "Well, perhaps I should run up and convince him to take a break." She minced across the wood floor. "Have fun!" she called gaily over her shoulder, her earrings tinkling.

Jamie mustered a wan smile. Some fun. She knew she would spend her entire evening wondering what Tiffany was doing with Hazard. She would be a horrible dinner companion for Brett. With a sigh, she picked up her purse from the end of the couch.

"Come on, Jamie," Brett said, heading for the front door. "We'd better hurry if we want to make that reservation."

He held open the door for her but she paused on the threshold. "Oh, I left my raincoat in my room." Jamie stuck her hand in her purse and pulled out her keys. "Why don't you warm up the car, and I'll be right down."

"Okay." He didn't object. Maybe he felt guilty for having kept her waiting so long.

Jamie hurried up the stairs. She didn't want Tiffany hanging around the lab and dropping cigarette ashes all over Mark's equipment. She also didn't want Tiffany hanging around Hazard. Yet she hadn't the faintest idea how to keep Tiffany away from either of them.

She grabbed her coat from her bedroom closet, draped it over her arm, and walked across the hall to the doorway of the lab. She could see Hazard seated in front of the computer, with a stack of papers beside the keyboard. Tiffany stood behind him, stroking his chest with her hands.

"Come on, Hastings," she entreated in a sultry voice. "You can do this tomorrow."

"It canna wait, Miss Denae."

"Call me Tiffany. I just love the way it sounds when

you say my name." She leaned over and pressed her breasts into his back. Jamie saw Hazard's hands drop from the keyboard onto his thighs.

"Tiffany," he said. "I must do this job for Mark. I canna come with ye, lass."

"But—" She stood up and tossed her hair. "But you said—"

"I dinna promise ye," he interjected. " 'Twas just your badgerin' tha' made me quit protestin'. Now if ye dinna mind, I'd like t' get back t' my work."

"Oh!" Tiffany fumed. "You're just like that Jamie. Work, work, work."

Jamie smiled to herself. Hazard didn't seem interested in Tiffany's plans. Perhaps his passionate kisses had been acting after all. A wonderful sense of relief passed through Jamie as she stood in the doorway watching them.

Then Tiffany changed tactics. She reached around Hazard, and without any warning scrambled her fingers over the buttons on the keyboard. Lines of gibberish filled the computer screen.

"Blister ye, woman!" Hazard barked, catching her wrists. Tiffany fell on him, laughing wickedly, struggling to pull her arms away but not struggling hard enough to succeed. Hazard jumped to his feet, turning as he rose, and yanked her arms over her head. The position accentuated the fullness of her bosom. For an instant he surveyed the thrusting points of her breasts beneath the black lace camisole she wore as a blouse. Tiffany laughed in his face and swayed into him, knowing that she had caught his attention at last.

"Are you going to punish me now, big boy?" she taunted.

"I'd like t' thrash ye! Ye just made me lose half an hour's work."

Tiffany clucked. "Oh, aren't I bad!" She snuggled against him. "If you promise to come out with me, I'll leave you alone for a while."

"Will ye now?"

"Yes, and I'll be very good." She stood on tiptoe and kissed him.

Jamie saw Hazard hesitate and then raise his hands to draw Tiffany into an embrace. The relief Jamie felt a moment ago froze into a chunk of disbelief and jealousy. She had misjudged Hazard. He was falling under Tiffany's spell after all. Jamie darted away from the doorway and stumbled down the hall. She berated herself all the way down the stairs, chiding herself for spying on them in the first place, admonishing herself so she would not have time to dwell on the way she truly felt—hurt and angry and betrayed.

9

DINNER WAS ABYSMAL. All Brett talked about was Hastings McDougall.

"We'll need a social security number or something," Brett said, taking a sip of wine. "Does McDougall have a green card?"

"I don't know." Jamie stabbed her salad with her fork. The turn in the conversation pinched her appetite. "I could ask him."

"How can he get paid otherwise?" Brett looked out the restaurant window to the bay. "He did the commercial yesterday and the one on the beach today. Plus that voice-over. We owe him a tidy sum."

"Isn't there some way we can work it out, Brett? Pay in cash or something? It's not like he's going to be doing this on a regular basis." Jamie's gaze wandered over the familiar line of Brett's profile—his wide forehead, turned up nose, and his thin upper lip that curled on one side. Often she wondered if Brett had practiced to make his lip curl in the style of Elvis Presley.

When she had first met Brett, the curled lip intrigued her. It gave Brett a sardonic look as if he knew all about the world and the way it worked. She realized when she got to know him better, however, that Brett was more cynical and slick than he was wise. He took little pleasure from life, and had no patience for simple things. Everything he did was for a competitive reason—his tennis, his running, his baseball card collection, and especially his work. He was an incredible businessman, sharp and cunning and doggedly persistent.

Half of Jamie's success was due to Brett's business acumen. She didn't doubt for a moment that she would have been just another photographer if it weren't for Brett. Now it was time to repay him, time to make their relationship permanent. They worked well together as business partners. Why wouldn't they do just as well as husband and wife? Surely, with Brett there would be no surprises jumping out of the wedding cake. Brett might not be warm and demonstrative, but he was steady and dependable.

Jamie glanced at Brett. She should reach across the table and lay her hand over his. She should tell him she would be his wife, that she would spend the rest of her life with him. She gulped down a swallow of wine and nearly choked. She couldn't say it. An awful flatness had developed between them, a flatness that had become painfully evident since Hazard had burst into her life. And Jamie wondered if any amount of logic, loyalty, or obligation could make that flatness disappear.

Brett watched the ferry plow through whitecaps on the bay. "What's McDougall do for a living, anyway?"

"I don't really know," she replied. She rested a forearm on the table beside her plate. "I think he's in shipping."

"You don't know?" Brett turned away from the window

and gave her an accusing glare. "I thought he was an old friend of the family."

"He is more Mark's friend than mine."

"Why didn't you ever mention him before?"

"I don't know." Jamie pushed a crouton around in a pool of blue cheese dressing. "I never thought about it."

"Mmmm—" Brett slipped his hand around the stem of his wine glass. "There's something about that McDougall, something that strikes me as odd. I just can't put my finger on it."

"You didn't get started on the right foot with him, that's all."

Brett squeezed the stem of the glass until his fingertips turned white. "What was he doing in your room that night, anyway?"

"He was fixing my window." The tips of Jamie's ears burned. She hoped Brett couldn't see them.

Brett scrutinized her. "I don't trust him. And I don't like him. I think you should steer clear of him."

She intended to do just that. If Hazard was the type of man who could succumb to the likes of Tiffany Denae, she would not waste her time worrying about him, or even thinking of him for that matter. Jamie forced her voice to be nonchalant. "He was just trying to protect my virtue."

"What—from me? Your virtue is none of his damned business." Brett leaned forward. "I still feel like belting him a good one, right on that perfect Scottish nose."

"Brett, don't. It isn't that important. Believe me."

"Well, I don't want you in the house with him. Not alone. When I go back to L.A., you're coming with me, like it or not."

Jamie bristled. She resented Brett's assumption that he could boss her around. He was accustomed to giving orders to people and sometimes made similar demands on Jamie. But Jamie didn't like being treated as his child or his employee. "Brett, I can't go anywhere, not when Mark's so ill."

"Then tell McDougall to hit the road. If you don't, I will." Brett's eyes glittered with anger.

In disappointment, Jamie pushed aside her plate. She hadn't meant for their intimate evening together to be spent talking about McAllister. She needed a friend tonight, someone to share her troubles. Her brother's condition worried her. She needed to talk about it. She had never felt so disconnected from Brett, and she was concerned about the gulf that had come between them. She needed to rekindle some intimacy between them. Yet McAllister was the single subject of their dinner conversation.

"Jamie, are you listening to me?"

She scowled. "Yes."

"Tell him to hit the road. What's he doing at the house anyway?"

"Oh," she replied, "he and Mark are working on a project." Jamie looked down. Brett's jealousy annoyed her. She was tired. She wanted to go home and go to bed. She didn't want to talk about McAllister. She didn't want to make up any more lies about him. She didn't want to be with Brett either, not when he was so crabby. She just wanted to fall into bed and sleep. "It means a lot to Mark to have him at the house."

"Mark." Brett finished his wine and put down his glass. "One of these days, Jamie, you're going to have to choose. Mark or me. And that day is coming soon."

Jamie stared at him. Was Brett simply impatient, or was he entirely unfeeling? How could he say such a thing when her brother was so ill?

*   *   *

That evening when Jamie and Brett arrived back at the house Jamie noticed an unfamiliar blue sedan sitting in front where the van usually parked. Curious, she called for Mrs. Gipson as she took off her coat. Brett hung it up for her.

Mrs. Gipson appeared from the kitchen with a magazine in her hand. "Yes, dear?"

"Do we have a visitor?"

"Some man came to see your brother. I told him not to disturb Mark, but he simply insisted. Claimed he had important news for Mark."

"Did he say who he was?"

"Lloyd Evans. Does that ring a bell?"

It did, but not loud enough for Jamie to attach a face to the name.

Mrs. Gipson rolled the magazine nervously. "Mark said it was all right."

"Mark would, you know him." Jamie frowned and glanced up the staircase. "I'm going to have to go up there and tell the man to leave. Mark needs his rest. He shouldn't be entertaining anyone at this hour." She glanced at her wristwatch. "Why, it's nearly ten."

"I'm sorry, dear. I shouldn't have let him in."

Brett poked his head into the deserted parlor. "Where is everybody?" he asked.

Mrs. Gipson brightened at the change in subject. "Oh, they all went downtown again. To that jazz club. All except for Mr. McDougall. He went for a walk."

This time the news of Hazard's absence was a pleasant surprise. Hazard had gone out alone, without Tiffany? Had he actually resisted her? Jamie didn't have time to dwell on the matter, however, and hurried up the staircase, aware that Brett trailed behind. When she reached the top of the stairs, she heard voices coming from Mark's room. One was Mark's, the other had an insistent whine. Jamie approached the door, which was half ajar, and paused at the threshold.

"You're crazy, Kent," the stranger said. "This will all be a waste, this will all be for nothing."

"That's my decision," Mark replied tiredly.

"Listen, they got the lowdown on your medical problems. If you don't let me in on this, everything you worked for will be lost."

"Some things are better lost than put in the hands of the wrong people, Evans."

"What do you mean? What kind of crack is that? I was in on this too, you know. It's not like this project is all your baby."

Mark coughed. "If you know so much about it, then you don't need me, do you, Evans? But you do. Because the hologram project is my baby. It has always been my baby. And it will be my baby until the day I die."

"But Kent, ten million. Think of it."

"At this point, money doesn't mean a helluva lot to me, Evans, know what I mean?"

Jamie froze. What did Mark mean? Had he been withholding the nature of his illness? Was he dying? Her knees suddenly felt weak. Jamie grabbed the woodwork for support as Brett strode up behind her and peered around her to see who was talking. He rapped on the woodwork.

"Mark," he called out. "Is everything all right in there?"

Brett swept into the room without waiting for a reply. Jamie followed, still dazed. She did recognize the man with the whining voice. He had been Mark's research partner.

"Is this man bothering you?" Brett asked.

"Naw, he's a candy striper from the hospital," Mark

drawled. "Jamie, Brett, this is Lloyd Evans, my ex-partner."

Evans nodded tersely, obviously upset at being interrupted. "I'm trying to talk sense into Mark," he explained. "He could make a lot of money if he plays his cards right."

Brett's lip curled. "Mark isn't interested in making money, just spending it—as long as it's his sister's." He stepped closer. "What's the deal? I couldn't help overhearing you say ten million."

"Ah! Finally, somebody with a bit of sense." Lloyd Evans turned toward Brett with a big smile.

Jamie stared in dismay at Brett and then looked at her brother, who was watching the two other men, his eyes flickering with anger.

"Jamie, get him out of here," he murmured weakly.

Jamie moved to block Lloyd Evans's path as he sidled closer to Brett.

"This project could get Mark fortune and fame, if he—"

"Just a moment, Mr. Evans," Jamie interrupted. "If you want to talk deals, you'll have to deal with Mark. And he is in no condition to talk to anyone tonight."

"You don't want to know how you can make ten million?" Brett asked in disbelief.

Jamie shook her head. "Mark said no. That's final. Now, if you please, Mr. Evans, let me see you to your car."

Evans frowned and leaned over the bed. "I'm warning you, Kent, one way or another they're going to get the hologram project. You can either profit from it, or suffer a great big loss. It's your choice."

"Who's they?" Brett inquired. "What's this project that's worth ten million?"

Jamie's heart sank. Brett would be dying of curiosity until he knew all about the project. Once he found out, he would make life miserable for her and Mark until he found a way to take advantage of the money-making aspect.

Jamie, silently cursing Brett for his nosiness, ushered Evans out of the room. Brett followed them down the stairs, firing questions at Evans.

"What is this project he's working on?"

"A hologram project," Evans replied. "Something that creates three-dimensional objects that have actual mass. He and I came up with the idea about five years ago when we were working together."

Jamie crossed her arms. "Mr. Evans, the project is no concern of anyone but my brother. Please, go."

Brett put his hand on Evans's sleeve. "Wait a minute. Who wants the project?"

"Who do you think?"

"Uncle Sam?"

"Maybe."

Brett narrowed his eyes. "Why? For what?"

"A hologram like the ones Mark and I were developing could perform tasks no human would be able to withstand. They could be sent to other planets to explore. They could do menial tasks and free humans to devote their time to greater works."

"No shit." Brett's eyes were glowing by the time Evans finished and his face was lit up by the fires of potential profits. Jamie knew that look well. It was the look Brett always got when he came across a business venture that challenged him. Jamie had to get Evans out of the house, out of reach of Brett's eager questioning. She didn't know what to do, other than use physical force to evict Evans from the house. Yet most of the damage had already been done. Brett knew about the hologram project. It was a secret no longer.

"That's not the reason the government wants Mark's project," Jamie put in. "Don't make it sound so lofty, Mr. Evans."

"What do you mean, Miss Kent?"

"The holograms could become the ultimate weapon of war. The ultimate soldier. Isn't that right?"

Evans glared at her for an instant, and then his expression eased. "Be that as it may, Kent stole the idea and developed it on his own. Now he's trying to cut me out of it entirely. I could sue him."

"Mark never stole anything from anybody." The edges of Jamie's lips were tight with rage as she turned to Brett. "Brett, see this man to the door."

"Wait a second, hon." Brett waved her off.

Jamie stomped to the door and flung it open. A blast of frigid air tore through her light blouse but she barely felt it.

"Get out, Mr. Evans! Right now!"

Evans smiled indulgently at her, knowing he had a captive audience in Brett, and was in no danger of being thrown out of the house by a woman.

"I said just a minute, Jamie." Brett glared at her.

Evans ignored the open door and turned back to Brett. "Like I told Mark, he could profit from our invention. But if he dies before he lets someone in on—"

"Mr. Evans—" Jamie shouted. "Get out!"

Suddenly, a dark form appeared in the open door. And out of the darkness thundered a deep voice. "Do what th' lass says."

Hazard stepped into the light of the main hall. Jamie had never been more relieved to see another person in her entire life. It gave her a great deal of satisfaction to watch Lloyd Evans turn at the sound of Hazard's voice and behold the tall hologram. She saw Lloyd's face slacken with surprise and fear, obviously aware that Hazard would have no trouble lifting him bodily and tossing him out on his ear. He was no longer dealing with her, a small female barely over a hundred pounds. He was facing a giant of a man who didn't look the least bit friendly.

"Okay. Okay." Evans held up his hands in a gesture of submission. "I'll leave. But if you change your mind, give me a call." He held a card out to Brett.

"Give the card back, Brett," Jamie demanded.

Brett laughed incredulously. "What?"

"Give the card back."

Brett looked at Jamie and then at Hazard. He paused.

"Give th' man his card," Hazard repeated, stepping toward Brett.

Brett slipped his hand in his trouser pocket. "Hey, this is a free country."

"But ye are no' th' master o' this house. Jamie is. Now hand o'er th' card so this gentleman can be on his way."

Brett slapped the card onto Evans's outstretched hand as he blew out a sigh of exasperation. He wasn't willing to pay the price for refusing to obey the tall Scotsman.

Hazard glared at Evans and indicated the door with a tilt of his head. "Now, out wi' ye."

Evans pulled his overcoat up around his ears as he hurried out of the door. Jamie slammed it behind him. Then she accosted Brett, her cheeks flushed with rage.

"You bastard, Brett!" she shouted.

Brett held up his hands. "Wait a minute. I'm just trying to swing a deal here."

"It's not yours to swing."

"Jamie, hon! I'm just looking out for your best interests. Ten million. Think what you could do with ten million."

"I'd like to spit on ten million." She was so angry she

felt as if a vein would burst in her temple. "How could you, Brett? How could you have the gall?"

"Listen, Jamie. My gall has got you where you are today. If I had listened every time you protested about a contract or a client's sensibilities, we wouldn't own the best studio in L.A., we'd be taking photos of snot-nosed kids in department stores."

Jamie stared at him, aghast at his vicious outburst.

"Yeah, look at me like that, Jamie. Look at me like I'm some sort of monster. I'm a businessman. Business requires a certain amount of ruthlessness. If you're too chicken-livered to take it, maybe you should just get out." He jabbed his hand to his neck. "I've had it up to here with your emotional trauma, with your sponging brother, your petty little grievances." He jerked his thumb at Hazard. "And your *friend of the family*, here, too."

Jamie felt as if she had turned to stone.

Brett strode to the stairs and put his hand on the bannister. Then he turned. "You know, the thanks I get for trying to help your brother and you—"

"You can honestly stand there and say you're trying to help Mark?" Jamie asked in a voice strangled by anger.

"You bet your sweet bippy."

Hazard crossed the floor to the stairs. He was still taller than Brett, even though Brett had gone up two steps.

"Honest?" Hazard remarked. "You're an honest man, Brett. I'm your brother. And that's two lies."

Hazard brushed past him and strode down the hall to the kitchen. Jamie was so close to striking Brett that it frightened her. She forced herself to remain at the foot of the stairs and watched Brett stomp up to the second floor. Then she followed, bursting into Mark's room. Mark sat up in surprise.

"What aren't you telling me," she shouted.

"What?"

Jamie slammed the door and strode to Mark's bed. "What aren't you telling me, Mark? What's really wrong with you?"

"Like the doctor said—" Mark shrugged "—pneumonia."

Jamie stared at Mark as if to glare the truth out of him. "Lloyd Evans seems to think it's much more serious. And what did you say to him—something about money not meaning much to you anymore. You're really sick, aren't you? And you don't want me to know."

"Jamie." Mark reached for her but she backed away, full of angry hurt because he had not confided in her. Mark sighed and sank back to his pillows.

"Listen, brat. You're making something out of nothing. I've got pneumonia. I'm weak. I'm feverish—but that's all it is."

"Evans mentioned your medical records, though. Why?"

"Who knows?" Mark shrugged again. "Maybe he's reading more into them than he should."

But Mark's gaze dropped from Jamie's as he spoke, leaving Jamie with a sickening suspicion that he was not telling her the truth.

"You'd tell me if you were really sick, Mark, wouldn't you—I mean dangerously ill?" She thought of his hemophilia, his numerous blood transfusions, and the accompanying fear that he might have contracted the AIDS virus before the implementation of careful blood screening.

"You'd tell me, wouldn't you, Mark?"

"Sure, brat." He glanced at her and smiled wanly. "Now will you let me get some sleep?"

10

JAMIE SAT IN THE PARLOR viewing the videotape she had made from the film footage. Sometime after midnight she had come downstairs to work. She had been too worried about Mark and too angry with Brett to go to sleep, and thought she'd make good use of her insomnia by editing the commercial. Now, at one-thirty, she viewed her progress on the screen.

The parlor was pitch black except for the television screen where Hazard and Tiffany kissed and embraced. How light Tiffany looked as Hazard held her aloft and kissed her. How perfectly Tiffany's figure melted into his. Tiffany seemed so delicate, so ethereal on film it was no wonder Hazard found her desirable.

Jamie glared at the screen, fighting the arousal she felt. No man had ever kissed her that way. Hazard's mouth was passionate, forceful, and demanding. The only man who had ever kissed Jamie was Brett, and his kisses were quick pecks or overly wet caresses after he'd had too much to drink. His lips had never stirred her, had never demanded anything of her. Jamie clicked off the remote control with a snap, unable to watch anymore.

The television screen was still glowing in the dark when Jamie heard someone walking down the stairs. She twisted around on the couch to see who approached. Hazard strode across the hall and stopped in the doorway. His tall figure never ceased to impress her. But this time a jitter of excitement fluttered inside her at the sight of him. Jamie had ceased to think of Hazard as a ghost or a hologram. She had begun to see him as the man in the commercial, a very real, very virile man.

"Hi," she ventured, trying to be casual.

"Jamie girl." Hazard sauntered into the parlor. "What are ye doin' sittin' in th' dark?"

"I was just watching television." She turned on the lamp near her elbow and watched his face turn to gold in the darkness. "Hazard, you shouldn't be going out so much."

"Why not?"

"If anything happens to you before Mark gets well enough to deal with you, he'll be devastated."

Hazard walked to the fireplace. "I have things t' do."

"What business could a hundred-year-old ghost possibly have in town?"

"Plenty. I want to find out who killed Nelle."

"How could you find anything after all this time?"

" 'Tis a problem, I'll admit. There's no trace o' her or o' me. Nothin'! Like we never existed." He strode to the fire. "I gave this town my heart, Jamie, my heart an' soul. A Highlander does nothin' halfway. Yet after all the effort, the sweat, the dreamin'—nothin' remains." He leaned on the mantel. "Do ye know what is located in th' McAllister Building now? Not a thriving shipping business, but a Laundromat! What th' devil is a Laundromat?"

"It's a place where you can wash clothes."

"A glorious use of that fine building," he said sarcastically. "And th' library I had built for this town. At least ye would think tha' would have remained as a testimony t' my dedication. But 'tis called somethin' else now, not a mention of th' McAllister name anywhere. 'Tis a bitter pill t' swallow, lass, a bitter pill."

"Well, at least there's this house. It's still called the McAllister House. In fact, it's rather famous."

"Aye. Because o' th' ghost of a supposed murderer." He scowled and straightened. "And Nelle, poor Nelle McMurray. All that's left of her memory is a gravestone in th' old section of a cemetery. And no one t' mourn her passin' or carry on her name."

Jamie watched Hazard run a hand through his hair. She felt comfortable enough with him now that she could question him about Nelle. She set the remote down on the table at the end of the couch.

"You've said that I resemble Nelle. What was she like?"

Hazard brightened immediately. "Ah, she was bonny! A Highlander's dream. Skin as creamy as milk, hair as rich as honey, eyes like emeralds. I loved her th' moment I set eyes on her."

"How did you meet her?"

"She sailed t' Port Townsend on my ship, th' *Phoenix.* She was comin' back from Boston, where she had been goin' t' school for quite a number o' years. She planned t' start a school for girls."

"You met her when she was a passenger?"

"Aye. An' we took t' each other like heather t' th' heath. The voyage from San Francisco t' Port Townsend was th' shortest voyage I'd ever taken. What a distraction she was! Lookin' back, I was never happier."

"So what happened?"

"When we got home, she told me I couldna see her."

"Why?"

"She had a previous understandin' with Richard Veith, one o' th' bigwigs in town. She had known him before she left town an' they had been corresponding over th' years." Hazard stuffed his hands in his pockets and slowly crossed the floor. "Well, she said she had t' honorably break it off with Veith before I could court her." He paused and sat down beside Jamie.

"And Veith didn't like the idea?"

"An understatement, Jamie. And when he found out tha' a scurvy Scotsman was involved, he liked it even less. He had no love for me, by God. I was makin' a name for myself an' Veith didn't like me cuttin' in on his profits or his lass. But Nelle wasna really his lass. Trouble was, he couldna seem t' get tha' through his thick head."

"What did he do?"

"Ach!" Hazard threw up one arm. "He threatened her. He tried t' buy me off. He wouldna take no for an answer an' made Nelle's life difficult. She couldna get money for her school. Veith saw t' that."

"He sounds like a real charmer."

Hazard laughed grimly. "Aye. A charmer. I never liked th' man, an' after I saw what he was doin' t' Nelle, I decided t' take matters into my own hands."

"What did you do?" Jamie leaned forward, captivated by his tale.

"Nothin', Jamie girl. I never got a chance t' help her."

"Is that when you—when you died?"

Hazard shrugged his wide shoulders. "As far as I know."

"Richard Veith killed you!"

"Perhaps, but why would he have killed Nelle an' Bill?"

"I don't know." Jamie thought for a moment. "Why go to all that trouble to win a woman and then kill her?"

"Aye." His voice trailed off and his gaze met hers. It appeared Hazard was a victim of the very crime of which he had been accused, or else he had gone to considerable trouble to think up a yarn just to trick her. If so, she had played right into his hands by helping him flesh out the story.

Jamie looked down. "I'll have to do some more research," she ventured, "to see if there's any evidence to support this new theory."

"D'ye mean t' say you're startin' t' believe me?"

"I wouldn't go that far—" Jamie interjected.

"But you're havin' second thoughts, aren't ye, lass? I might not be a murderin' lyin' villain after all." He grinned. "And look at ye, sittin' here next t' me without fearin' for your life."

"Not completely—" When she rose, Hazard closed his left hand around her wrist.

"Nay now, Jamie. Dinna run off."

"Mr. McAllister—" She tried to pull away but he held her firmly.

"Sit down, lass. Come, sit down!" He gently pulled her back to a sitting position. "You're startin' t' trust me, aren't ye? A miracle like tha' calls for a celebration." He jumped to his feet. "Do ye have a drop in th' pantry?"

"I think we have some wine."

"Wine it is."

"There's probably some chilled in the fridge." When he hesitated, she added, "You know—the icebox." Hazard nodded and motioned for her to remain where she was. He strode from the room and returned with the fumé blanc that Brett had purchased. Jamie derived a certain amount of satisfaction in watching the wine poured into glasses to share with Hazard, not Brett.

Hazard gave her a goblet and then reached for another, raising it up in the air. "Here's t' th' heath, the hill, an' th' heather, th' bonnet, th' plaidie, th' kilt, an' th' feather."

Jamie chuckled at his toast and raised her glass to touch his, but he drew back.

"An' here's t' th' lassie who knows I'm not lyin' 'bout bein' a murderer, killin' and dyin'!"

Jamie grinned. "And here's to the Scotsman whose charm is so thick, he can get me to believe in any old trick."

"Ach, lass," Hazard exclaimed. "Ye cut me t' th' quick." But he was delighted with her impromptu toast. He clinked her goblet with great relish and then took a sip of wine, all the while gazing at her as his eyes danced with merriment.

Jamie broke away from his gaze, disconcerted by his magnetic stare. "Would—would you like to see the tape of your commercials?" she stuttered.

"What's a tape?"

"It's a—well, it's like a bunch of photographs strung together one after another. Here, you'll see." She used the remote to activate the television and videocassette recorder and started the videotape.

"I've edited them. But they still may need some revisions. We'll do final editing in Los Angeles."

Hazard sipped his wine while he watched the commercials unfold on the television screen. Jamie watched him. Awe spread across his face as he saw himself stride to the stairs and embrace Tiffany.

"It looks so bloody real!" he exclaimed in wonder.

Jamie grinned and nodded. There was the kiss again.

She caught herself succumbing to the passion of that moment and stared at the screen while her heart flip-flopped wildly.

"Ach, you'd think I really missed th' woman," Hazard commented, nodding toward the television.

"Yes," Jamie replied. "You're quite an actor." The tape ended in a grainy blur.

"Can I see it again?"

"Wait. Here's the second one, the one we did on the beach." Jamie clicked the remote to fast-forward the tape.

"Fascinatin'. Bein' a nineties man is just fascinatin'."

Jamie located the second commercial and sat in silence as the tape ran. The ending came a moment later, with a kiss and the wind in their hair. Jamie shut off the VCR and switched on the radio instead. Soft jazz hummed in the background. Jamie sat back and tipped her wine glass to her lips, wishing the alcohol would make her feel more at ease.

"I wonder if Tiffany knows she is kissing a ghost," she mused.

Hazard put his empty goblet on the tray. "I dinna think she can tell."

"You don't think she can tell the difference between a hologram and a real person?"

"Nay. She likes it." Hazard turned and his gaze settled on Jamie. His glance wandered over her hair, down her nose, and over her lips. Jamie's skin tingled as if he had touched her.

"I canna tell th' difference either, Jamie. I experience all th' sensations of a real man."

"Oh?" Jamie's skin turned to goose flesh.

"And I've been wonderin' if ye could tell th' difference yourself."

She stared at him for a moment, shocked by the impli-

cation of his words. Did he expect her to kiss him? Did
he think every woman would jump at the chance to kiss
him? Not everyone was like Tiffany Denae, ready to take
on any male that passed a screen test. Jamie rose slowly
to her feet, flushing.

"What did you say?" she breathed, her voice cracking.

Hazard rose also, straightening up to his full height. In
wild distraction, Jamie glanced up at him, ignoring the
voice deep inside that urged her to do his bidding, to kiss
him as she longed to kiss him. But only fools acted on
such impulses. Besides, she wasn't certain at this point
whether the wine or her head were making choices for
her.

Hazard spoke, his voice low and full of intimacy. "Ye
know what I mean, Jamie."

Jamie retreated a step backward. "I don't believe a kiss
reveals much about a man one way or another."

"Then ye must not have kissed enough men t' find out
differently."

"Like the song says," she replied, attempting to hide
her embarrassment with a witty remark. "A kiss is still a
kiss." Jamie turned, anxious to extricate herself from the
sudden intimacy Hazard had initiated, but he slid his hand
around her elbow to keep her from leaving.

"Th' song is wrong then, Jamie girl. A kiss is like nothin'
else when ye kiss someone ye have feelin's for."

"You mean like the kisses you share with Tiffany?"
Jamie's voice was frozen and harsh and she felt Hazard's
grip tighten.

"Tha's just an act with Tiffany."

"So kisses can be part of an act."

"Sometimes. But ye can tell when a kiss is real." His
eyes smoldered down at her and Jamie sucked in her
breath.

"Tiffany thinks it's real."

"Tiffany wants it to be real. But her wind shakes no corn, if ye know what I mean."

Hazard's gaze lingered on Jamie's lips and then raised to her eyes. Jamie stood frozen in place, hypnotized by the nearness of his body.

"Jamie, I've seen your work. I've seen your Real People. Ye know what's real an' what isn't. Ye can see through all th' trappin's t' th' core o' things."

Jamie gaped at him in wonder. No one had ever given her a greater compliment.

"That's why I'm askin' ye, lass, t' verify my presence. You of all people can tell." He reached for her hand, dwarfing it with his own, and placed it on the flaring line of his jaw exactly where she had longed to touch him. His blue eyes glinted at her, bits of lapis lazuli in the firelight.

"Touch me, Jamie," he murmured, his voice rumbling in his chest. "Tell me what I am. A real man or some God-forsaken shade."

She could not break from his gaze. She could not deny him either. His words were more command than request. Falteringly she ran her palm over his jaw and then his cheek. He was warm and vibrant. A splash of vermillion blossomed on Hazard's cheekbones as her fingertips glided over his lips, but his eyes never wavered from her face. Jamie, with her heart hammering away, continued her exploration, running her fingers down the cleft in his chin, down the powerful column of his neck.

Jamie paused at the neckline of his sweater and looked down as Hazard covered her hand with his own. He guided her hand to his chest. She placed her other hand beside it and closed her eyes as she spread her fingers across his chest. She could feel the solid planes rising and falling as quickly as her own. Fighting back a burgeoning wave of arousal, Jamie caressed his torso, tracing the contours. Hazard reached out to touch the dark-blonde hair of her lowered head and murmured her name. His rich voice, resonating beneath her hands, melted her resolve.

Jamie could no longer deny the voice inside that screamed at her to kiss him. She wanted to touch Hazard just as Tiffany had touched him in the commercials. She wanted to feel his hair, his back, his mouth. She wanted his jaw to clamp over hers and his eyes to close in glorious oblivion as their lips came together.

In one fluid movement Jamie's hands curved up and over his shoulders. And when she looked into his eyes, he clutched her upper arms and pulled her into his chest. Her head fell back and his mouth came down upon hers, claiming her with a shattering, rapturous kiss.

Hazard gathered her into his arms, crushing her against the hard planes of his body while he caressed her back and ran a hand into her hair. Jamie stood on tiptoe, nearly lifted off her feet by his embrace.

"Ah, Jamie," he whispered against her lips when the kiss finally ended, "canna ye tell I'm a man?"

"Hazard—" she breathed, stunned. She could feel her legs trembling and her heart banging against her ribs. Brett had never affected her like this. She pulled back and stared at him, full of confusion and desire. She wanted to kiss him, crawl all over him, brand him with kisses so passionate she would turn him into a man regardless of his original form. But Hazard was a ghost. She must not forget that he was a ghost.

"Jamie," he murmured again, smothering his words as his mouth sank upon hers. He was hungry and insistent and he consumed her lips. His tongue plunged into her mouth, circling her teeth, twining around her tongue, flitting over her lips as if he couldn't get enough of the taste of her. Jamie moaned against him, unable to fight his passionate onslaught and her own delirious appetite.

"Hazard!" she cried, pulling away from his mouth before he took her very soul away. "Hazard, I can't—"

"Ye canna tell, can ye, Jamie?" he asked, his eyes blazing into hers.

"No, but—"

" 'Tis no act. Not with ye, Jamie."

His words struck her. Did he harbor feelings for her? Or did he want to make her think he cared for her to gain her sympathy and support. Or was he really kissing Nelle? Jamie pushed against his chest. She should break away before his kisses dissolved her doubts, before she ceased to think altogether. But Hazard's mouth and hands imprisoned her. His lips were everywhere—on her mouth, her jaw, her eyelids, her throat. And his hands were everywhere—in her hair, on her back. Jamie had never felt such strength, such frenzy. She closed her eyes, caught up in the mad thrill of his passion. Shivers of delight rippled across her skin where his mouth touched her flesh, and a throb of want knotted deep inside her belly when his hands drew her hips against his. Maybe Hazard was right about kisses after all.

Flames of desire blasted through her, laying waste to her notions of chastity and flushing her with visions of his naked shoulders. She grew frantic for his lips, frantic to feel his flesh against her own. Jamie arched against him, pressing her breasts into his sweater. Through the thick knitted strands she could feel the heat of his body. He kissed her neck, forcing her backward in his arms so that he could press kisses at the neckline of her sweater. His right hand eased around her rib cage and over her breast. His thumb dragged across the tip. Jamie's nipple went rigid at his touch, while at the same time the throb in her belly tightened, stabbing her with a force so strong that she moaned.

"Ah, lass—" Hazard exclaimed, his voice thick with passion. He didn't finish his sentence, but clutched her rump with both hands and pinned her against him while his breath came hot and fast on her throat. Jamie could feel every inch of him. The throb inside her became an ache so intense that she whimpered out loud.

"Lass, I'm still hotblooded!" he whispered in her ear. His voice was like thunder.

"Oh, don't!" Jamie croaked. Her hands spread across his chest as she pushed against him slightly. But she was losing the battle, she was falling under his spell. If he kissed her again she would be utterly lost to him. Her hands swept up the sides of his face and into his hair. The tawny waves ran through her fingers like silk. Then his head moved, reminding her of the dangerous power of the man that strained beneath her hands. If Hazard could throw Brett across the room, he could do anything he liked with her. If he wanted to take her, there was nothing she could do to stop him. It would be hopeless to try to resist. Yet she wasn't sure if she wanted to resist Hazard.

Trembling, Jamie pulled back. What was she doing? Had she lost all control of herself? Hazard had probably said the same words to Tiffany. She could just imagine what Tiffany had done with Hazard.

Well, she was not Tiffany. And she was not Nelle. She was not about to succumb to Hazard so quickly. Jamie, horrified at her lack of control, pushed against his chest when he stooped to kiss her again.

"Hazard, no!" She struggled against him, terrified of her own weakness and his power of seduction. "I can't!"

She had to get away. She had to get away from Hazard and stay away.

Hazard let her back away to arm's length without releasing her. "You're shyin' away," he panted. "Why?"

She yanked down her sweater, feeling disheveled. "Because!" she exclaimed. "Please, Hazard, let me go."

He let his arms fall with a sigh. Jamie stepped back, smoothing away the wrinkles in her sweater.

"Did I scare ye again, lass?" he asked softly, raking his hand through his hair. Jamie glanced at him. He looked feverish. His eyes smoldered and his face glowed with raw desire.

"I don't know what came over me, Hazard. I shouldn't be with you like this."

"Because I'm not a real man." The bitterness in his voice made her lower her head. "But I felt like a real man to ye, didn't I?"

"I should never have let you kiss me."

"Why? What's th' crime?"

"Because I'm kind of committed to someone else."

"Committed?"

"Nearly engaged."

"Engaged?" Hazard bellowed in amazement. "Not t' that Brett fellow!" When she nodded, Hazard stared at her, outraged. "Ye canna be serious."

A deep blush raced across her face and spread into her hairline. "I've known Brett for years, much longer than I've known you."

"Aye, but ye don't love him, do ye?"

Jamie squared her shoulders. "I don't believe that's any of your business, Mr. McAllister."

He scowled. "Ye couldna love th' man and kiss me th' way ye just kissed me. You're starving, lass. 'Tis plain as day."

"You're the one who's starving. You're the one with the century-old libido."

Century-old *what?*"

"Libido. Sex drive."

"So I'm a lecherous old bastard, eh?" McAllister stared at her, incredulous. "Is that what ye think o' me?"

"Yes. I look like Nelle to you. You probably fantasized that I was her the whole time." She turned away from him. She couldn't bear to see the offended expression on his face.

"It goes deeper than tha', lass, much deeper," he called after her as she walked away. "And ye know what I'm sayin'. We're like two magnets, Jamie, pullin' at each other."

She turned at the parlor doorway. "McAllister, that line is as old as the hills."

He crossed his arms. " 'Tis no line, Jamie. There's somethin' about ye tha' strikes me right here." He touched his heart with a closed fist.

"Somethin' akin t' my own nature. I know ye, by God. Somehow I've always known ye."

Jamie stared at him. His words were dangerously similar to the way she felt about him. But she wouldn't admit that, not when she felt so confused. "How could you possibly know me?" she sputtered.

"I dinna know, Jamie. It's just a feelin' I have."

"One of those gut feelings?"

"Aye."

Jamie put her hand on the door and pulled it open. "I told you before, Hazard, I don't put much store in gut feelings."

11

JAMIE FLED TO HER ROOM and began to prepare for bed. As she took off her sweater, she thought of the way Hazard's hands had caressed her. She never should have let him kiss her, and she never should have kissed him back. She was a fool. As she crawled into bed, she promised herself not to be alone with Hazard again.

That night, Jamie again had the dream of the woman in the blue dress. Again the woman led Jamie to the edge of the bluff. Again the faceless figure pointed and said, "*Tree of Heaven.*" But Jamie could not see any tree. She could barely see at all because of a swirling mist that rose up from the cliff. *Tree of Heaven.* Jamie tried to resist the pull of the mist, tried to back away. But she fell over the edge, into the foggy gray depths, screaming and screaming as she plunged to the bottom.

She jerked awake. Her nightshirt was wet with sweat and stuck to her breasts in damp patches. Even her hair felt damp. Then she heard an unfamiliar voice shouting. The muffled voice came from an unearthly distance that made her wonder if she were still dreaming. It was like hearing an argument in a neighboring room. The deep male voice yelled at someone, raging in words so garbled that Jamie couldn't make out any intelligible sounds. All she could tell from the tone of the voice was that it was unmistakably menacing.

Jamie slid from her bed as her hand groped for the night light. She glanced wildly around. No one else was in the room. She stumbled for the door and flung it open, running into the hallway. Suddenly, she realized the hall was quiet, the noise had ceased. Jamie, breathing heavily, paused on the carpet runner and hugged her arms. The chill of the dark house was nothing compared to the strangling iciness she felt inside.

What was happening to her? Was her dreaming becoming a problem again, making her sleepwalk? She could have sworn the voice was real, yet out in the hallway she heard nothing but the grandfather clock ticking near the foot of the stairs. Jamie glanced at Mark's door, hoping he might be awake, but his door was shut and no light shone underneath. She looked in the lab, wondering if by some chance Hazard was still up, but the room was shrouded in shadows.

Jamie returned to her bedroom and carefully closed the door. As soon as she latched it, she heard a roar of sound, the same male voice shouting, admonishing, threatening. Jamie fell against the door, her heart pounding in her chest. The voice terrified her. She reached behind her, grasping for the doorknob, wrapping her shaking hands around it. But she did not have a chance to turn the knob before she caught sight of a movement in the full-length mirror on the door of her closet.

Someone was in the room after all! Jamie, forgetting that she was unarmed and half dressed, plunged into the center of the room, determined to find out what was making the horrible noise. She peered at the mirror, a bright plane in the shadows. Something moved, something reflected in the mirror. Jamie glanced over her shoulder, but no one was behind her making the movement. She stepped closer.

The shape of a woman was in the mirror. But the shape was not Jamie's, and she knew by all laws of nature that she should be able to see her own reflection. She took a hesitant step forward as the figure grew more distinct. Before her was the lady in the blue gown, the same lady she had seen in her dream! Terrified, Jamie gaped at the figure as the voice in the room thundered and roared. The lady in the blue dress rushed to the very front of the mirror and pressed her faceless head against the other side, thrusting her profile into the silver surface as if it were plastic wrap, stretching it around a nose, a brow, and a mouth that opened in a scream.

Jamie fell back in horror, afraid that the lady would stretch the mirror until it ripped and spilled her headlong into the bedroom. Still the man raged. The lady in the blue dress moved her lips and Jamie thought she heard another voice, a faint female voice. She leaned closer. The lips moved again, and the clawlike fingers of two hands stabbed down the mirror as Jamie heard a cry of anguish and then uncontrolled, heart-wrenching weeping.

"Who are you!" Jamie demanded.

Again the hands clutched frantically as if the woman were being dragged away. Jamie ran forward, realizing that the woman in the blue dress was in trouble and was vainly trying to get away from someone, probably the man who yelled at her. Without thinking, Jamie reached for the hand that stretched the surface of the mirror. Her arm sank up to her elbow, finding nothing but chilled emptiness like the dank air in a pump house. Horrified, Jamie snatched her hand back in revulsion.

Suddenly, the man stopped raving, as if Jamie's intrusion into the world behind the mirror had interrupted him. The lady in the blue dress retreated from the surface of the mirror. But Jamie could still hear her weeping. The sobs tore at her heart, as if someone she loved were grieving.

"Who are you?" Jamie asked the flickering shape. "Who's hurting you? What's happening?"

Then she saw the lady look up, her hair blowing back from her horribly blank face.

"Hazard!" the lady wailed in a voice so plaintive, so haunting that it branded Jamie's memory forever.

"Who are you?" Jamie cried again, intent on answers, frantic to know how to help the woman. "Tell me who you are."

The lady leaned closer, one of her fingers pushing through the mirror. Jamie watched in dread fascination as the figure wrote out letters with her finger, tracing from right to left in characters that appeared backward to Jamie. Jamie followed the figure's hand as she formed the characters Ǝ-⅃-⅃-Ǝ-И. Jamie stared in astonishment. The lady in the blue gown, trapped in a horrible spirit world of her own, was Nelle McMurray.

"You're Nelle!" Jamie exclaimed. The blank face turned to Jamie, flickering and glimmering. Suddenly, Jamie could see an eye. Then the other eye. Soon a nose materialized and then a set of full lips and a round, feminine chin. Jamie stared, her hands slowly raising to her cheeks. Nelle McMurray had a face now. But her features were Jamie's!

Tree of Heaven.

Instantly the figure in the mirror vanished, leaving behind the letters she had drawn on the mirror. Jamie read the characters from left to right as they would appear to her if not written backward—E-L-L-E-N—the letters of her given name. Jamie felt as if she had plunged into the mirror, into a cold so deep, so black that she would never come to the surface again. Jamie screamed. She couldn't stop herself. A cry ripped through her lips, tearing out of her throat, shattering the stillness of the big house. And she was falling . . . falling . . . falling.

When Jamie woke up she was back in bed. Light poured through a crack in the drapery at the window. She squinted and turned to look at the clock on her night stand. One o'clock! She had slept past noon! The day was half gone. How could she have wasted the day and everyone's time by sleeping through the morning?

Jamie threw off the covers just as Brett came through the door. Brett was the last person she wanted to see. She was still angry at him for the Lloyd Evans incident.

"You're up!" he said, smiling. "Finally!"

"Hi," Jamie replied in a raspy voice. She put a hand to her neck, wondering why her throat felt raw and sore. Then she noticed the reflection of her arm in the mirror across the room. The sight of the mirror sent a chill down the back of Jamie's neck as a vague recollection of a dream pricked her.

She rose to her feet. "Why did you let me sleep so long, Brett?"

"You needed the rest. I guess I didn't realize what a strain it was for you to be in this house."

Jamie glanced at him briefly and then staggered into the bathroom, feeling groggy and disoriented, while Brett trailed at her heels.

"Jesus, you had a good one last night!"

"Oh?" Jamie squeezed blue gel onto her toothbrush, held the brush under the faucet, and turned on the tap. She wished he would leave her alone.

"Don't you remember?" He watched her brush her teeth in the mirror while he leaned in the doorway. "Maybe not. I gave you a bunch of sleeping pills so you'd sleep. Maybe you got blitzed from those."

Jamie rinsed her mouth. "I had a nightmare?"

"You were screaming. I found you on the floor screaming. You were totally incoherent. I mean totally!"

Tree of Heaven.

Jamie jerked around so fast that Brett looked over his shoulder to see what had caught her attention.

"What is it?" he asked.

"Did you hear that?"

"No." Brett's eyebrows drew together as he studied her face. "I didn't hear anything. What did you hear?"

Jamie glanced back at the room and then hung her toothbrush on the stand. "Nothing," she replied, feeling dizzy. Bits and pieces of the dream rushed back to her in a jumbled array of images and sounds, triggered by the phrase she had just heard. She put a hand to her forehead, as if to block out the visions, the voices.

"Jamie, are you okay?"

She nodded and walked into the room, looking around her as if she had never been there before. Brett watched her in concern. She wandered over to the mirror and stared at it for a moment.

"I had a dream about this mirror."

"Oh, yeah?"

"And there was someone in it, but it was me."

"Of course it was you." Brett laughed and squeezed her shoulders. "Who else would it be?"

Jamie continued as if she hadn't heard his words. "And

I heard this awful man yelling, and then—" She broke off when she saw the letters still scratched in the mirror.

"What is it, Jamie?"

She put out her hand and very gingerly touched the letters with her fingertips. "It wasn't a dream," she whispered in awe. "I knew it! It wasn't a dream! She actually came to me!"

"Who actually came to you? What is all this?" Brett grabbed her wrist and pulled her around to face him. "Jamie, what are you ranting about?"

Jamie tugged backward, trying to break free. "It wasn't a dream, Brett! I did hear those voices! Look at the mirror."

Brett glanced over her shoulder at the glass. "What of it?"

"Don't you see those letters?"

He looked closer, tilting his head to avoid the glare. "I see something, some kind of scratches." He released her wrists and leaned close to the glass. "What is this, Jamie? Some juvenile trick?"

"What do you mean?"

"Scratching your name on the mirror. Look at it! You've ruined it! You know, you could really do some serious damage during your sleepwalking. Have you ever thought of what you might do?"

"But I—"

"This is getting out of hand. I'm going to get you out of here, and I mean soon. Before you hurt yourself, or somebody else."

"But Brett—"

"Listen, Jamie." He took her shoulders forcefully. "You can't stay here. I don't care what you do, as long as you come back to L.A. Bring your brother, bring Mrs. Gipson, bring whatever—but you'll make yourself crazy staying here."

Jamie realized Brett would never believe her or understand her. He hadn't even looked closely enough to see that the letters on the mirror had been scratched in the silver material on the back of the mirror, not on the surface of the glass. It would have been physically impossible for her to have scratched the letters. She let her arms drop to her sides in resignation. Brett didn't believe a word she said, and he certainly wouldn't believe her tale about Nelle McMurray.

"You're right, Brett. As soon as we're finished filming, I'll leave Port Townsend."

"Good." He kissed her cheek and picked up her robe. "That's my girl." He draped the robe around her shoulders and gave her a hug, nuzzling his face into her tousled curls. "You've been acting so weird lately. It's a relief to hear you making sense for a change."

After coffee and a bite of breakfast, Jamie hurried up to her room to dress. There was more work to be done, more shots for the commercials to be taken on the beach. Jamie stepped into her jeans and pulled on a turtleneck sweater and a tapestry vest. She brushed her hair and pulled it into a long ponytail. She had no energy to fuss with it.

When she put down the hairbrush she caught a glimpse of her face in the mirror. The events of the previous evening had drained her of color. She was white and peaked. She looked every inch a ghost herself. Jamie brushed across her compact of blusher and swept some color onto her cheeks. She bit her lips, trying to bring some blood into them. Still she looked pale. Her eyes were huge and haunted and tired. Brett was right. She had to get away from this house.

Her observations were interrupted by Mrs. Gipson's voice in the hall. "Marcus Aurelius Kent, what do you think you're doing?"

Jamie jerked away from the mirror. What had Mark been up to this time? Why had he been out of bed? Jamie rushed out of her room.

Hazard McAllister stood in the doorway of the lab with Mark in his arms. Mark was dressed in robe and pajamas, but he held a piece of paper in his hand and was studying it while the housekeeper regaled him.

For an instant Jamie's glance locked with Hazard's over her brother's head. He didn't smile. Jamie didn't either, but she felt a hot blush burn her cheeks.

"What's going on?" she demanded.

Mrs. Gipson turned to her, hands on her ample hips. "I came up here to get Mr. McDougall, and where should I find him but in the lab with your poor brother!"

"Mark!" Jamie admonished.

Her brother glanced at her briefly and then looked back at the paper. "The matrices are wrong, that's what it is. The matrices."

"Mark!" Jamie planted herself in front of Hazard and her brother. "Why are you out of bed?"

"I just had to check something. I'm close, sis, really close."

"Yes, you're close to landing in the hospital. Would you take him to his room, Mr. McDougall?"

"Aye." Hazard brushed past her and strode into Mark's room. Mark's bed was a mound of books and notebooks and computer printouts. Jamie sighed and pushed a book out of the way while Hazard lowered Mark to the sheets. Mrs. Gipson hovered in the background shaking her head.

"Men!" she exclaimed.

"I can't believe it, Mark," Jamie added. "What makes you think you're well enough to get out of bed?"

"I'm onto something, Jamie. It's driving me crazy. I can't just lie here like a lump."

Hazard stacked the books on the night stand as Mark talked. Jamie tried to ignore the presence of McAllister, but was maddeningly aware of his tall figure behind her. She snatched the paper from her brother's hand.

"Mark, you don't seem to realize how sick you are. You can't keep pushing yourself like this. Nothing is that important."

"It is to me." Mark reached for the paper, but Jamie raised it over her head. Mark sighed in defeat and closed his eyes. He licked his dry cracked lips. "It is to me," he repeated softly.

Mrs. Gipson stepped closer. "Excuse me, Mr. McDougall, but Mr. Fittro wants you downstairs. He's ready to make some kind of recording."

Hazard glanced at Jamie and raised an eyebrow. Jamie's knees felt weak just from looking at him. "The other voice-over, Mr. McDougall. Remember? He wants you to be the voice on the second commercial, too."

"Oh, with that accent of yours, it will be just wonderful." Mrs. Gipson beamed. "I just love the way you say things, Mr. McDougall."

"Thank ye, Edna." Then Hazard turned to Mark. "I'll be back, Mark." In reply, Mark raised a hand and let it flop to the blanket.

Mrs. Gipson clasped her hands beneath her sagging breasts. "Can I get you anything, Mark?" she inquired in her usual fashion before departing. Mark shook his head. Jamie leaned forward. "Any mail today, Mrs. Gipson?"

She shook her head. "No, dear, not from New York."

Disappointed, Jamie mumbled her thanks. Then Hazard walked out of the room with Mrs. Gipson chattering away at his elbow.

Jamie sank to the bed beside her brother. She sighed and surveyed his wan face, more worried than angry at him.

"That McAllister—" Mark smiled shallowly. "What a guy!"

"He should know better than to drag you around."

"Ah, don't blame him, sis. I asked him to. You know the man never sleeps? He doesn't seem to require rest. He stays up all night reading, helping me."

"You're joking."

Mark shook his head. "He's quick, too. You know, I tell him a thing once, just once, and he's got it, just like that. You should see him whip around on the old computer."

"Really?" Jamie adjusted his blankets and tried to appear uninterested. "He can grasp the technology?"

"No problem. The man was born in the wrong century. He learns more in a minute than most people learn in a year. He's like a twentieth-century version of a Renaissance man. He's got an amazing memory. I'd like to do some tests on him, see if his energy transfer altered his intelligence, his recall abilities."

"What kind of tests could you do?"

"I don't know, I've been thinking about it, though."

"Do you think—" Jamie looked down. "Is McAllister here to stay, Mark? Do you think his new form is permanent?"

"I have no idea, sis. We're forging completely new territory. Digital pioneers! I love it!" He smiled and looked at her. "It's hard to even tell that he's not a normal human. Except for his quick mind. But then there is a possibility that the guy is just naturally gifted and was like that a century ago."

"You like him, don't you?"

Mark shrugged his scrawny shoulders. "He's easy to be around."

"That says a lot, coming from you."

"Well." Mark crossed his arms. "Most guys are more interested in beer and football. Hazard doesn't have a clue about the Forty-Niners or Bud Light, thank God! So do me a favor, Jamie. Don't let him watch television."

Jamie smiled. "He doesn't have time. He's too busy cutting commercials and keeping you up all night."

Mark reached over and put his hand on Jamie's forearm. "Brett doesn't suspect anything, does he? He hasn't asked you any weird questions about McAllister, has he?"

"So far, no."

"Good. Keep it that way. Brett's another one of those people that would exploit a situation like this. The sooner you accept that, the better it will be for you. Is he going back to L.A. soon?"

"When we get done with the filming. Maybe in a few more days." She patted the covers. "Meanwhile, big brother, stay in bed, get your strength back. Don't push yourself like this."

Mark swallowed and put his forearm over his eyes. "I need to rush, Jamie. I may never finish this project if I don't."

"Nonsense. The project isn't going anywhere."

Mark didn't move his arm from his face. All Jamie could see was the end of his nose and his lips. "It could be. I expect any day to have it pulled out from under me."

Jamie stared at him. "What?"

"People want this hologram technology. They want it bad. Maybe bad enough to kill."

He raised his arm and gazed at her. His face was all hollows and shadows. Jamie grabbed his arm before he could cover his face again. "They'd kill you for it?"

"Or you. That's why I didn't want you to come here or even know I was here. I feel safer now that McAllister is around. But not much. And to get so damn sick at a time like this—"

Jamie released his arm. "Mark, you've got to forget about the hologram project and concentrate on getting well. Then we'll get you out of Port Townsend to somewhere safe." She noticed his frown of protest and shook a finger at him. "I'm serious, Mark. If you don't stop driving yourself like this, I'll have that doctor admit you to a hospital. Then you'll be forced to quit working. I mean it!"

"Sis, you don't understand—"

"I do too." She rose. "If I don't see improvement in your condition in the next two days, I'm going to have your equipment boxed up and shipped to Chicago."

"Over my dead body."

Jamie glared at him for his particular choice of words. "You think you're joking, don't you? Well, I don't think you're a bit funny."

12

THE REST OF THE DAY was spent filming on the beach. Though the weather cooperated magnificently, Jamie could not concentrate on her work. Thoughts of Mark kept crowding in and she had to struggle to keep her worries to herself. If Mark did have AIDS, it was not something she could casually mention to anyone except the closest of friends. And who could she name as a close friend at that moment? Brett? Hardly!

Jamie was also full of thoughts about Hazard and the vision of Nelle McMurray. She tried to avoid Hazard during the shoot, and when she filmed him she put a cool wall of professionalism between her eye and his face.

By the time Jamie returned to the McAllister House, she had another headache. She dropped her equipment in the drawing room, feeling emotionally and physically drained, and stood in the hall massaging her temples while the rest of the crew bustled past her, anxious to clean up and grab dinner downtown. Brett passed her, ruffling her hair, oblivious to her condition. Jamie still burned with

152

anger over their argument about Lloyd Evans and the hologram project. She watched Brett stride up the stairs, calling for Tiffany. Somehow the Lloyd Evans episode seemed a million years away now.

Jamie's pills were in the kitchen. She could hear Hazard talking to Mrs. Gipson in there. Though she had promised herself to steer clear of Hazard, Jamie padded to the kitchen, certain she would be safe as long as Mrs. Gipson was in the same room with them.

When she got to the kitchen, however, she was dismayed to find herself alone with Hazard.

Jamie paused, undecided what she should do. Hazard hadn't heard her approach, and for a minute Jamie watched him make coffee in the automatic-drip coffee maker. He leaned over to put the used filter in the trash, but couldn't see how to open the lid. Jamie smiled to herself and leaned against the doorway. He could handle a computer, but he couldn't figure out a trash can. Some genius.

"Step on that little pedal," she suggested.

Hazard looked up, startled.

"Down near the floor." Jamie pointed to the bottom of the trash can. Hazard stepped on the pedal and the lid popped open.

"Faith!" he exclaimed in surprise. He dropped the soggy coffee filter into the waste can and smiled at her. "Even th' trash needs a—what do ye call it—a remote control."

Jamie smiled thinly, too spent to manage more. He inspected her face as she stood before him, and his voice was full of gentleness when he asked, "What's wrong, lass?"

"Oh, nothing." At his question, something caught in Jamie's throat and she choked on a huge sob. She covered her eyes with her right hand, embarrassed that Hazard might see her crying. But once the sob began she could not stop its course. "Oh, everything!" she finished, breaking down.

Hazard reached out for her and drew her to his body, slipping a hand into her fawn-colored curls. She clung to the front of his sweater, sobbing, too wary of him to wrap her arms around his chest and embrace him. Her shoulders shook as she wept.

"Jamie," Hazard murmured. "Ah, lass!" He stroked her hair. The gesture was incredibly comforting to someone who had received very little physical contact in her life. Just as before, Hazard's touch healed her. Slowly, her tears subsided and she moved away from him, pinching the last of her tears back with her thumb and forefinger.

"Sorry!" she said.

Hazard still held her shoulders. "No need t' be sorry, Jamie."

"I don't usually lose control like that."

"There's nothin' wrong with losin' control once in a while." He smiled at her kindly and Jamie's heart flopped. "Now tell me, lass. What's got Jamie Kent feelin' so low?"

Jamie sank onto one of the kitchen chairs while Hazard poured coffee and set a mug in front of her.

"Thanks," she mumbled. Her eyes stung.

He leaned against the edge of the sink and gazed at her. "Tell me what's ailin' ye now."

"I guess for starters it's my brother."

"He is seriously ill, isn't he?"

"Yes." Jamie sniffed. "And he seems to be hiding something from me. What if he's really ill? What if he's dying? If Mrs. Gipson hadn't called me, I might never even have known he was sick."

He nodded gravely. "Maybe he didna want t' worry ye. T' spend your valuable time nursin' him."

"That's crazy. What if I had stayed in L.A., not knowing he was up here in Washington? And—if something happened to him? I might have never seen him again." Jamie gulped her coffee, nearly overcome again by tears. Then she set down the mug and stared at her hands. "Why doesn't he confide in me?"

"Mark's a scientist, Jamie. He thinks differently from you or me. He weighs what's practical an' what's sentimental, and makes his decision from there. Ye canna fault him for followin' his nature."

"Well, still—" she stared at Hazard. "Mark should tell me if it's serious."

"Aye."

Jamie sighed. There was more to her anguish than just Mark's state of health. The visions of the night were still raw and ragged, and she battled with the possibility that her sanity was really slipping this time. Her relationship with Brett had run aground and she wasn't sure if she wanted to continue with him or not. Moreover, she could not bear the strain of avoiding Hazard for another day.

Jamie swallowed and looked at Hazard. Her eyes flickered in hesitation for a moment, but she plunged ahead. "There's something else that's bothering me." She stood up and stuffed her hands in her back pockets. "Hazard, I want to apologize for last night—"

"Last night?" He held up his hand. "Nay. Ye dinna have t' apologize, Jamie."

"But it wasn't right. I shouldn't have let it happen. It was my fault."

Hazard shook his head. "I'll not listen t' such drivel, Jamie girl."

"But it wasn't proper. I'd like to blame it on the wine,

but I can't entirely." Then she added solemnly, "I take full responsibility for what went on."

"Oh, ye do, do ye?" Hazard straightened. He had never seemed so tall. "Ye dinna think I have any say in th' matter? Ye're th' only one tha' can make a move, are ye?" He scowled and his sunny face transformed into thunderclouds. "Ye treat me like a child, by God, like I canna account for my own actions!"

Jamie looked down. The throb had begun to pound inside her head.

"Ye modern women want t' do all, be all, and take all th' responsibility. No matter how th' man feels."

Jamie's ears burned. She couldn't look up at him.

"Aye, ye modern women with your modern women's liberation dinna think ye need men a'tall, do ye, Jamie? That's th' fashion these days."

Jamie was startled at the hard ring of bitterness in his words. She had never heard such a tone in Hazard's voice before. Somehow she had relied on him to be charming and congenial at all times, no matter how she behaved in return.

Hazard banged his coffee cup down on the sinkboard. "It must be gratifyin' t' be sae independent. Lonely as hell aflame, but gratifyin'."

Jamie, desperate to escape Hazard's wrath and her raging headache, reached for the Percodan tablets on the windowsill. But Hazard's hand shot out and caught her forearm in a tight grip.

"Nay, now. No pills. A strong woman like you doesna need any pills. All ye have t' do is quit fightin' your nature."

His blazing eyes challenged her. Jamie shrank back, consumed with confusion and indecision.

"Hazard, why are you being like this?"

"Because ye trample my feelin's, lass. Ye trample them like ye trample your own. And it's not somethin' I take lightly. I know what I feel. And I'll not have a wee slip of a woman tellin' me otherwise." He let her arm drop.

"Hazard, you've got it all wrong."

"Have I?" He crossed his arms over his chest and glared down his nose at her. "I willna catch ye unaware again. I never had t' force mysel' on a woman, and I'm not about t' start now. Especially with a lass tha' doesna think I'm a man. Ye dinna need t' give me th' cold shoulder, Jamie, like you've been doin' all day."

"Cold shoulder?" she protested. She had avoided him, but she hadn't been rude, had she?

"I'm not a block o' wood, lass. All ye have t' say is, 'Mr. McAllister, leave me alone. Your attentions are not appreciated.' That's all ye have t' say, Jamie. Just be honest wi' me. I'll have no more o' th' malarky ye've dished out today."

"But I—"

"Just say th' words, Jamie. 'Tis simple. Unless, o' course, what you've been tellin' me isna th' truth."

Jamie massaged the sides of her head, barely able to think past the pounding in her temples. But she knew without thinking that she did appreciate Hazard's attentions. She appreciated them far more than she cared to admit.

"Well?" Hazard demanded when she remained silent.

She took one look at Hazard's stormy expression and quickly glanced away. "That's not exactly what I would say."

"An' what would ye say then, Jamie? Tell me."

"I don't know," she retorted, full of anguish and sick at heart. "It's all so confusing."

"Aye and it will be 'til you become captain o' your own soul."

"I've never been good at knowing what to do. I've never known what to say to people."

"Ach, more drivel. You've been listenin' to tha' Brett too long. He's got ye believin' ye need him t' tell you what t' do, when ye dinna need him at all."

"I know he seems like a jerk sometimes, but without him—" Jamie broke off, no longer certain how to end the statement. For the first time in years a whole new facet of her life had opened in which Brett played no part whatsoever.

"Without him, what, lass? What would life be for Jamie Kent without her lover Brett?"

"He is not my lover!" Jamie colored.

"What is he to ye then?" Hazard grasped both of her wrists and pulled her against him. Jamie closed her eyes as he drew her to the hard frame of his body. The touch of him, even the mere thought of touching him, made her heart race. She pressed her eyelids together against the pain, against the confusion, against the wild surge of desire that bolted through her. "I don't know anymore, Hazard! I just don't know!"

"Well, ye canna go through life avoidin' every question that's put t' ye! Ye canna be a citadel, hidin' away from yoursel'." He paused and studied her while she struggled with her thoughts. Then he added in a more moderate tone of voice, "You're a bonny lass, Jamie. I'm not just chasin' the cheese. But 'til ye can accept your own feelin's, 'til ye know your own mind—" Hazard slowly released her wrists and sighed. "Well, I've said enough."

Jamie backed away. "Hazard, things are happening too fast."

"Time means nothin', Jamie girl," he replied softly. "Nothin' a'tall."

That night Jamie avoided going to bed. She did not want to face the mirror and the possibility that the events of the previous evening might be repeated. Brett suspected that she was frightened and volunteered his own room, saying he would be happy to keep her company. Jamie turned down the offer. She hated to admit to Brett that she was frightened. She promised she would turn in soon, but said she simply wasn't tired yet because of sleeping in so late that day.

She sat through the eleven o'clock news. She sat through Johnny Carson and the late movie, and fell asleep on the parlor sofa holding a pillow to her chest. She woke up to the deep tones of a male voice and the sensation of someone picking her up, lifting her from the couch.

"Jamie, lass, wake up."

Hazard had hoisted her into his arms.

"What are you doing?"

"I'm puttin' ye t' bed, lass." He strode out of the parlor. "You'll freeze down here in tha' cold parlor. Look at ye. Ye're hands are like ice."

"Oh." Jamie wrapped her arms around his neck for support as he climbed the stairs. The closer they got to her room, the tighter she grasped his neck. He shot a questioning glance at her when she turned her face into his chest. Then he stepped into the room, closing the door with his foot.

"Ye're stiff as a board, Jamie. Dinna ye know me well enough t' realize I willna harm ye?"

"It's not that," she mumbled.

"Then what is it?" he inquired, gently sitting her on the bed.

Jamie looked around him to the mirror on the closet door. "I just had a nightmare last night, that's all." She lowered her head.

Hazard knelt on the floor beside her. He picked up her left foot and slipped off her shoe. Jamie watched him without objecting. She was too tired to protest, and the touch of his hands was too comforting to resist.

"Ye're frozen, lass." He removed her sock and massaged her pale toes and heel. Jamie closed her eyes and sighed as his strong hands kneaded her flesh. Delightful warmth spread across her instep and flowed up her ankle. Hazard did the same to her other foot. Jamie opened her eyes when he stopped rubbing, to find him smiling at her.

"Ye like tha'?" he asked.

"It's lovely."

"Warmer now?"

"A bit. Thanks."

Hazard remained on his knee, still holding her foot. "Well, ye get yourself a decent night o' rest, now, lass. Ye were lookin' pale today."

She nodded and swallowed. "Hazard?"

"Aye?"

"Could you just stay here for awhile?"

Hazard's hands quit caressing her foot and he glanced up in surprise.

Jamie blushed. "I'd feel a lot safer."

"Ye're spooked, aren't ye, Jamie?"

She nodded, her eyes imploring him to stay. "Just for a while?" she added in a small voice.

Hazard smiled. "I never could say no t' a beautiful woman."

"I didn't mean that I want you to—" Jamie broke off, pulling her foot away.

"Sae ye want just a bedtime yarn, then?" Hazard rose

to his feet. "Ach, lass, ye know how t' wound my male sensibilities."

Jamie drew up her feet and hugged her knees, glad that Hazard did not press her for more than she was ready to give.

"Get in your nightclothes, then." He waved her off the bed. "I'll make ye a warm fire."

"Thanks."

Jamie scurried to the bathroom to change while Hazard bent to build a fire. At the bathroom door she paused and glanced back at him. Had Brett been the one to carry her to her room, he would have insisted upon a kiss and whatever else he could wrangle out of the situation. Jamie's eyes darted over the powerful lines of Hazard's body and her mouth curved into a smile. She could trust Hazard not to overstep his bounds, not until he knew she was ready. A warm sensation poured over her, and she knew at that moment that she was falling in love with him.

Jamie brushed her teeth, ran a comb through her hair, and splashed water over her face. Then she changed into her flannel nightshirt and walked over the cold floor to the bed. Hazard, leaning one forearm on his knee, glanced over his shoulder at her approach. His eyes took in her green flannel shirt and then his glance flashed up to her face.

"Ye modern women wear th' strangest get-ups," he commented.

Jamie looked down at her practical attire, seeing it for the first time as woefully unfeminine.

"'Tis not a garment t' drive a man wild with desire," Hazard added.

"Good!" Jamie grinned and threw back her covers.

Hazard chuckled and replaced the fire screen, striding to the other side of the bed.

"I suppose ye want me t' sit on a chair halfway across th' room."

"No, the bed is fine, Hazard." She patted the comforter that covered the extra pillow. "I trust you."

He scowled and lowered himself to the bed, which shook when he sat on it. He bent over and took off his shoes. Jamie flushed, suddenly unsure whether having him so close was such a good idea. He was so large, he filled up the other side of the bed and seemed much closer than she had imagined. He rose up on one elbow and gazed at her, his eyes sparkling.

"Shall I tell ye a story, Jamie?"

"I might fall asleep," she lied. She was so keyed up by the proximity of his body that sleep was a remote possibility.

"Sleepin' is th' whole idea." He smiled quietly and reached over and touched her hair, letting a curl slip through his fingers.

"I was never wi' Nelle this way," he murmured. "I never knew th' touch of her body under all tha' wire and whalebone, never felt her tender thigh under all those petticoats."

Jamie flushed with pleasure as his hand caressed the side of her face and the back of her head. "You never knew her intimately?" she breathed, wondering why she found it so easy to accept his caresses as long as they were speaking of Nelle, as if what he was doing to her was being done to someone else.

"Nay. 'Twas difficult t' arrange. She had a reputation tha' could not be compromised if she were t' have her school. We were both well-known in town. 'Twas not easy t' escape th' public eye."

His hand slid down her neck, down her back, over the slender curve of her hip, easing down the coverlet. Jamie closed her eyes and let the warmth of his hand send ripples of heat across her skin.

"Ah, lass, ye feel like heaven," he whispered. In one strong movement, he pulled her to his chest, wrapping his arms around her slight frame. Jamie ran her palms up the sides of his chest until her hands rested above his shirt pockets. When he made no attempt to disrobe her, Jamie slowly relaxed, letting her body mold into his as if she were fashioned to lie beside him. Jamie buried her face in the warmth of his chest and curled against him, feeling more safe and secure than she could ever remember.

"How long did you know Nelle?" she asked quietly.

"A few weeks," he murmured into her hair. "Only a few weeks." He sighed. "But 'twas as if we had known each other forever. I canna describe it. 'Twas no flirtation. No inconsequential affair. We both knew it."

Jamie closed her eyes, listening to his voice rumble deep in his chest.

"It's like th' way I feel for you, Jamie girl."

"How can you be so sure?"

"I just am." He kissed her briefly. "Now sleep, lass. Ye just close your eyes an' sleep."

Someone shook Jamie awake. She opened her eyes, blinking, trying to focus on the shape sitting beside her on the bed.

"Lass, wake up."

Jamie rose up on an elbow and brushed back her hair. "What's going on? What time is it?"

"Seven-thirty." Hazard, fully dressed, took her shoulders and squeezed them tightly. "Ye must get up now, Jamie. Up, lass."

She nodded and yawned and sat up, throwing the covers back.

"Why didna ye tell me about th' mirror?" he demanded.

"The mirror?"

"Aye!" Hazard pointed across the room to the closet door. "What do I see th' first thing this morning, but tha' mirror with those letters scratched on it."

"Oh." Jamie squinted and yawned.

"How th' devil did th' letters get there?"

"Nelle scratched them in the mirror."

Hazard stared at her. "What?" he thundered.

"I've been having dreams about her, only I didn't know who she was. When I saw her in my dream, she didn't have any face. And then last night—or I guess it was the night before last—I heard voices. I thought I was just dreaming, but I wasn't. I woke up because the voices were so loud. And then Nelle tried to get out of the mirror, but someone pulled her away. A man was screaming at her, yelling at her. It was awful. I couldn't make out what he was saying, but he did something to Nelle. She was crying hysterically."

"My God!"

"She called your name, Hazard."

Hazard collapsed on the bed. "Ah, God!" he cried, anguish contorting his face.

"I asked her who she was. That's when she scratched the letters in the mirror."

"She's in a livin' hell, a hell worse than mine!" Hazard exclaimed. "Ah, Nelle!"

Jamie reached out and touched his shoulder, deeply moved by the desolation in his voice. "Hazard, maybe it was just a dream."

He shook his head. "Nay. She's not at rest. She's relivin' her murder over an' over again. Oh, God." He dropped his head in his hands. "I canna do a thing t' help her."

"Maybe you can."

Hazard's head shot up. "What d'ye mean?"

She glanced at him and licked her upper lip, uncertain whether or not to add the last bit of information. "I think I am Nelle, Hazard. I know it sounds crazy, but I think I've come back to you somehow. The other night, after Nelle scratched those letters in the mirror, she looked at me. Finally her features appeared. She had my face, Hazard, my face!"

" 'Tis true ye look just like her, but wi' different hair."

"And those letters—do you realize that Nelle spelled backward is Ellen? That's my real first name."

Hazard stared at her. " 'Twould explain a lot o'things, Jamie. A lot o'things."

"If I am linked to her, maybe there is some way to find out how we can help her."

He nodded. " 'Tis tha' Richard Veith, that bastard!"

Jamie let her arm drop.

"How can I kill the bastard when he's already dead?" His blue eyes flashed with a cold hard fire when he looked at her.

When Jamie went down for breakfast she found Tiffany, Brett, and Bob talking in the kitchen. Brett glanced at her as she entered the room, and he watched her walk to the table. Casually, he stirred his coffee.

"Sleep well?" he asked.

Jamie wondered if he knew Hazard had spent the night in her bedroom. She didn't want to give him the satisfaction of seeing her blush, so she pulled out a chair and did not hesitate to answer. "Yes. Like a baby, Brett."

"No nightmares?"

"Not one dream."

Jamie sat down and watched Tiffany slide her hand off Brett's thigh.

"Good morning, Tiffany," Jamie greeted, "Mrs. Gipson."

"Good morning, dear," Mrs. Gipson answered. "Would you like something for breakfast?"

"No, thank you, Mrs. Gipson. Just some coffee, please."

"Where's that handsome Mr. McDougall?" Tiffany purred.

Jamie shrugged and pulled her coffee mug into her hands. Hazard had left her bedroom, threatening to bring hellfire and damnation on the entire Veith clan. "I don't know where he is," she answered finally.

Brett and Tiffany exchanged glances as if they had discussed Hazard's whereabouts before she arrived. Tiffany smiled crookedly. The expression made Jamie's stomach knot. Did they suspect something? Did they know that she and Hazard had been together during the night? Jamie stared at her mug, feeling as if Tiffany had contaminated their innocent friendship.

"Jamie," Bob Fittro interjected. "We had an idea this morning. Since tomorrow's Halloween, we thought we'd have a party, sort of a cast party for the commercials."

"That sounds all right." Jamie didn't care about parties one way or another. The events in her life had become an intense dull throb that she could no longer ignore.

"If it would be okay with you and Mark we could have the party here. I think we could get a band. I know a bunch of guys in Seattle that would come over."

"We could dress in costumes," Tiffany added. "Wouldn't it be fun?"

"Sure, if it's okay with Mark." Jamie forced a smile. "Is it all right with you, Mrs. Gipson?"

"As long as the house doesn't suffer any damage."

"We'll help clean up, too." Brett sipped his coffee. "Then we'll say good-bye to Port Townsend and fly back to reality."

Your reality, Brett. Jamie frowned and then turned to watch Mrs. Gipson wash the breakfast dishes.

"Why don't we take the ferry over to Seattle today and look for costumes? We can plan the party on the way over." Tiffany took a drag on her cigarette and gazed at Brett through the smoke she exhaled. "How does that sound?"

"Sounds great. I haven't been to Seattle for years. Jamie, why don't you take a break and come along? You could use the change of pace."

Jamie shook her head. "I really can't, Brett. If I leave Mark alone for a day he'll probably overdo again and wind up in the hospital."

"That's where he belongs anyway," Brett retorted. "I mean, do you expect to spend every minute at this house with him?"

"Right now, yes."

"Fine. Don't go with us," Brett snapped.

Mrs. Gipson walked to the table, wiping her hands. "Oh, Jamie, I almost forgot. This came for you in the morning mail." She held out an envelope and Jamie saw the logo of the Taft Gallery in the left corner. Her heart thumped as she took the letter.

"Thanks, Mrs. Gipson."

"Isn't that the letter you've been waiting for?"

"I hope so!" Jamie smiled at the housekeeper and then noticed that everyone at the table was waiting for her to open the envelope. Carefully, she broke the seal and drew out a heavyweight bond paper. For a moment she scanned it and then placed it on the table. Brett watched her closely.

"Well?" he asked.

In reply, Jamie shoved the paper over to him.

Brett mumbled the words of the letter out loud until he hit important phrases such as "former manager liked your work very much," then "gallery has been purchased by a European shipping tycoon," and "must wait to see if new owner decides to display your photographs." Brett shook his head as he lowered the letter to the table.

"What do you think?" Jamie asked.

"It's a polite way of saying thanks, but no thanks."

Tiffany nodded. Jamie noticed the barest hint of a smile on Tiffany's lips.

Brett sighed. "When are you going to give up, Jamie? When are you going to see the futility of it? There are a thousand photographers out there trying to break into the New York scene, trying to say something. It's not for you. Your place is in Los Angeles, with commercial work. Why don't you just face it?"

Jamie's shoulders slumped. "I just wanted more, Brett."

"More? What more could you want than the Noel Condé account?"

Jamie stared at Brett's incredulous face. He actually believed that the Noel Condé account was the pinnacle of their careers. Nothing she could say would convince him otherwise.

She knew after last night that she would never be able to marry Brett, not after spending the night in Hazard's arms, knowing the feeling of being held by a man she truly loved. She had to give Brett's ring back and tell him the truth. She did not love him. And she knew now that marriage without love would be like a prison sentence with no parole.

Yet Jamie knew it would be difficult to break the news to Brett. His ego and competitive nature would be affected even if his heart remained untouched. He would probably fly into a rage and make life miserable for everyone around him. The least she could do was wait until after the party to inform him of her decision. Then he could have his temper tantrum without spoiling the celebration. The question was, could she bear another day of withholding the truth?

13

JAMIE WATCHED THE CREW leave for Seattle from the window in Marks' room. Mark, having had a full day and night of rest, was looking the best he had appeared since her arrival in Port Townsend. He was actually dressed and had eaten breakfast. Jamie smiled at him over her shoulder. Maybe her threats to pack up his equipment had convinced him to attend to his health.

"You'll be happy to know that everyone is leaving for Seattle this morning."

"Great. When will they be gone for good?"

"The day after tomorrow, I believe." Jamie idly watched a young woman in a windbreaker approach Brett and hand him a piece of paper before he got in the van. She spoke with him briefly and then hurried to the house across the street, leaving a paper stuck in the crack of the door.

"You should have gone with them, sis. You've been cooped up in this house for nearly a week."

"That's all right. I've been busy. I've hardly noticed."

She walked away from the window and picked up Mark's tray full of empty dishes. "Since you're feeling better this morning, Mark, I may run downtown."

"Fine."

"As long as you promise to keep out of the lab."

"You know I can't make a promise like that." He coughed and Jamie glanced at him in alarm. But the coughing spell was brief.

"If you don't stay out of the lab, I won't go."

"Okay. Okay. I'll read. I've got some articles to catch up on."

She smiled and whisked out of the room, nearly colliding with Hazard. He caught the outside edge of the tray while the cup and saucer clattered.

"Whoa, lass!"

"Sorry." She laughed. His hands touched hers and the warmth of his flesh sent a wonderful shiver through her, reminding her of the hours she had slept cradled against his chest.

"Well, now, Jamie, 'tis a pleasant sound, hearin' ye laugh."

Had she never laughed before? Had she been so glum that Hazard had never heard her laugh? She couldn't believe it. Yet she didn't doubt that he was right.

"It's amazing how good you can feel after a decent night's sleep," she replied.

"Sae ye slept well?"

"Never better." A smile blossomed outward from her heart to her face. Hazard's eyes seemed to melt with pleasure. Jamie wanted to tell him how she felt about him right then, wanted to shout at the top of her lungs that she loved him. But she could see Mark watching them from his bedroom. Her declaration would have to wait.

"Hazard, I'm going downtown. Would you like to come along?"

"Aye, why not?"

"Good. I'll just take this to the kitchen and meet you on the porch."

Minutes later, Jamie hurried out the front door, pulling on a cardigan. Hazard stood near the top of the stairs, reading something on a piece of paper while a breeze rattled the bottom of the page. He glanced up at the sound of the door closing.

"What's that?" Jamie asked, striding across the porch. The tap of her boots echoed under the vast empty space beneath the floorboards of the veranda.

"A notice tha' was left in th' door." Hazard held it out as they walked down the steps.

Jamie glanced at the paper. It bore a headline Save Our Tree. A crude drawing of a gnarled tree took up much of the paper. She didn't glance at the text below the illustration.

"It looks like another one of those environmental issues."

"I canna believe anyone would want t' cut down tha' tree. Why, it's been part o' Port Townsend for a long time."

Jamie gave the paper back to Hazard. "It's a particular tree?" she asked.

"Aye. A tree given as a gift to Port Townsend by th' Japanese emperor. The sapling was planted before I—well just before I passed on."

Jamie took his arm and hugged it, offering her silent support. Hazard pulled her close as they walked across the bluff toward Water Street.

"Th' tree must be huge now, a century old. Why would they want t' cut it down?"

"Maybe it's standing in the way of progress. Usually that's the case."

Hazard folded the paper with his free hand and stuffed it in the rear pocket of his jeans.

"Old things gettin' in the way o' progress. In wi' th' new an' out wi' th' old."

Jamie leaned her head on Hazard's upper arm. She loved the feeling of his firm muscles and the closeness of his broad shoulder. Her hair blew into her face and she swiped it away, smiling and happy.

"Just like Hazard McAllister," Hazard continued. "If it serves no purpose, get rid of it. Hazard McAllister and the Tree of Heaven, ancient relics both."

Jamie stopped in her tracks. "What did you say?"

"Hazard McAllister and the Tree of Heaven ancient relics both," he repeated. "Why?"

"Tree of Heaven—you mean that's the name of a real tree?"

"Aye. Th' tree that I've been talkin' about all this time."

"The Tree of Heaven is here in Port Townsend?"

"Aye, lass." Hazard chuckled and pointed over the bluff. Jamie pushed her hair back and looked in the direction in which he pointed. " 'Tis right there, Jamie. Tha' big old spreadin' affair at th' foot o' th' stairs."

Jamie stared down the wooden walkway. The stairs angled along the face of the bluff to the bottom of the cliff where shops and restaurants nestled along the waterfront of Port Townsend Bay. The tree stood in the rear lot near an old brick building, its intricate pattern of branches reaching toward the sky. Around the tree was a cordon of yellow rope and a ring of people carrying protest signs. To the left was a bulldozer, backhoe, and a crane, and the beginnings of a new building foundation.

Wind tugged at Jamie's sweater and flattened the pant legs of her jeans against her calves, pulling her toward the edge of the bluff, just like in her dream. A cold sweat broke out on the back of her neck.

"Jamie, you're as white as a sheet." Hazard wrapped an arm around her shoulder. "What's wrong?"

"The Tree of Heaven," she gasped. "It's been in my dreams, too." She grabbed for Hazard's sweater. His sturdy body would keep her from going over the edge of the bluff. Surely, this time she would not plunge over the cliff as she did in her nightmare.

"In my dreams, Nelle takes me to the bluff and points. She says, 'Tree of Heaven.' But I never see any tree. All this time I thought the Tree of Heaven was just a figment of my imagination."

"Maybe Nelle was tryin' t' tell ye somethin'. Maybe she knows somethin', Jamie."

"Let's go down and see what's so special about that tree."

They clumped down the wooden stairs and walked over the brick cobbles to the protesters. Jamie surveyed the tree which looked like a bonsai project growing out of control. The tree had hundreds of tiny twisting branches attached to a huge knotted stump that reached torturously upward, as if stretching for the bluff. The leafless tree, bare and black in the misty harbor atmosphere, appeared unearthly and alien to Jamie. Yet something about the tree fascinated her and kept her searching the filigrees of twigs as if to find an answer to the puzzle of her dream.

"Save our tree! Save our tree!" chanted the protesters. One of them leaned close to Jamie.

"Have you seen our flyer?" the man asked, waving a paper under her nose.

"Yes."

"Why in blazes does someone want t' chop down this tree?" Hazard inquired.

"Because"—the protester stuffed the flyer into his half-zipped jacket—"Frank Veith wants to put in a video store here. The tree's in the way."

"Frank Veith?" Hazard questioned, eyeing the brick building next to the empty lot. "Aye. O' course. His great-grandfather Richard must have bought this parcel o' land."

"Who?" the protester asked, confused.

"Richard Veith. He once owned half th' buildings this side o' Water Street. Except for tha' brick one there. Tha' one belonged t' Hazard McAllister."

"Who?"

"Hazard McAllister."

The protester shrugged, unfamiliar with the name. "Well, you sound like a history buff, sir. Surely you realize how important the Tree of Heaven is to the heritage of this city."

"Aye," Hazard replied, still fuming about his name going unrecognized. "I do, lad."

"We can't let people like Frank Veith destroy this landmark."

"What can we do to help?" Jamie asked.

"Write letters to the newspaper. Complain to the mayor. Call your congressman."

The protester was interrupted by a loud honking. Jamie looked over her shoulder to see a late model Honda Prelude jerk to a stop. Behind it was a big-wheel truck hiked so far off the ground, Jamie wondered how a person could get in and out of the vehicle. She watched the Honda's door swing open and a man in a wool overcoat jump out. Four men dropped from the truck to the ground behind him. Jamie felt Hazard stiffen as the man in the wool coat approached, his gloved hands in the air.

"All right, everybody. Break it up. The party's over."

"Who is that?" Jamie asked.

"Frank Veith," Hazard said. "I'd bet a bottle o' scotch on it."

The man in the coat strode toward the tree while the wind ruffled through his thinning hair, revealing a bald spot on the top of his head. He was tall and wiry, and wore a pair of tinted wire-frame glasses that concealed his eyes. Though his clothes were expensive, his posture was bad, and he held his left shoulder lower than his right, ruining the fine lines of his coat.

The protesters ignored him. In fact, the closer he approached, the louder they chanted. "Save our tree! Save our tree!"

"Listen, people. This is your last chance," Veith shouted. "You're on private property."

"Save our tree! Save our tree!"

"Work will resume here this morning! You have one minute to leave!"

The protesters ignored him and circled the tree waving their signs.

"I have a permit here." He reached in his pocket and pulled out a white envelope. "I've got permission to cut down that tree. It's rotting. It presents a danger to citizens using the stairway."

"Bull!" retorted the protester who had spoken to Hazard.

"This is an official document. Ignore it and you will be arrested for trespassing and disturbing the peace."

"Go ahead. Have us arrested!" a young woman shouted.

"Save our tree! Save our tree!"

Veith frowned, his lips puckering into two thin lines. He motioned with an abrupt wave of his hand for his companions to step forward. "Get these damn trespassers off my land," he commanded.

Jamie clutched Hazard's arm. She hadn't really looked at the other men until that moment. They were tough construction workers with burly arms and hefty legs like linemen on a football team. They wore hard hats and insulated vests and steel-toed work boots. And by the looks on their faces, they relished the idea of a brawl and a beer after breakfast.

At first Jamie thought that Veith was only bluffing. Surely, he didn't mean to harm the protesters. They weren't bothering him enough to warrant physical violence. He probably intended to scare them. Yet, his men stomped forward, intent on the job at hand, and would have barged into the ring of protesters if Hazard hadn't stepped in their path.

"Wait a blisterin' minute!" Hazard roared.

"Out of my way, bud," the largest of the men replied. "Or you'll be first."

"Leave 'em be!" Hazard retorted, shaking off Jamie's hand. He took a menacing step forward.

"This don't concern you, Jack." The man spit on the ground near Hazard's shoe. "Now fuck off."

Jamie realized the chanting had ceased and everyone was watching Hazard. Onlookers collected on the sidewalk and a few shopkeepers hung in their doorways, curious to see what would happen. Jamie hugged her sweater around her and prayed Hazard wouldn't do anything rash. He was only one man against four big brutes. They could inflict serious damage, even to Hazard.

Hazard planted his feet and raised his fists. That was all the excuse the big brute needed. He swung at Hazard, but Hazard dodged the blow and retaliated with a powerful left hook that caught his opponent under the chin. The brute's head whipped backward and for a moment he wobbled on his feet. Then he plunged backward, unconscious before he even hit the ground. The protesters cheered and whooped.

Hazard had barely recovered his balance when the other three men surged forward.

"Hazard!" Jamie screamed.

Her cry was a useless warning. The men fell upon Hazard, but they couldn't knock him down. Instead, two of the construction workers pinned his arms behind his back, and a third was about to pummel him in the stomach when a police car arrived, screeching to a halt before the Tree of Heaven.

Two policemen sprang from the squad car. "Okay, boys! Hands in the air! Right now!"

The construction workers shoved Hazard away so roughly that he stumbled trying to get his footing in the mud. Jamie ran to him and clutched his arm while Frank Veith approached the policemen.

"Officers, thank you for coming." He held out his hand and shook one of the officer's hands.

"What's going on, Frank?" the elder of the two policemen inquired.

"This man," Veith nodded toward Hazard, "is trespassing on my property. He refuses to leave. And I have a court order stating—"

"We know all about your court order, Frank." The policeman glanced at Hazard. Jamie's grip tightened around Hazard's arm as if to lend support to his physical being while he was scrutinized by the officer.

"Okay, Frank. We'll take him in."

"What about them? The protesters? I can't get a thing done here when they're marching around."

"They weren't fighting, were they?"

"Well, no, but—"

"We'll take this guy in first. We'll deal with the protesters later."

Jamie listened to the officer as he informed Hazard of his rights. Then she followed him to the squad car, protesting all the way that Hazard had only been protecting the protesters.

The younger officer wouldn't let her get into the squad car with Hazard.

"You mean I can't go with him?" she asked.

"That's right, m'am."

"But—"

"You can see him at the police station."

Jamie watched, helpless and worried, as the police car made a U-turn and headed out to Water Street. Many of the onlookers booed the action of the police officers as the car drove away. Jamie crossed her arms over her chest and frowned. How would she ever get Hazard out of jail in time so that he could leave Port Townsend with her and Mark? She had no intention of lounging around in this town waiting for someone to steal Mark's project or do him bodily harm.

Then her eyes caught the movement of a man in front of the brick building on her left. The man, dressed in nondescript jeans and a plaid shirt, had just lit a cigarette and inhaled. He blew out smoke through his lips while he watched the police car turn the corner and disappear. A strange smile stretched his lips back over his teeth. Jamie didn't like the predatory look of that smile. Besides that, what did the stranger find so amusing about Hazard McAllister's arrest?

Jamie walked to the police station at the end of Water Street and found Hazard standing at the counter.

"I can go, then?" Hazard asked Officer Baeth, the older policeman who had apprehended him.

"Yeah, but I don't want to see your face again." Baeth shook a yellow pencil at him. "You understand, McDougall? You're lucky Veith isn't going to press charges."

"But those men were going to attack the protesters," Jamie countered.

"Those protesters were on private property. Besides, you only thought they were going to attack the protesters. They hadn't really done anything by the time we showed up. Frank was just trying to get some business done, that's all."

"When did Frank Veith take possession o' tha' piece of land?" Hazard asked tersely. "It was public right o' way in my—well, at one time, anyway."

"He bought that strip a few years back. He owns the whole block. And it's his to use."

"But the tree is a historical landmark," Jamie said.

Officer Baeth waved her off. "That tree is bug infested and half dead, Miss Kent. No one ever looks at it. The tourists don't even know it's there, the way it's tucked behind the Veith building like that. I think this whole deal happened because a bunch of Seattle activists got wind of it and saw a way to raise a ruckus about construction. You know how they're building over on the mainland, packing houses in like sardines in a tin can. Those activists will try anything to halt construction or get a little media attention."

"But if tourists knew about the tree, if the area were made more accessible—"

"Miss Kent, I'll tell you what. I'll have Veith hold off. Now you go on home. And don't get into any more fights,

McDougall, or I'll have to book you for disturbing the peace."

Jamie thanked him while Hazard took her elbow and guided her through the door.

"We still didn't find anything out about the Tree of Heaven," Jamie declared as they walked along the sidewalk from the police station. "And after today, I doubt Frank Veith will let us look around his property."

"Aye. You're right. Sae we just won't ask for his permission."

"What do you mean?"

"We'll have t' come back later. At night. When Veith's big boys are all tucked in for th' evenin'."

"You mean break in?"

"Not necessarily, Jamie girl. There are ways t' get into tha' old building o' mine if no one's messed with th' original design. And it doesn't appear likely tha' anyone has."

"You're turning me into a regular ne'er-do-well."

Hazard laughed and winked at her. "Come on, lass. Let's go back t' th' house."

They hurried up the street to one of the staircases leading to the top of the bluff. Jamie kept pace with Hazard, and not until she reached the top did she realize how quickly he walked. She gained the last step, her legs burning with the effort, and took a deep breath of relief. The rest of their walk would be on level ground. She could manage that.

Jamie's breath caught short in her chest, however, when she saw a car parked next to the sidewalk at the top of the bluff. A man leaned against the front door of the car, the same man Jamie had seen smiling at Hazard an hour ago. He was still smoking. But this time he had a gun in his right hand, not a cigarette lighter.

Hazard stopped short. "What th' devil!" he gasped.

The man with the gun smiled and waved his weapon. "Into the car, McDougall. You, too, Miss Kent."

"Who are you?" Jamie asked.

"Your tour guide. Now get in."

His smile vanished and Jamie stumbled forward into the back seat of the sedan. Hazard was pushed in beside her so roughly that he knocked her into the lap of another man. He had a gun, too, and kept it trained on Jamie as she struggled to sit up. The man outside slammed the door near Hazard, threw his cigarette to the ground, and jumped in the car. The sedan pulled away from the curb and sped through the residential neighborhood of Victorian mansions and bed-and-breakfast inns. Jamie was oblivious to the scenery.

"Where are you taking us?" she asked.

"We're going for a little ride," the man answered, turning in his seat. He pointed his gun at her but looked at Hazard. "And if you try anything, McDougall, I'll shoot the little lady here. "We know *she's* flesh and blood."

Jamie's heart sank. Whoever these men were, they obviously knew about the hologram project and Hazard McAllister.

14

JAMIE GLANCED AT THE DRIVER and the other two men, who were dressed in jeans and wool shirts. All of them had short, closely cropped hair and expensive wristwatches. The watches and the outfits seemed incongruous. Were they the men that Mrs. Gipson had told her about? She studied them, settling back into the car seat next to Hazard. She found his hand and held it tightly. There was nothing else she could do but go along for the ride.

The car drove past Kai Tai Lagoon on Kearney Street, through the light at the base of the bluff, and then south on Highway 20. Jamie watched the marina go by, then Safeway, the Manresea castle, and the Ford dealership on the city limits. No one spoke a word.

Finally, the car turned off the highway and followed a narrow road to Glen Cove. They passed the small marina there and drove along a gravel road until Jamie saw a large cruiser pulled up at a private dock. Hazard peered out the window at the long white ship with the radio dish atop the pilothouse. Jamie wondered what Hazard thought of the modern vessel, but didn't say anything to him.

The car door opened. "All right, McDougall. Out of the car."

Jamie and Hazard were taken to the ship, which got underway as soon as they were aboard. Two of the men accompanied them belowdecks, where they were shown to a huge cabin in the aft section. One wall of the cabin was glass, which looked out on a magnificent view of the harbor. At the window end of the room was a seating area of couches and chairs, and at the other end was a huge conference table. Along the wall near the door was a wet bar and standing near it was a man with white hair. He smiled when the door closed behind Jamie.

"Come in. Come in!" he motioned. Though he looked briefly at Jamie with a man's eye for beautiful women, he reserved his close scrutiny for Hazard. Jamie glanced at him, realizing the prematurely white hair had tricked her into thinking the man was old. He was not more than fifty, and his bright blue eyes snapped with smug intelligence.

Hazard did not step forward. He crossed his arms and stared down his nose at the short, white-haired man. "What is th' meanin' o' this!" he thundered.

"You speak! You can actually speak!"

Hazard glowered. "Of course I can speak, ye bloody bastard."

The older man beamed and pressed his hands together as he walked around Hazard, inspecting him as if he had just unwrapped a Christmas present.

"They said you could talk, but I didn't believe it." He laughed, his voice full of tight energy. "Amazing!"

Hazard lunged for the white-haired man, but the two

men behind Hazard grabbed his arms and jerked him back.

"Now, now, Mr. McDougall!" the older man exclaimed. "Behave yourself. If you don't, we'll have to take out our displeasure on Miss Kent. You wouldn't like that, would you?"

"Bastard!"

"Such language, Mr. McDougall!" Dr. Hamilton clucked his tongue, but all the while he surveyed Hazard with an avid gleam in his eye.

"Ye know my name," Hazard snarled. "How about tellin' us yours?"

"Gladly. I'm Dr. Hamilton." He nodded with a curt bow. "And I've been anxiously waiting to meet you. I just can't understand where the Scottish accent comes from. Was Dr. Kent trying out different dialects for some reason?"

"Th' accent's mine." Hazard wrenched free of his captors.

"And how does he control you from a distance? Or are you programmed to respond to certain verbal and visual stimuli?"

"No one's controllin' me. And if it weren't for Jamie, there, I'd thrash ye."

"I don't doubt you would." Dr. Hamilton smiled. "You're a strapping fellow, Mr. McDougall. I'd be interested to learn whom Kent used as a model for you."

" 'Tis my body and my brain, I'll have ye know. And if ye dinna tell me what's goin' on, I'll tear this scum bucket apart, fore t' aft."

Dr. Hamilton laughed with glee, which infuriated Hazard. He lunged forward. The guards scrambled to grab hold of him, but not before Hazard seized the front of Dr.

Hamilton's suit. Instantaneous fear drained the color in Dr. Hamilton's face.

Hazard whipped the crook of his elbow around the doctor's throat, lifting him off the ground and choking him. But at the same time, one of the guards snatched Jamie, cruelly clutching her hair and snapping her head backward while he held his pistol barrel to her neck. Jamie stared at Hazard, her eyes huge with fright as the cold circle of steel pressed into her throat.

Hazard's eyes flashed in anger when he realized the futility of the situation. He could never endanger Jamie. He sighed in disgust and shoved the doctor away from him. The guards regained their stance by Hazard's side while Dr. Hamilton stumbled away, pulling down his sleeves and the hem of his jacket, trying to hide his momentary lapse of poise. It took only a second for him to regain his composure and turn back to face Hazard with a smile. This time, however, the doctor did not stand quite so close.

"So you want to know what's going on?" Dr. Hamilton asked. "Poor soul. You're like a modern-day Frankenstein, aren't you? A tragic pawn."

"I'm no man's pawn."

"And like that unfortunate monster, you're a bit violent. Violence didn't work too well for Frankenstein or his creator. I'd think about your penchant for violence, Mr. McDougall, if I were you."

"What d'ye care, Hamilton? What's your angle?"

"My angle?" Dr. Hamilton crossed his arms. "I'm a businessman, Mr. McDougall. In the old days I would have sold arms and munitions to those in need of them. However, in this day and age, I am forced to be more creative. Nuclear arms are not practical. Biological warfare is environmentally unsound, and we all must cultivate an environmental conscience these days. So, when I heard about Mark Kent's wonderful new development, well—" he smiled and extended his palms upward. "I simply had to be the first to see it."

"How did you find out?" Jamie asked.

"My dear, I've been waiting for your brother to finish his project for months now. My finger is on his pulse. Though I must say I am concerned that his pulse is weakening."

"You're the one that offered to buy the project?"

Dr. Hamilton nodded. "I can take Kent's project and fly with it. I have a lab in Canada that could get the hologram project up and running in weeks. But since your brother is being so stubborn about ethics and such, I was forced to take matters into my own hands."

"So you're takin' us t' Canada, are ye?" Hazard put in.

"Correct."

"Leave Jamie be," Hazard added tiredly. "Let her go. She canna help ye."

"She's a behavior modification device, Mr. McDougall. Where you go, she goes. Besides, with Jamie on board, we might just convince her brother to sell us rights to his little project after all."

"Ye'll not harm her?"

"Heavens, no. And when we're all finished, she can go home, safe and sound." He gave Jamie a reassuring smile, but she was not fooled. Once Dr. Hamilton discovered what made Hazard tick and how to reproduce the hologram, there would be no need for a modification device or a witness to Dr. Hamilton's crimes of kidnapping and industrial theft.

Jamie detested Dr. Hamilton's smugness and his condescending tone of voice. He was the type of man who was certain of his superior knowledge and power and gloated

over the powerlessness of those inferior to him. Jamie was
grimly aware that under Hamilton's smiling facade, he was
probably deciding how to dispose of her.

As Hamilton chuckled his way back to Hazard, he drew
a syringe out of his pocket. This time Jamie lunged forward.

"No!" she cried. Dr. Hamilton ignored her outburst.
The guard yanked Jamie backward, nearly pulling her
arms out of their sockets.

"You're a bit on the feisty side, Mr. McDougall. I'm
afraid I'm going to have to administer a tranquilizer. I
have some tests to perform on you, and I don't want you
giving us a hard time."

Hazard reared back as the doctor held up the syringe,
priming it.

"No!" Jamie shouted. "You don't know what it will do
to him."

"Quiet!" Dr. Hamilton snapped, his face suddenly
hard. "Hold him down, boys," he ordered. While Hazard
writhed, trying to break away, the doctor jabbed him in
the shoulder. A moment later Hazard fell limp, hanging
lifeless between the men at his side.

"Take him to the lab and undress him," Dr. Hamilton
instructed. Then he turned to Jamie with a smile, his de-
meanor changing instantly. "And you, Miss Kent. Would
you like some lunch, my dear?"

"Go to hell!"

Jamie's stomach growled as she paced across the small
cabin. When she had refused lunch, she had been taken
to a cabin forward of the conference room and had been
locked in with a warning to keep quiet. Hazard had been
dragged to the lab, but she wasn't certain of its location.
What were they doing to him in the lab? She hoped and

prayed they wouldn't kill him. Hazard was no ordinary hologram, and they might harm him out of sheer ignorance. They weren't aware that Hazard was more than a product of Mark's equipment. Jamie stared out of the small porthole, worrying about Hazard's condition. She saw nothing but blue-gray water. How far had they sailed toward Canada? And how would they ever escape from a boat in the freezing water of the Straits of Juan de Fuca?

Hours later, the man that had sat in the back seat of the car brought her a tray of food. Jamie ignored him as he put the tray on the small table and tried to make conversation. She did notice, however, that he had entered the room without a gun in his hand. Perhaps he felt no threat from a small woman. Jamie turned her back until he gave up trying to get conversation out of her and left, locking the door behind him.

Jamie stood with her back to the tray, determined not to eat any food offered by Dr. Hamilton. She wanted nothing to do with that man. Then she reconsidered. If she were to keep up her strength and try to help Hazard, she would have to eat something. She consumed everything on the plate.

Hours passed. Jamie rattled the door, tried in vain to open the porthole, and searched the cabin for an object she could use as a weapon. She found nothing. The drawers beneath the couch-bunk were empty. The built-in wardrobe contained nothing more dangerous than a hanger. The small table near the door was attached to the wall and the flimsy chairs would shatter to pieces before hurting anyone. Frowning at her lack of success, Jamie wandered into the bathroom. Shower stall, toilet, and sink. Nothing removable. What about under the sink? Jamie crouched on her haunches and opened the door, hoping she would see a toilet plunger lying in the cabinet. But all she found was extra soap and three packages of tissue. She stood up and sighed. Great idea while it lasted.

Jamie was just about to turn to leave when she looked at the toilet a second time. Wait a minute. The top of the toilet tank was removable. In fact, it was a heavy ceramic lid that could knock a man senseless. Jamie grinned and lifted the lid. She took it over to the table and set it down. Then she dragged a chair to the side of the doorway. The next time a guard came to feed her, she would be ready and waiting, toilet tank lid in hand.

Time dragged. Jamie spent hours waiting, listening intently for the sound of footsteps in the hallway. By nightfall she was stiff from sitting near the door and weary from the strain of monitoring every small noise, tensing each time she anticipated the approach of a guard.

The guard finally arrived sometime after seven o'clock. She could hear him whistling as he came toward her. Jamie jerked to attention and scrambled onto the chair seat. Carefully, she lifted the toilet tank lid and raised it above her head, ready to bring it down the minute the door opened.

A key rasped into the lock. The button clicked open. Jamie's muscles tensed, sending a bolt of fear and apprehension through her. The door swung wide and a man came over the threshold. Jamie swung down the lid, slamming it against the crown of the guard's head.

He didn't cry out. He didn't make a peep. He just wobbled for a moment and then pitched headfirst into the cabin, sending the tray of food flying across the floor. Tomato soup splattered against the wall panel like blood, dripping down the wall in thick red fingers.

Jamie froze, aghast, thinking she had killed him. Then she jumped off the chair and raced to his side. He was breathing, but she supposed he might be unconscious for a while, considering the blow he had just suffered. Jamie reached down and slipped the gun from the waistband of the back of his pants. Then she rummaged around in the broken dishes and silverware for the ring of keys he had put on the tray. In only a matter of seconds she was in the hallway, locking the door behind her.

She leaned against the door, marshaling her thoughts. She had to think and think quickly. How long would it be until the guard was missed? How long until he regained consciousness and alerted his buddies? What was that bastard Dr. Hamilton doing to Hazard? And where in the name of Hades was the blisterin' lab? Jamie smiled grimly as she clutched the gun. She was beginning to sound like Hazard McAllister.

She looked down the hall. The lab was probably not in that direction. The large conference room had taken up most of the space in the stern of the ship. She looked up the gallery and saw numerous doors on both sides of the corridor. Most likely this side of the ship was designated as cabin space. That left the starboard side and the corridor that bisected the ship a few feet away. She scampered to the corridor and nosed around the corner to see if the coast was clear. The corridor was empty.

Jamie crept along the hallway, alert for the slightest sound. She kept the gun pointed directly in front of her, ready to shoot at any moving target, while sweat popped out in little beads on her forehead. If anyone appeared, she wasn't certain if she would shoot the gun or wet her pants.

When she got to the intersection with another corridor running fore to aft, Jamie heard voices coming her way. She flattened against the wall, her heart slamming against her ribs. The voices grew louder. What if they turned and saw her? One gunshot, and the entire ship would know she had escaped.

Jamie held her breath as the men came abreast of the corridor. She waited, stiff on the outside but trembling like crazy on the inside. Surely, they could hear her heart pounding. Yet, the men passed down the hall without even looking to the side. Jamie closed her eyes and muttered a silent prayer of thanks.

She waited until their voices faded and then stuck her head around the corner. There was the lab. She could see what looked like an intensive care ward through a long band of windows in the hallway. Dr. Hamilton walked across the brightly lit room and took off a white lab coat. One of the guards leaned against a doorway, chatting with him. Jamie saw Dr. Hamilton stride toward the door. She skittered backward, into the corridor from which she had just emerged.

"Good night, Reeves," she heard Dr. Hamilton say as the door whisked open. "Call me at the first sign of any change."

His footsteps tapped a brisk staccato on the vinyl floor as he left the lab. Once again Jamie flattened against the wall, hoping the doctor wouldn't come her way. Once again her presence went undetected. Now all she had to do was take care of the guard in the lab.

Jamie wiped the tip of her nose with the back of her hand. Then she bent over so no one could see her through the lab windows and scrambled across the hall. She squatted by the door, wondering how she could get into the lab without the guard knowing. She craned her neck, inch by inch, just enough to look through the door, moving unbearably slow so she wouldn't catch his eye.

The guard paced the main room while he drank a can of Diet Pepsi. A television flickered nearby on a wall mount. Jamie couldn't see Hazard anywhere. She wondered if he was still drugged and unconscious.

The guard stopped his pacing when a sports brief broke the regular programming. He paused with his back to Jamie. She put her hand on the door to push it open just as a strange blue light flared at the forward end of the lab. Jamie watched in horrified amazement as the blue form moved toward the guard, taking the shape of a man as it got closer. The guard gaped at the human form, and for a moment he froze with surprise.

Jamie took her chance and burst into the lab, slapping both hands around her gun. "Freeze!" she cried, just like policemen shouted on television.

The guard swung around to look at her at the same instant the blue light transformed into a human arm. A punishing left hook whipped the guard's head around, and he plunged to the floor, his eyes rolling to the back of his head. His Pepsi flowed around his head in a fizzing brown puddle.

Jamie stared as the rest of Hazard McAllister materialized out of the blue light. He was stark naked, magnificently stark naked. Jamie's arms drifted downward as she took his measure. Some men might have looked ridiculous standing there without a stitch of clothing. But Hazard bore his beautiful nakedness like an impenetrable suit of armor, all hardened brass and sturdy leather thongs. Jamie had never seen anything like it. And when he turned to her, she saw his blunt manhood flop against his thigh. She tore her eyes away from his midriff, blushing hotly inside and out.

"Good work, lass!" Hazard exclaimed, grinning as if unaware of his nudity.

"Get your clothes, Hazard," she replied, stumbling forward. "I'll tape his mouth and tie him up somehow."

Hazard turned and loped away. Jamie stared after him, still overwhelmed by the sight of him. How must it feel to touch that body! Jamie felt her legs trembling as she knelt beside the unconscious guard. She shoved his gun away from him and then found some duct tape in a cabinet. She was ripping off a piece of the tape with her teeth when Hazard returned, stuffing his shirttails into his pants.

After they left the guard bound and gagged and locked in a small closet, they crept out of the lab.

"What now?" Jamie whispered.

"Saints know." Hazard grabbed her hand and ran up the hallway just as an alarm blared, pulsating in short, ear-shattering blasts.

"They know!" Jamie shouted.

"Come on!" Hazard pulled her up the companionway to the next deck. She could hear shouting and someone running behind them. Hazard scrambled over the deck, dodging bullets. Jamie stumbled in the darkness after him, tripping over a cleat, but Hazard kept her from falling.

Then all the lights on the ship came on, flooding the deck. Two more guards burst from the pilothouse.

"Stop!" one of them yelled. Hazard ran aft, dragging Jamie with him.

"Get him!" another guard cried.

Hazard threw a leg over the rail and Jamie pulled back, realizing that he meant to jump.

"C'mon lass!" Hazard shouted breathlessly.

"I can't!"

"Ye can." He grabbed her hand in a vicelike grip. " 'Tis our only chance."

Jamie crawled over the rail and before she could say

another word, she was pulled over the side into a black windy void. Bullets whirred past her head and hissed into the water. She was falling, falling! Then she hit the water with a smack and went under.

15

JAMIE CLAWED HER WAY to the surface of the water with one hand while she clutched Hazard's big hand with the other. Bullets whizzed past as the guards continued to fire at them, but the night was as black as the water, and Hazard and Jamie were nearly invisible in the waves.

Salt water slapped Jamie in the face, choking her, while she treaded water and stared at the long white ship. What could they do? What would happen to them? Hazard might not be affected by the chilly water, but Jamie knew that a human being could perish from hypothermia in less than half an hour. She felt something brush her leg and hoped it was just a long strand of kelp floating near the surface and not a shark looking for a quick meal.

After a few minutes, the guards stopped shooting and the lights blinked off, leaving only the night signal lights illuminated.

"What are they going to do?" Jamie gasped through lips already stiff with cold. "Why have they quit firing?"

"A vessel's comin' up behind us."

She turned to look for the ship and saw the faint silhouette of a large ship, perhaps a ferry, bearing down on them. "They'll never see us!" Jamie cried. "They'll run over us!"

"Maybe not." Hazard let go of Jamie's hand, and she whipped her head around in terror, flailing her arms to grab hold of him again. She found it hard to drag her arms through the water. The cold sucked the energy from her limbs and dulled her mind. Then Dr. Hamilton's ship sped away, nearly submerging them in the frothy wake.

"Hazard," Jamie sputtered. Her hair dripped in her eyes, burning them with salt water.

"Dinna be afraid, Jamie. I'm goin' t' let myself turn back t' light."

In seconds, Hazard transformed from a human shape into a blue beacon of indefinable shape, sparkling like a spotlight in the black expanse of water. The approaching vessel blew two blasts, signaling that something had been spotted off port bow.

"They've seen us," Jamie barked hoarsely. Her hands and feet were growing too heavy to move and more than once she went under.

"Just hold on, lass," she heard Hazard say. She wondered how he had spoken to her, but couldn't figure it out. It was too hard to think when she was so cold and so terrified.

"Hold on, lass!"

Jamie woke up to the heavenly smell of coffee. She opened her eyes. She was lying in a bunk with a mound of wool blankets covering her. Her wet clothes had been removed and she lay beneath the covers as naked as a baby. Hazard stood above her, watching her, a deep crease between his eyebrows. His wet clothes had been replaced by a white terry-cloth robe with an emblem sewn on the breast pocket. Another man stood behind him. The stranger wore a blue uniform and a hat with braid on it. She was in another cabin on another ship.

"Jamie! Thank God!" Hazard grinned and sat down beside her on the bunk. She tried to grin back but her lips wouldn't obey her. "How are you feelin'?" He took her hand and squeezed it.

"Okay."

The man in the uniform leaned closer. "We were worried about you for awhile. You got mighty cold out there."

"Where are we?" Jamie murmured.

"On the *Princess Maria*, a cruise ship out of Seattle."

"We were lucky ye were passin' by, captain."

The man shook his head sagely and fingered his beard. "I've heard about ships sinking in a matter of minutes. But I never witnessed it first hand. Good thing you had that light on or we never would have seen you two."

" 'Twas not an experience I want t' repeat," Hazard replied. Jamie glanced at him. Hazard had made up a story to explain their predicament and still keep the authorities from finding out about the hologram project. She was grateful for his quick thinking.

"Well, Mrs. McPherson, you drink some hot coffee and take it easy. We'll be in Seattle in about an hour and a half." The captain stepped to the door and opened it. "If you need anything, just use the buzzer. And when your clothes are dried, I'll have them sent down."

"Thank you, captain," Jamie smiled. "Thank you so much."

He saluted and closed the door.

Jamie rolled her head on the pillow so that she looked at Hazard. He bent over her, the robe gaping open at the chest to reveal his muscular torso and the red-gold hairs upon his chest. He gazed down at her, his eyes dark blue with concern.

"Jamie, I thought I'd lost ye," he murmured, fervently kissing her hand without taking his gaze off her face. She watched as his lips pressed her skin. Her breasts immediately reacted to the contact of his lips. Her nipples hardened beneath the sheet and a jab of desire jolted through her. She shuddered involuntarily.

"D'ye want some coffee, lass?"

"No." She shook her head while she reached up for the strong column of his neck. Her fingers quickly traced the line of the robe until she found the curls of his hair at the nape of his neck. "I just need you to hold me, Hazard."

She sat up and the covers fell away to reveal her slender torso. Hazard glanced at her, drinking in the sight of her beautiful naked body, creamy ivory dipped in rose. He eased his hands around her, just under her arms. His thumbs framed the round curves of the outsides of her breasts while his fingertips nearly reached her shoulder blades. For a moment his glance swept over her taut breasts and then he pulled her against him, pressing his face into her hair.

Jamie clung to him, drawing strength from the wide girth of him, the warmth of him, and the sound of his voice as he murmured her name. She had almost lost Hazard. And never, never in a million years would she let this chance go by to show him how much he meant to her. No matter what the consequences might be, no matter how inhuman Hazard McAllister was, she loved him and wanted to join with him and meld him to her soul.

She raised up to kiss him and his mouth met hers with a hunger sharpened by a narrow brush with death. Each kiss was precious, each caress a gift bestowed by fate or luck. Jamie opened her lips to him and this time plunged her tongue into the warm cavity of his mouth, pressing her breasts against his robe, and shoving her hands under the fabric until she had pushed it off his shoulders. His skin stretched tightly over a blazing expanse of muscle and sinew. Jamie thrilled to the feeling of the power that moved beneath her fingers as she dragged the robe down his arms. His back felt incredibly wide and smooth, like a wedge of heated flint. She caressed him, murmuring his name against his lips, chanting a hymn of heat and need.

Hazard pulled his arms out of the sleeves, one at a time so he did not have to release her. Frantic with desire, Jamie drew the belt ends apart and threw them aside. The robe sank around Hazard's hips, parting in the middle as his erect manhood jutted out of the folds and pressed against her belly. Jamie gasped and glanced down, forgetting to breathe at the sight of him.

He raised her chin to force her to look at him. His eyes were swimming with desire, pools of molten turquoise. "Jamie, lass," he said huskily. "We must finish what we start this time, or I'll go stark ravin' mad."

"Then start," she whispered. "You hotblooded Scot."

Hazard stared at her for an instant, wondering if he had heard her correctly. Then he grinned, a grin full of love and lust so plain that Jamie went wet between her legs. She slowly lowered to the pillow without breaking from his gaze, ready and willing to accept him. Still smiling, he threw off the blankets and bent over her, straddling her knees with his own. He planted his right hand near her head and with his left he smoothed back her hair from the side of her face in a gesture fraught with tender possession.

Then, without tearing his eyes off her, he gradually lowered his weight upon her, pushing one of her legs aside. Jamie gasped at the heat of his body. For the first time in her life she felt the touch of a man's naked body against her own. It was a feeling like no other, all solid heat, much more dense than her own flesh. She ran her hands up and down his back, following the muscular planes of his torso. Her heart thudded with joy, with anticipation. And with a sudden clarity of vision, she knew that what she was about to share with Hazard was the culmination of two lifetimes, hers and Nelle McMurray's.

Hazard kissed her collarbone, her neck, her chin, and then her lips.

"Ah, Jamie!" he exclaimed. "I canna wait another moment."

Jamie's heart pounded in her chest as he raised above her and drew up her knees. Her hands posed in midair as he kissed her again and guided his length to her. With a growl, Hazard claimed her.

Jamie cried out, first in pain and then in astonishment as he forced his entire length into her, burrowing to the root of his shaft. He moaned, holding back a century of need while Jamie held his hips to hers. She didn't want him to pull away. She wanted to feel him at the very center of her being. She wanted to hold him there and keep him there forever, deep inside her, deep enough to fill the black void that had eaten away at her for years.

But Hazard was driven by his own desires. He drew her hands over her head, laced his fingers with hers, palm to palm, and kissed her, slowly moving against her at first. Gradually, Hazard's tempo increased and he broke from the kiss, breathing heavily. Jamie held onto his shoulders, caught up in a new wave of desire that had come with his quickening pace. She arched into him, tipping her hips to meet his, frantic to reach a strange and compelling height just beyond her grasp.

"Jamie!" he gasped. The sheen of sweat on his back

suddenly turned cold. "Ah, lass!" His plunging grew deeper and wilder as his voice grew higher and tighter. "Ah, God, lass!" Then Jamie saw beneath her fingers a layer of light blossoming on Hazard's skin, as if he effervesced. But she had no time to wonder at the light. She was soaring, soaring, soaring to the edge of a cliff, riding on a wave of frenzy so fierce she was consumed by it, unable to break away from it.

"Jamie!" Hazard cried in a strangled voice. But Jamie could hardly hear him. Blood pounded in her ears. She felt something burst inside her, something hot and molten. Heat shot through her arms and legs, and for a moment she was lost to an incomparable sensation of fulfillment and bliss. Hazard hung above her, rigid and shuddering, with his eyes shut and his lips parted as he sucked in great gulps of air without exhaling.

Jamie, glowing like a firebrand, finally opened her eyes. She gasped. Hazard was swamped in light. Jamie stared in shock as she saw light pouring out of her body. Shafts of yellow and blue and magenta streamed from her, and a glowing pink aura shimmered on her belly and thighs.

Still tense, Hazard had not yet come to his senses. He seemed to be lost from reality. "Oh, God!" he moaned, forcing out the words between his gritted teeth. Light shot skyward from the bed, illuminating the room as if a flare had gone off. Jamie could do nothing but gape in horrified amazement. Then Hazard let out his breath in a burst and threw back his head.

"Hazard!" Jamie cried, struggling up to her elbows.

He rolled away from her and landed on his back with one arm flung over the side of the bunk. He panted and trembled, and Jamie was suddenly afraid.

"Hazard!" she cried again, sitting up in alarm. Her desire had vanished in an instant. She stared at him. He seemed utterly exhausted and unusually pale. He hadn't opened his eyes, either, and wasn't aware of the light that danced across his skin. Jamie hesitantly reached out, wondering whether she should touch him. She brushed back his hair.

"Hazard, open your eyes."

He swallowed and licked his lips. "Jamie—I—"

"Hazard, you're glowing!"

He opened his eyes and looked down at his chest and then raised his hand. "Saint Andrew!" he breathed as he inspected his arm. Then he let his hand drop and his eyes closed again.

"Are you all right?" she asked.

He smiled faintly. "I dinna know. I think my century-old what ye may call it's got me in its grip."

"You look pale." She felt his forehead. "And you're cold. Do you feel okay?"

Hazard turned his head and gazed at her with feverish eyes. Then he pulled her to his lips and kissed her to reassure her. She felt his hand shaking.

"Jamie, I never felt anythin'—not anythin'—near this. It's walloped me." His hand slid from her hair. "Give me a minute t' gather my wits, lass."

Jamie embraced his chest and looked at the underside of his jaw. "You were full of light, Hazard. Light lit up the entire room."

His hand rose and caressed her back. "Are you all right, though?"

"Yes!" She stroked his cheek.

"Did I scare ye, love?"

She hugged his wide chest and smiled. "I'm a big girl now, Hazard McAllister," she replied softly. "You can't scare me."

But Jamie *was* scared. She watched Hazard closely,

worried about his condition. His speech had been slurred and his breathing shallow, and for the longest time he did nothing but absently stroke her back.

"How did you do it?" she asked at last, when his breathing had returned to a steady rhythm.

"Do what, lass?" he replied, his voice rumbling against her ear.

"Turn to light in the sea."

He breathed in deeply, raising her up with his chest.

"I found out I could transform myself after tha' Dr. Hamilton drugged me. 'Twas a fortunate occurrence. He couldna test a thing then. 'Twas mad as a hornet he was."

"So you can go back and forth at will?"

"With considerable concentration, lass, especially t' come back from bein' light."

"Maybe you shouldn't do it that often." She ran a worried glance over his face. "Maybe it's dangerous for you to transform."

"Aye. I'd hate t' lose this body now." He raised up and kissed her. The color was beginning to flood back into his face and Jamie felt a great sense of relief. "Now that I've had the pleasure of knowin' yours." He rolled onto his side and draped his leg across her thighs. Then he drew her into his arms and squeezed her, surrounding her with his large frame. "Ah, Jamie, my bonny little sparrow, ye've got a body tha' makes me thankful t' be a man." He nuzzled her neck. "An' now, Jamie girl, I'll make ye glad t' be a woman."

She reached up and touched the hand that cupped her left breast. "You already have, Hazard."

"Nay," he chuckled, pinching her nipple. A shaft of exquisite pain ripped through her. What other tricks did Hazard know? "Th' first time was for my pleasure," Hazard went on. "This time will be for yours."

Could there be a greater pleasure than she had just felt in his arms? Before she could ask, Hazard lowered his head and took her breast in his mouth, suckling her like a babe. Jamie cried out and closed her eyes, surrendering to an exotic ache that spread like liquid fire from her breasts to somewhere deep inside her belly.

Hazard ranged over her body, tasting and biting nearly every inch of her flesh, from the lobes of her ears to the ends of her toes. Jamie lay on the bunk, suspended in a world of ecstasy, her skin tingling as if every nerve were alive and pulsating. Then Hazard took her once more—slowly, sweetly, maddeningly until she cried out for mercy.

Afterward she lay devastated, satiated, and glowing, unable to speak. Hazard lay beside her, with a hand on her flank. Jamie sighed as he nestled against her, and she suddenly felt a horrible emptiness as a new realization hit home. Hazard would never spill his seed in her, never give a child to her, never complete the timeless cycle of birth and death, never culminate their lovemaking as it was meant to be culminated. Jamie turned in his arms and clung to him, hugging him until her arms ached. More than anything, she wanted a part of this man, a part of him that would be hers forever. Yet she would have to settle for whatever portion fate would allow.

"What's th' matter, Mrs. McPherson?" Hazard murmured.

"Nothing, Mr. McPherson," she replied. "Nothing at all."

16

JAMIE AND HAZARD DID NOT GET BACK to Port Townsend until the next morning, after a night spent in a motel in Seattle and a ferry ride back to the peninsula. Though Jamie had never spent a more exquisite night than the one she had shared with Hazard, she was anxious to get back to her brother to warn him of Dr. Hamilton's intentions to steal his project. She had called Mark from Seattle to explain what had happened so he wouldn't worry needlessly, but had left the bulk of the story untold until she saw him face to face.

Mrs. Gipson met them at the door, skittering about in excitement.

"Jamie! Mr. McDougall, there you are!" She closed the door after them and followed them to the stairs. "Mark will be wanting to hear all about your kidnapping. Are you all right?"

"We're both fine, Edna, thank ye." Hazard pulled Jamie close and he squeezed her shoulders.

Jamie smiled up at Hazard.

"Would you like some lunch?"

"That would be great, Mrs. Gipson."

The housekeeper bustled off to the kitchen, and before Jamie had taken more than three steps up the stairs, she saw Brett appear in the drawing room doorway. He glared at Jamie, then at Hazard, and strode across the room, dragging a roll of black crepe paper.

"Where in the hell have you been?" Brett demanded. "I was worried sick about you." Impatiently, he rolled up the loose end of the crepe paper.

"We took a swim in the Straits of Juan de Fuca," Jamie explained.

Brett glanced at her face, thinking she was joking, and then looked over at Hazard. "What's going on, McDougall?"

"We were kidnapped by one o' Mark's admirers."

"What?"

"Tried t' take us t' Canada. We jumped ship an' got picked up by the *Princess Maria.*"

"You expect me to believe that?" Brett snarled. "I know goddamn well what you were doing. You were probably holed up somewhere, screwing yourselves blue."

Jamie gaped at Brett, aghast that he could say such a thing. Then anger flooded her, filling her with hot, raw rage. She'd had enough of Brett. She couldn't take another one of his remarks. She stalked down the stairs to Brett and slapped him soundly. His head snapped to the side with the force of her blow. He held his cheek, astonished that she would strike him. Jamie remained standing in front of him, shaking with rage. When he said nothing, she slapped him again and then whirled around and strode up the stairs with hard, pounding steps. She rushed down the hall, rapped on Mark's door, and burst into his bedroom.

Mark looked up in surprise at her tumultuous entrance. "Jamie! What's going on?"

"It's a long story," she said, holding up her hands. "Suffice it to say that you are in danger, Mark. Some guy named Dr. Hamilton knows all about you and Hazard. We've got to get you out of here."

"You're serious."

"Dead serious, Mark."

She relayed the events of the past day and a half, leaving out the personal details. Mark listened, his face growing dark with anger.

"Why can't they just leave us alone?" he cried. "And what do they think they're going to learn from Hazard? He's not a true product of the hologram project."

"I want you to pack up, Mark," Jamie answered. "We've got to get you away from here. Tomorrow."

"What about Hazard?"

"He can come with us."

"Do you think he'll want to?"

Jamie thought back to the last hours she had spent with Hazard. "He'll come," she replied.

Jamie returned to her room after lunch with Hazard and Mark. She picked up the engagement ring from her night stand and slipped it into the pocket of her jeans. Then she ran a brush through her hair and glanced at her reflection in the mirror. Though she had decided earlier to wait until after the party to talk to Brett about their relationship, she could not adhere to her plan. A burning sensation gnawed at her. Jamie knew the cause. She was angry at Brett, livid in fact, and had been livid for a long time. She could either let it burn or do something about it. For once Jamie did not gulp down a Valium to subdue her feelings. She decided to use anger as a shield against Brett, for he would surely lash out at her. Jamie breathed in resolutely and made a face at herself. Do it now, Jamie Kent, she told herself. Wait another hour and you'll go mad, really mad this time.

She knew Brett was in his room alone. He had just returned from town with boxes and bags and an assortment of food and booze for the party. She had heard him tell Tiffany he was going to shower before dinner.

Jamie closed her door and walked down the hall. Breaking an almost-engagement should not be an impossible task, especially since she had never accepted a marriage offer from Brett in the first place. He had forced the ring on her, expecting her answer to be affirmative. Yet Jamie knew the confrontation would be a struggle. Brett would demand reasons for the breakup. He would try to make her feel guilty and responsible for their problems. He was not one to accept refusal with grace.

Before she was aware that she had walked any distance, Jamie was standing before Brett's door. Determined to get the scene over with, Jamie straightened her shoulders, lifted her hand, and knocked on his door.

"Come in!" he called.

Jamie opened the door to find Brett dressed in a towel and slippers. He grinned at her expression of surprise.

"Hey, Jamie! Just the person I wanted to see."

He bent over the profusion of bags on his bed and pulled up a bouquet of flowers wrapped in tissue paper.

"For you, hon. I, uh, I got to thinking about what I said. I was kind of a—well, a total jerk."

Jamie was doubly surprised. Was she hearing correctly? Was Brett admitting that he was wrong? She was so surprised she didn't respond until he shook the flowers at her. "Come on, don't you like roses, Jamie?"

His callous behavior brought her to her senses. He could have at least approached her with a friendly gesture instead of standing in the middle of the room shaking his peace offering at her. She felt her anger flare pure and strong again. "Which incident are they for, Brett?"

Brett's smile dissipated. "What in hell is that supposed to mean?" The flowers drooped in his hand.

"I'd simply like to know which incident the flowers are for—today, the Lloyd Evans incident, or the other night when you were drunk?"

Brett threw the flowers on the bed. "Does it matter?"

"Are the roses a blanket apology, then? A kind of generic 'I'm sorry'?"

He glared at her. "They're nothing! Forget it!"

Jamie stepped into the room and closed the door. "That's what's wrong with us, Brett. You seem to think you can fix everything with a purchase—an expensive ring, flowers, tickets to the ballet. But that doesn't make me forget your behavior. That doesn't do anything for me at all. It doesn't take much to go out and buy something. But it does take a lot to speak from your heart. I'd like an apology from you, Brett, some actual words to let me know how you really feel."

"Actions speak louder than words," he retorted.

"Not always, Brett."

He stared at her, the resentment so strong on his face that Jamie felt a prickle of fear. "You're a cold bitch," he said between his teeth. "You've always been a cold bitch. Cold and calculating. Standing behind that camera, watching. Sucking other peoples' emotions up like some Goddamn vampire."

"I am not cold."

"Yes, you are. You don't even know it, that's how bad it is. How long have we known each other—four years? And how many times have we got it on since we started dating?" He strode up to her. "How many times, Jamie, have I come on to you, and you turn me off—click!" He snapped his fingers. "Just like that!"

"I was saving myself." She hugged her arms.

"No, you weren't. That's just an excuse. I can see through you, you cold bitch. You just don't want to lose control."

"That's not true!"

"It is and you know it." He grabbed another towel off the dresser. "Well, listen up, Ice Queen, the real world doesn't work like a camera." He threw the towel over his shoulder. "You can't stand around just watching. You have to participate. You have to interact with other people. Or those other people go somewhere else to have their film wound—know what I mean?"

"I'm not in the film-winding business, Brett, not for you, not anymore."

He jerked around. "What do you mean?"

"I might have been once had you ever told me that you loved me."

"Wait a minute—"

"No, you wait a minute." Jamie strode up to him. "I don't think you know the difference between love and sex. I don't think you have the faintest idea what love is. You certainly don't love me. You don't listen to me when I talk to you. You don't care how I feel about things. Sex is all you want from me. If I hopped into bed with you right now, you'd be perfectly satisfied. No, let me amend that—" With a yank, she pulled off his towel. He gasped in surprise. "You'd be perfectly happy if I serviced you right here."

Jamie dared not look at his nakedness, afraid that she would lose her resolve altogether. Her legs were shaking as it was. A movement caught her eye, however, and she glanced down. Impossible as it seemed, her anger and the actions she had hoped would humiliate him, had aroused him. She glared at him in disbelief. He shrugged.

"Hey, I've never been stripped before," he explained, grinning. "It turns me on."

"You're disgusting, Brett. You really are." She turned for the door.

"What's the matter, Jamie? Don't you know what to do? Didn't they teach you how to please a man in art school?"

Jamie pivoted at the door.

"Here's your ring back," she dropped it on the chair beside the door. "Why don't you give it to Tiffany? She seems to like you."

"Hey, just a minute." Brett snatched his towel off the floor. "What's this all about? It's that McDougall, isn't it?"

Jamie put her hand on the doorknob but said nothing.

"He's got to you, hasn't he?"

Jamie heard Brett pad closer.

"God, Jamie. Don't fall for that foreign accent, that line of gab."

"McDougall has nothing to do with it."

"It's this place that's coming between us. That's what it is. It's this place. Once we get back to L.A. you'll change your mind. I know you will."

"No, I won't." She opened the door.

"Jamie, if you give back the ring, we're through. We're finished. That means the business, too. Everything you've worked for."

"Fine." She stepped through the doorway.

"Jamie!"

Slowly Jamie turned. An awful calm had come over her. She felt as if *she* were being directed by a remote control. "I don't love you, Brett. I can't marry you. That's all."

"You'd better think about it, hon. I'll give you a few days to think it over because if you break our engagement, our partnership is over, too."

"You said that already."

"Jamie, you'll be nothing without me. Do you understand what I'm saying? I made you."

"Did you?" she asked coolly.

"You better believe it." He put a hand on the door as if to keep her from going. "Don't do this to yourself. Wait until you're back in L.A., back to reality."

"Brett, L.A. is your reality. Not mine. I don't need more time to think about it. It's over between us." She strode through the doorway.

"Think of your options, Jamie," he called after her. "You'll change your mind."

Jamie fled to Mark's room after her scene with Brett. She needed to be with someone, and Hazard had left the house. She found her brother in the lab, boxing up his equipment.

"Almost packed?" she said, leaning against the doorway.

Mark looked over his shoulder at her. "Just about. Hazard said he'd help with the heavy stuff later." His glance lingered on Jamie, as if to discern why her color was abnormally high. But he didn't ask any questions, for which Jamie was grateful.

She stepped forward. Mark wrapped an electrical cord around his arm. "So what are you going to be tonight?"

"Tonight?" Jamie asked. "Oh, you mean at the Halloween party?"

"Yeah, what are you going to be?"

"I don't know. I haven't even thought about it."

"What are you—some kind of party pooper?"

Jamie stared at him. "Mark, I've had a lot on my mind lately. This party is not a top priority. You're not thinking of going, are you?"

"Sure I am. I love Halloween."

"Do you think you can take it?"

"Heck, I can sit around downstairs. I'll get McAllister to help me down."

Jamie unplugged a videocassette machine from the surge protector. "What are you going to wear?"

"Remember that costume we used to make—you know the table top with the head on a plate?"

Jamie chuckled. "That always was a favorite of mine."

"Would you bring me up the stuff for it? The paper plate, the ketchup and all that? I've got a box in the lab I can use."

"Sure."

Mark dropped the coil of electrical cord into a box. "So what costume are you going to wear?"

"Oh, I don't know. Maybe a ghost. That would be appropriate."

"Not original, though, sis. Hazard's going as Hazard McAllister."

Jamie straightened. "What?"

"I think it's great. He's going as himself."

"What if anyone suspects?"

"Get real, sis. No one would believe Hazard is really a ghost. None of them has enough imagination for it."

Leaving Mark to nap for the remainder of the afternoon, she returned to the drawing room where the studio equipment was stored. She packed her gear into the appropriate cases, making sure that everything was locked and secure. She glanced at her watch. It was three-thirty. She had little time left to come up with a costume for the party that evening.

The party had become more an inconvenience for her than an event to anticipate. It was the final hurdle before her escape from Port Townsend. She had no wish to be in the same room with Brett, and she worried what would happen when Hazard showed up as the ghost that supposedly haunted the mansion. Parties had never been easy for her to endure; she was too shy and retiring. Jamie assumed this Halloween party would be the same as all the others. She would sit on the fringes nursing a glass of wine, praying that no one would force her to dance, while Brett flirted with the prettiest women guests.

As she walked to the door of the drawing room she nearly tripped over a trunk that had been left sticking out beside the antique sideboard. Swearing under her breath, Jamie regained her balance and glanced down at the case that had caught her pant leg. She recognized it as the one containing the costumes used in the commercials. Perhaps she could find something inside that she could wear.

Jamie knelt and opened the trunk. Tiffany had worn a blue satin gown in the commercial. But there were three other dresses that were folded carefully between tissue paper. Jamie pulled out an evening gown of white satin with bands and bows of teal-green velvet. The sleeves were huge puffs that narrowed to tight cuffs below the elbow. My, won't this look ridiculous on me, Jamie thought with a smile. But at least it was a costume. She rummaged around and found a fan, some gloves, and a pair of pearl earrings in a teardrop shape. If she could arrange her hair to look like that of a woman of the 1890s she might just pull it off.

Jamie didn't eat dinner, mostly because she did not want to run into Brett at the table. She had also nibbled at enough hors d'oeuvres to take the edge off her hunger. After she helped Mark with his costume, she hurried to her bedroom to dress. She could hear the band setting up one floor below.

Jamie flipped through her history books until she found a decent example of a female hairstyle at the turn of the century. The style of the day seemed to be a chignon worn high on the head with fringes at the hairline. She had never fussed with her hair much and wasn't certain she could copy such a hairdo. But she would give it a try.

It took longer than Jamie anticipated. After an hour of curling her dark-blonde hair with a curling iron, she finally achieved a decent chignon. The fringes would have to be deleted, however. She wasn't about to cut her hair in front to create little curls.

She wiggled into the gown, thankful she didn't live at a time when women had to be laced into corsets and hung with all sorts of wired and padded foundation garments. Jamie was slender enough to fit in the gown without being cinched. It fit her well, and the square neckline trimmed in velvet accentuated her slender neck and delicate jawline. Jamie tilted her head and glanced at the bustle on her backside. Granted, she wouldn't want to wear such a dress every day, but the style was peculiarly flattering to her figure.

Ready at last, she flowed from her room, checking to see if Mark had already gone down to the party. His room was empty. Jamie felt a flutter of stage fright. What if everyone looked at her when she went down the stairs? What if she tripped on the gown and fell? She wished someone were upstairs to accompany her.

Jamie chided herself for being a coward and walked to the stairs. The loud music blared down below. She put her gloved hand on the bannister and took a step downward. The hall was full of guests, some coming in the house and some strolling into the parlor and drawing room, which had been cleared to serve as a dance floor. The flash of Jamie's white gown caught more than one glance, and she felt many eyes as she descended. The farther down she floated, the hotter her blush flared on her cheeks. When she was halfway down, she glimpsed a tall figure standing in the parlor doorway.

Hazard was dressed in an old-fashioned black tuxedo with long shiny lapels, a white waistcoat complete with a gold watch fob and chain, and white tie. He gazed up at her, thunderstruck. A thrill shot through Jamie and she paused. She saw him thread his way through the crowd. By the time Jamie gained the bottom step, he had arrived at the staircase with a radiant smile on his lips.

"Jamie! My God, lass!" He stuck out his gloved hand and Jamie accepted it, glad to have his company. The tuxedo flattered the lines of his body more than any modern clothes he had worn. He looked magnificent in black. His hair glinted in shades of gold, amber, and copper, and his eyes gleamed and glittered like shards of sky-colored crystals.

Jamie did not step off the last stair. She couldn't move. Instead, she stood before Hazard, unintentionally regal in her shimmering gown, astonished that she had rendered him speechless. Spellbound herself, she returned his gaze and felt truly beautiful for the first time in her life.

"What a lovely gown!" a woman remarked near her elbow, breaking the spell.

"Thank you," Jamie replied.

"Who are you? Cinderella?"

Jamie smiled and stepped down to the floor. "Not really. But I feel like Cinderella."

Hazard drew her close to him and bent over her hand. "Jamie, ye stunned me."

"Really?" Jamie beamed with pleasure.

"Ah, lass." He kissed the back of her hand. "Ye look grand."

"You look fetchin' yourself, Hazard McAllister. That's who you're supposed to be, isn't it?"

"Aye. I'm McAllister all right." He winked and held out his arm. She draped both hands around his elbow, proud to be escorted by the tall and elegant Scotsman, and loving the sound of his chuckle as he guided her to the dance floor. Her heart burst with happiness. She belonged with this man. She knew his walk, she knew the pace of his breathing, she knew his smile and the cadence of his voice. Somehow she and Hazard had been fashioned for each other, and she belonged on his arm as she had never belonged to anyone. For the first time in her life Jamie walked into a party and did not feel alone.

"They can dance t' this music?" Hazard asked, bending down so she could hear him over the din.

She nodded.

"Why is that guitar player wearin' those black glasses at night?"

"He thinks he's cool."

"Cool?"

"You know—attractive. Stylish." She smiled and squeezed his arm.

Hazard guided her to the dance floor and turned to face her. "How about a dance, Jamie?"

"I've got to warn you," she replied. "I don't dance very well."

"Drivel!"

17

HAZARD TOOK JAMIE'S HAND and raised it formally while his other hand curved around the small of her back. He did not bring her close, but held her firmly away from him. "Just follow my lead, Jamie girl. And relax. Ye look ravishin'."

"I'll try. But I've never danced in a get-up like this."

Before she knew it, Hazard was gliding her around, expertly guiding her through the other couples. His confidence freed her. She let him take her and forgot to worry about stepping on his feet or bumping into other couples. She could tell by the pressure of his hand on her back or the dip of his hand holding hers which way he would turn. After a few minutes his signals became second nature, and before she knew it, she was actually enjoying the music. He twirled her round and round until she was dizzy with happiness, until she was completely enchanted. She closed her eyes and smiled, enraptured and delirious. When the ballad ended, she opened her eyes, slowly emerging from the dream, only to be startled by the sound of applause. Jamie blinked. She and Hazard were on the dance floor alone. Everyone else stood in a ring around them, clapping.

"Ye canna dance, eh, Jamie?" Hazard smiled down at her.

"It was you," she answered, breathless.

He led her off the floor, nodding and smiling at the clapping guests as they made way for the couple. He didn't speak again until they gained the bar in the corner next to the fireplace.

"Hazard, are you always like this?"

"Well, I've never been shy, if that's what ye mean." He grinned. "And I've always liked a woman tha' can kick up her heels."

"I've never danced like that. Dancing was always awkward for me."

"Ye never were with me before, Jamie, that's why." His arm lingered behind her, supporting her. "Ye read me well out on th' floor. You're a natural."

"Hardly." Yet she had been a natural in Hazard's arms and she knew it. A rush of satisfaction raced through her and brought a smile to her lips.

"What can I get for you?" the bartender asked.

Jamie couldn't keep from grinning. The bartender grinned back, infected by her ebullient mood.

"How about a champagne cocktail," she said.

"Champagne cocktail it is. And you, sir?"

"Scotch."

"On the rocks?"

"Nay. Straight, if you please."

They sipped their drinks and Jamie made a face as Hazard took a hefty draft of his whiskey. "How can you stand to drink it like that?" she asked, grimacing.

"There's two things a Highlander likes naked, Jamie,"

he replied. "And one o' them's scotch." He winked at her, and before she could blush at the inference, he took her elbow and guided her back to the dance floor.

This time Jamie approached the dance floor with a thrill of anticipation instead of dread. Hazard took her in hand again and swept her away.

"I notice a different style o' dancin'," Hazard said as they moved across the floor. "Couples are more intimate in th' nineties."

Jamie glanced at the dancers nearby. Most of the women were draped over their partners. Some people were even kissing each other while they danced.

"Yes, they are."

Hazard's hand tightened around her fingers. " 'Twas considered poor manners t' touch a woman's back without gloves in my day."

"We've done away with manners it seems."

"I wouldn't mind dancin' closer to ye, Jamie. 'Twould allow for more space for others on th' dance floor, wouldna ye think."

Jamie chuckled. "You are incorrigible, sir."

Hazard's arm brought her against him until her breasts pressed into his lapels and her hips grazed his trousers. For a minute they danced with their right hands still extended in a formal pose while Jamie tried to master the jolt of desire that shot through her. She slid her hand from the top of Hazard's sleeve and up over his shoulder until her palm came to rest at the side of his neck. She loved the solidity of his torso. His silken hair grazed her fingertips at the nape of his neck. Gradually, their right hands drew closer and closer until Hazard curled her wrist over his heart.

"You don't get as much exercise this way," Jamie ventured, trying to ignore her racing pulse.

His arm tightened around her and he bent down until his cheek pressed against her hair. " 'Tis not about exercise I'm thinkin'." For a while he danced in silence, holding her against him, feeling the touch of her body molding into his. Jamie could tell by his breathing that he was growing more aroused with every second they moved against each other. His hand swept across her back as his lips brushed her ear. "Ah, Jamie girl." He sighed. "Ye dinna know what ye do t' me."

She pulled back at his words and he relaxed his grip. When she glanced at his face she saw dark hungry lights in his eyes that even his slow smile could not disguise. Jamie slid her hand back to his upper arm and drew away from him with a sigh, as hungry for him as he was for her, but not wanting to make a spectacle of their attraction for each other.

The music ended and he backed away from her, clapping. Jamie glanced at the side of his face as he applauded and was surprised to see how quickly his expression had changed. His mouth was set in a hard firm line and his blue eyes glinted like bits of ice as he observed something across the room. Jamie followed his line of sight, wondering what could have changed his mood so drastically.

There, across the room was Tiffany leaning over the coffee table in front of her. Brett sat beside her, laughing, with his arm draped across her bony back. Tiffany's head and hand dipped and moved along the top of the table and then she raised up and flung back her hair.

"What in blazes are they doin'?" Hazard asked.

"Snorting," Jamie replied, taking Hazard's arm.

"Snortin'?"

"Yes. They're drawing a white powder called cocaine up through their noses. It's a drug."

"What effect does it have?"

Jamie frowned. "It is supposed to make you feel splendid and all powerful for a few minutes."

Hazard chuckled. "Ye dinna need a drug for tha'."

His innuendo was not lost on Jamie, and she smiled vaguely as her gaze lingered on Brett and Tiffany. She watched Brett lean over and kiss Tiffany. Jamie wondered what she had ever seen in him. In L.A. she had considered him conservative in comparison to the people they knew. But in this house he had changed from Dr. Jeckyl to Mr. Hyde.

Hazard tugged on her arm. "Looks like th' musicians are takin' a break. Shall we get your brother a drink?"

Numbly, Jamie nodded and let him lead her to the bar. By the time they had got their cocktails and pressed through the crowd to the sidelines, Jamie saw Brett and Tiffany standing next to Mark's chair. Tiffany was appropriately dressed as a cat, with black tights and black cat ears and a long black tail that she had draped over her arm.

Brett watched Jamie approach, his gaze bright with the effects of the cocaine. Jamie hoped he would not make a scene. Sometimes he could get mean when he was high, and she didn't want him to spoil the party with his bad temper. This was one party she was enjoying, and she didn't want anything or anyone to burst her bubble of happiness.

"Well," Brett called out, his voice overloud. "Aren't we the dynamic duo!" Jamie glared at him, wishing he wouldn't talk so loudly. Brett leaned forward. "Did you two go to the same tailor, or is this just a happy accident?"

" 'Twas happy 'til you showed up, Brett," Hazard replied.

"I'll bet it was." Brett barely concealed the snarl in his voice. Tiffany drew on her cigarette and slowly blew the smoke out as she regarded Jamie's finery. Jamie unconsciously raised up to her full height as Tiffany appraised her. Tiffany's eyes glittered and her lips stretched back into a smile.

"Enjoying yourself, Jamie?"

"Yes. And you?"

Tiffany linked her arm through Brett's elbow. "Darling, I always enjoy myself. It's my credo." Jamie caught the stormy look Tiffany shot Hazard. He must have said something to her, something that had put her in her place. Jamie would have liked to hear what he'd said.

Brett, who was dressed in a Union Army uniform, took a drink and eyed Jamie over the rim of his glass. Then he glared at Hazard.

"Why don't you go and mingle with the other guests for awhile, McDougall? Give it a rest."

"I might later."

"Now. I want you to leave Jamie alone."

Hazard narrowed his eyes. "I'll go when I please an' not a minute before."

"Listen, buddy." Brett stepped closer. "Don't cut into my territory. I don't like it."

"Ye mean Jamie?" Hazard asked, baiting him.

"She's my girl."

"Is she now?"

"You're damn right she is." Brett slammed his glass on the table beside Mark's chair. "And I don't want you sniffing around her."

"Brett!" Jamie cried, embarrassed.

"Listen, McDougall," Brett jabbed his finger into Hazard's chest. "Jamie and I have an understanding. But you're putting wild notions into her head. You're getting her confused. And you have no right barging in on our relationship."

"Ye dinna have a relationship." Hazard glared at Brett's hand until he dropped it to his side.

"Just keep away, McDougall. Or else."

"Or else what?" Hazard casually slipped a hand into the pocket of his trousers. His nonchalance made Brett even angrier.

Brett scowled, grasping for a threat that might scare off the Scotsman but found none. "Just keep away. I'm warning you."

Hazard replaced Jamie's hand upon his arm and turned as if to leave. But he paused and looked back at Brett. His gaze swept over Brett's moussed hair, over the ornate uniform with the fake medals, and the shiny tasseled boots. His lip curled with derision. "If you canna bite, man, dinna show your teeth."

At midnight Jamie returned from the bathroom to find Mark and Hazard gone. She inspected the crowd, searching the dozens of strange faces for one she might recognize, but saw no one but Bob Fittro. Desolation passed through her when she realized she had been left alone. With the absence of Hazard, the glitter of the evening dulled instantly. She retraced her steps and peeked into the kitchen, wondering if Hazard might be there. But the kitchen was empty.

"Looking for your escort?" Tiffany appeared at Jamie's elbow.

Jamie turned, taken by surprise. "Do you know where Mark is?" She ignored Tiffany's reference to Hazard.

"It seems he got tired and asked Mr. McDougall to carry him upstairs." Tiffany brushed past her and strolled to the counter near the coffee pot. She picked up a pack of cigarettes.

"What's with McDougall, anyway?" Tiffany continued. "He seems unusually devoted to the both of you."

"He's just an old friend," Jamie replied. "Of the family, you know."

"I don't trust him. Nobody's that devoted without a reason. It's not natural." Tiffany pulled out a cigarette and regarded Jamie steadily, without a hint of friendliness in her eyes.

Jamie broke from the stare and poured a glass of water from the tap, aware that Tiffany was still looking at her.

"Take a bit of advice from the voice of experience," Tiffany said and drew on her cigarette. "Don't burn your bridges."

"What do you mean?"

"I can see what's happening. I saw the way you looked at McDougall tonight. Don't be a fool, Jamie. Don't let yourself be taken in by him. He's one of those charmers. I've had hundreds of them. Sure, they look good and they sound good, but they're no-good. Not when the glow wears off."

"Oh?" Jamie gulped her drink.

"You'd be a fool to give up Brett." She tipped her ashes into the sink and Jamie moved aside slightly. "Brett's a rock. He's every girl's dream. He'll be a millionaire by the time he's forty."

"Money isn't everything."

Tiffany laughed her dry mirthless laugh. "It is when you're an actress and get to be my age. When you wake up in the morning and can't get rid of the lines under your eyes, then you start to think of money and what you'll have to do to keep it coming in."

"But you're not that old. You're younger than me, aren't you?"

"Yeah, and just about ready to start playing character

roles instead of the lead." Tiffany puffed away, agitated. "In our business, careers are too damn short. There's always some cute little model waiting in the wings to take your place." She narrowed her eyes. "But before I give over my crown to some debutante, I intend to make it big, Jamie, and you're not going to screw up my chances."

"How could I do that?"

"Look, this perfume series is your ticket, Brett's ticket, and my ticket. You and Brett will be playing with the big boys once you prove yourselves to that insufferable Noel Condé."

"And how will that help you?" Jamie asked, putting her glass in the sink.

"I'll get international exposure. Plus I'll be working in Brett's little project"—she lifted her chin—"as the star."

"What little project?" Jamie had not been informed of any new enterprises to be undertaken by JK Productions.

Tiffany blew smoke and studied Jamie's reaction. Then she smiled. "Haven't you heard? Brett's going to make a movie."

"He is?" Jamie couldn't hide her surprise.

"Come back to reality, dear. Come out of the cloud you've been living in. There's nothing worthwhile to keep you in Port Townsend, believe me."

"I'm staying in Port Townsend because of my brother."

"Sure you are." Tiffany laughed again. "Sure you are, Jamie."

Jamie's scalp tightened with the first symptom of an oncoming migraine. She steeled herself, fighting the sensation, well aware her suppressed anger at Tiffany's remarks was the source of her headache. Hazard's words came back to her in a rush. *"Until ye become captain o' your soul, Jamie—"*

Jamie breathed in. *I am captain of my own soul. I'm not*

a citadel. I am captain of my own soul. She faced Tiffany, resolute in her determination to confront the redhead.

"You can think what you like, Tiffany. But my feelings for Mr. McDougall are none of your damn business. So butt out."

"Well." Tiffany gaped at her and then took a drag on her cigarette. "Temper, temper, Jamie."

"I don't need your advice."

"But think of your career, Jamie. You can't stay here. You can't shirk your responsibilities. A lot of people are depending on you."

"I'm tired of being depended upon. Just for a change I'd like to do what I want."

"You picked a damn fine time for it!" Tiffany spat. Then she paused and breathed in, as if to collect herself. Slowly, she walked to the door of the kitchen. Before she left the room, however, she glanced at Jamie over her shoulder. "There is more than one way to skin a cat," she remarked acidly.

"What do you mean?" Jamie took a step toward her.

"Use your imagination!" Tiffany swung her tail around and then pivoted smartly, leaving Jamie puzzled and angry in the center of the kitchen.

Jamie whirled, her long dress swishing on the floor, and hurried out of the kitchen using the other door. She threaded through the dancers and climbed the stairs, anxious to leave the noisy crowd behind her. She hoped Mark hadn't overtaxed himself and intended to make sure he would retire early. Jamie flowed through the open door of his room and saw that he was already in bed, although he had a drink in his hand.

Hazard stood at the fire. He held a bottle in one hand and a glass in the other. He was laughing at something Mark had said when Jamie entered the room. Jamie glanced at him. The fire flickered over Hazard's face, patterning his skin and hair with blocks of shadow and light, accentuating the sharp straight lines of his nose and brow.

"Jamie!" he greeted, raising the glass. "There ye are."

She looked askance at the bottle of scotch. "I wondered where you two went," she replied, walking to the bedside. "Are you all right, Mark?"

"Sure. Thought I'd just turn in. Hazard and I were having a nightcap. You want a drink?"

"No thanks."

"So, Brat," he tried to look into her eyes. "What was that all about with Brett this evening?"

"Oh, he's just being a jerk lately." Jamie took a pile of books off the end of his bed and set them on the chair near the night stand.

"He's always a jerk as far as I'm concerned." Mark buttoned his pajama top.

"Well, he's outdone himself this time."

Hazard strolled up to the other side of the bed.

"So did you tell him off?"

"Yes." Jamie looked Mark in the eye. "I called it quits with him."

"Hallelujah!" Mark grinned and turned to Hazard. "It's a miracle, McAllister." Hazard nodded and sipped his drink. Mark put a hand over his sister's. "That's why Brett was so mad at Hazard. He needed someone to blame—besides himself."

"Something like that." Jamie shot a glance at Hazard standing across the bed from her. The firelight illuminated just one side of his face, leaving the other in darkness. All she could see in the shadowed portion was the flash of his eye. Solemnly, Hazard observed their conversation as if waiting for Jamie to declare her feelings for him to her brother.

Jamie, worried what Mark would think of her whirlwind romance with a ghost, placed her hand on Mark's wrist and attempted to explain the situation without admitting everything. "Brett thinks Hazard is a bad influence on me."

"Look who's calling the kettle black." Mark laughed and sank back onto the pillow. "If Brett only knew what Hazard is, he'd die. Blaming his romantic problems on a hologram, a ghost—it kills me. No offense, McAllister."

"None taken," Hazard replied wryly, finishing his scotch. "Well, not much anyway."

Jamie frowned. "That's enough insults for one evening, Mark, and quite enough to drink." She took the glass from his hand and placed it on the nightstand. Then she pulled the covers over him and straightened. "We've got a long drive ahead of us tomorrow."

"Well, everything's crated up. All we'll have to do is load it and go. Does Brett know?"

Jamie shook her head. "He still thinks I'm flying back with him tomorrow."

"Good. The less he knows the better."

"I'll rent a van first thing in the morning." Jamie leaned over the bed and patted Mark's bony hand. "Good night, Mark."

"Good night, sis. See you tomorrow. You, too, McAllister."

"Good night, Mark." Hazard finished his drink and smiled.

Hazard followed Jamie out of the room. When he closed the door behind them, Jamie turned to him. "Would you like to go back to the party?"

"Sure. Lead on, McDuff." He slapped her fanny.

Jamie glanced at him sharply. He raised an eyebrow and grinned. In silence they walked past her bedroom door toward the stairs, but near the stairwell Hazard wavered and leaned against the wall, swinging his head back and forth as if to clear his thoughts.

"Hazard!" Jamie lay her palm on his shoulder. "What's wrong?"

" 'Tis queer." Hazard raised a hand to his head. "I just felt lightheaded for a moment."

"Maybe it's the liquor."

"Aye. After not havin' a drop for a hundred years, maybe I canna hold it like I used t'." He pushed away from the wall and wavered. In alarm, Jamie grabbed him, shoring him up on his left side.

"You're in fine shape," she admonished. "You're drunk!"

"Nay, not after th' little I've had."

"Then why can't you stand up?" She dragged his arm over her shoulder. "You're in no condition to dance."

"The devil ye say."

"Come on, McAllister. I'll help you upstairs."

She struggled to the stairs while he protested, waving his bottle. But Jamie didn't listen to him, and hobbled up the stairs half-supporting his heavy frame. She pushed open his door with her foot and pulled him into the room, nearly falling with him to the bed. He sprawled against the pillows. "Saint Andrew," he sputtered, laughing. Jamie took off his shoes.

"Give me those." Jamie thrust out her hands and snatched away the bottle and glass, which she put on his desk. When she turned around, she found Hazard studying her.

"You're bossin' me," he said.

"You're drunk," she retorted, keeping a safe distance from his bed.

Hazard gazed at her, his eyes glittering. Jamie wondered

what he was thinking. She knew she should leave, but couldn't seem to break away from his gaze.

"Jamie." He pulled himself up on his elbows, slipping once in the process and chuckling at his own clumsiness. "Come here, lass."

"I don't think that would be wise." She meant to take a step backward but paused, captivated by the sight of him in his elegant tuxedo. The stiff tips of his collar jabbed into his bronze jawline, the tie at his throat bobbed up and down as he spoke, as if powered by the rich vibration of his voice, and the sleek, shiny lapels of his jacket flowed like ebony streams of satin down the muscular field of his chest. Each time he took a breath, his gold watch chain glinted, capturing her eyes and reminding her of the magnificent armored stomach that lounged beneath his waistcoat.

"So ye aim t' desert me tonight?"

"Hazard, you're in no condition—"

"At least give me a kiss then, before ye trot off." Hazard patted the edge of the coverlet beside him. "Come here, lass." When she hesitated, he scowled. "Well come on, then."

"Just a kiss," Jamie warned as she approached the bed. Hazard reached out and grabbed her, pulling her to his side. She lost her balance, tumbling onto his chest. He burst out laughing and rocked her in his arms, growling at her neck and nuzzling her ear until goose bumps broke out all over her body. His legs tangled in her white satin skirt as he wrestled her onto her back.

"Hazard! No fair," she cried, giggling, pressing against his chest. But her puny strength had no effect on the ceiling of muscle that hovered over her. And when she pushed against the hard columns of his arms, he only chuckled and pecked her lips.

"I'll resort t' anythin' when it comes t' having ye, lass."

"You scoundrel!"

"Ye drive me t' distraction on th' dance floor an' then expect me t' let ye go without a fight?" he said. His hot breath tickled the inside of her ear. "Ye're inhuman, Jamie."

"No—you are."

"Now who's playin' dirty!" he retorted. "You're a cruel woman, Jamie Kent, makin' such a joke as tha'."

He stared down at her, his eyes dancing with merriment and inebriation. "Saint Andrew, but ye're beautiful."

Jamie watched him narrow his bleary eyes as he struggled to continue, but his words slurred together incoherently. Suddenly, his arms crumpled and he collapsed upon her with a heavy sigh, smothering her with his weight.

Jamie closed her eyes and grimaced while she patted his back. "I love you, too, you big drunken ox." Then she squeezed out from under him, loosened his tie, and dragged his legs onto the comforter.

She stood for a moment and watched him as he slept. She did love him. Even though she knew it was hopeless and foolish, she loved that hotblooded Scotsman with all her heart and soul.

18

TREE OF HEAVEN. Tree of Heaven.

Jamie jerked awake. She heard Nelle McMurray scream again and thought she was still in her dream until someone pounded down the hallway past her door. Could the scream have been real and not part of her imagination?

Jamie flung off her covers and scampered to the door. She heard the cry again and doors slamming. What was going on? Grabbing her robe, Jamie flew out of her room, stabbing her arms into the sleeves of her robe as she ran.

In the hall she saw Bob Fittro disappear down the stairs just as Brett popped his head out of his room.

"What in the hell is going on!" he demanded. His hair stood up in stiff points all around his head.

"I don't know!" Jamie hurried to the stairs and saw Bob Fittro grab hold of a naked woman and pull her into the parlor. The woman was ranting and waving her arms, crying and blabbering. Jamie felt a chill race down her spine. She had heard such ranting before, in her thoughts and her nightmares.

With Brett close behind her, Jamie ran downstairs. By the time they reached the parlor, Bob Fittro had covered Tiffany with his robe. She was trying to wiggle out of his tight grip.

"Let me go! I've got to get out of here," she screamed.

Jamie stared at her, reliving the horror Tiffany was experiencing. Yet what had Tiffany seen? Hazard? Had something happened to Hazard? And why had Tiffany been naked?

Tiffany wrenched away from Bob and tore at the robe, frantically wiping her skin. "Help me!" she cried. "Oh, God! Help me!"

Brett swept forward, grabbing both of her arms, and shook her as if he could rattle some sense into her. Tiffany's tousled head rolled back and she gaped at Brett as if she didn't recognize him.

"Get hold of yourself, Tiffany," Brett demanded. "What in the hell happened?"

Tiffany wiped her throat and her arms, unaware that the robe had come open and most of her naked torso was in view. Jamie averted her eyes.

"Tiffany!" Brett shouted.

"Light," Tiffany raved. "I've got to get out of here!" She scratched at her throat and struggled to break free. Brett tightened his hold on her arms. "Let me go. I've got to get out of here."

"What was it? A bad dream?" Bob Fittro asked.

Tiffany stared at him and then laughed maniacally, as if she would never stop. She rolled terrified eyes toward Jamie, and her cackling broke off. For an instant their glances held. And then Tiffany began to babble about light, the blue light.

What had happened to Tiffany? The answer hit Jamie like a blast of frigid Puget Sound air. Tiffany had been with Hazard. In his bed. The bottom fell out of Jamie's heart. She couldn't breathe, she couldn't think. Hazard had taken Tiffany to his bed! Yet, what had he done to her?

"Jamie, get one of your Valiums!" Brett ordered, fighting to keep Tiffany from scratching him.

Jamie rushed to the kitchen. When she returned to the parlor she and Bob managed to force the pill between Tiffany's clenched teeth. She choked but the pill slipped down her throat.

"I've got to get out of here!" Tiffany's tangled red hair flopped against her straining white neck.

"Should I call someone?" Bob Fittro said. "Nine-one-one or something? She seems pretty upset!"

Tiffany sank to her knees, sobbing hysterically. Brett could not believe the huddled mass at his feet was Tiffany Denae. He glanced at Jamie, his eyes full of questions.

Then Tiffany spoke in a muffled voice. "He's—he's a monster."

Jamie's skin went cold.

Brett dropped on one knee and tried to pull Tiffany off the floor, but her slumped weight was too much for him. "What did you say?"

Tiffany raised her head. "He's a—monster. Inhuman."

"Who is?" Bob Fittro asked.

"McDougall!" She broke into sobs again.

"I knew it!" Brett jumped to his feet. "I knew it!" He ran to the foot of the stairs and then checked. "He raped you, didn't he, Tiffany?"

Blubbering, she nodded. Jamie gaped at her and then at Brett. Hazard had raped Tiffany? Or was Tiffany just acting? If she were acting, however, it was the performance of a lifetime. No one could look as genuinely terrified as Tiffany.

"I'm going to kill him!" Brett tore up the stairs with Jamie at his heels.

Brett burst into Hazard's room on the third floor. Jamie rushed in after him, and, helpless, watched Brett lunge for the bed where Hazard lay face down, naked. He hadn't even moved when his door was opened. He was probably too spent and satiated after his escapade with Tiffany.

"Get up!" Brett yelled, shoving him in his right shoulder. Hazard propped himself up on a forearm and squinted at Brett in disbelief.

"Brett, no," Jamie protested. "Leave it to the police!"

"Stay out of this," Brett snarled.

"Jamie?" Hazard asked, his voice slurred.

"Get up!" Brett shoved him again, but this time Hazard deflected his arm.

"Hands off, ye bastard!" Hazard said.

In answer, Brett flung himself on Hazard, rolling with him across the sheets. They crashed to the floor on the other side and struggled to their feet. Jamie stared at Hazard's naked body as Hazard shoved Brett against the wall. That beautiful body had been given to Tiffany. That beautiful body had moved over Tiffany's, joining with her as he had joined with Jamie. She had misjudged him, misjudged him thoroughly. Had he whispered words of love to Tiffany? Had he seduced her with that damnable Scottish voice of his? Jamie felt a betrayal so great that tears sprang up in her eyes.

Brett crashed against the wall and then immediately propelled himself away from it, using his momentum to hurl himself into Hazard's stomach. The impact knocked the wind out of Hazard, and he doubled over. Brett whirled, kicked Hazard in the side of his chest, and followed it up with a strike to the face. He checked, assuming one of his karate poses, while Hazard stumbled back, coughing and sputtering.

Jamie stood in the center of the room, frozen. She knew she should want Brett to beat the living daylights out of Hazard. She wanted Hazard to feel the awful pain she was feeling in her heart. Yet watching Hazard take blow after blow gave her no gratification whatsoever.

What was wrong with Hazard? He was a bigger stronger man than Brett. He had picked Brett up and thrown him across the room a few days ago. He had held his own with four of Veith's men. Why wasn't he fighting back? Yet did she want him to fight back? Did she want him to beat Brett? Where did her loyalties lie anyway?

Before she could straighten out her muddled thoughts, Jamie saw Brett spin and lift his leg for a deadly slam to the head. A hit like that could kill a man.

"Hazard!" Jamie screamed.

Somehow Hazard gathered his faculties enough to reach for Brett's foot. He caught it in midair and wrenched Brett off his feet. With a thud, Brett crashed to the floor. Hazard struggled to his feet, brushing back his hair as Brett rose unsteadily. Brett shook his head to clear his vision and swung for Hazard but missed. Hazard feinted with his right fist and then belted Brett on the right side of his face. Brett's head snapped back while his hands came up in front of him. Hazard punched him again and then slugged him in the gut. Brett staggered backward, blood streaming from his nose.

Hazard pursued him, but he was tiring. Jamie could see the strain on his drawn face. He continued to fight, however, and rained blows on Brett's face and torso until Brett, exhausted, finally fell against the door and slid down to the floor. Hazard stood above him, his magnificent chest heaving. When he was certain that Brett was not going to get back on his feet, Hazard took a step back-ward.

"Give it up, Brett," he panted. "Jamie's mine."

Brett didn't look up. His head hung down on his chest and his arms and legs sprawled haphazardly around him. Blood splattered his pajamas. But he started to laugh, and Hazard stared at him in amazement.

"Jamie doesn't want you now, McDougall. Not after what you did."

"Speak plainly, man."

"You know—to Tiffany."

"What?" Hazard roared, lumbering backward. His knees seemed to give out and he swayed for a moment before he plunged to the ground. As he fell, he hit the desk, knocking the whiskey bottle and glass to the floor with a clatter.

"Hazard!" Jamie screamed as she saw him collapse. She fled to his side. He lay on his back, one arm across his chest, one arm flung outward near his head. "Hazard," Jamie croaked as she saw that his eyes were closed. She bent near his mouth and felt his breath coming in shallow gasps. At least he was breathing. Out of the corner of her eye she saw Brett struggle to his hands and knees. He crawled across the floor while she elevated Hazard's feet, desperate to do something to help. Maybe he had just blacked out from the fight.

"Do you know what you just called him?" Brett ex-claimed through swelling lips. "You called him Hazard. What in the hell is going on?"

Jamie ignored Brett. With shaking hands she brushed back Hazard's hair, patted his cheek, and called his name, frantic with worry.

Then she saw an odd blue light. It flashed across Haz-ard's neck and over the planes of his face. In horror, Jamie watched the light sparkle and fade. The light had never faded like that before. Was Hazard losing more and more of his energy?

"Jesus! Look at his hand!" Brett gasped, his voice tight with alarm. "Look at his hand."

Jamie glanced at the hand that lay across Hazard's chest. The blue light still sparkled on his fingers. As she watched the light, she suddenly realized she could see through Hazard's hand. There was no bone and no flesh—nothing but blue light shimmering in the outline of a human hand.

"Jesus Christ Almighty," Brett swore. "Look at him!"

Hazard's entire body glowed while Jamie watched in distress. In the background she heard the whine of an approaching police car.

In what seemed like moments, and then again hours, Jamie looked up to see a policeman appear in the doorway of Hazard's bedroom. She pushed to her feet as Brett strode across the floor to the man in uniform.

"Would you like to tell me what's happened here?" the policeman inquired, pulling a pen from his pocket. He carried a metal clipboard and a form on which to jot down information. Jamie stared at him, wondering how they would explain everything. He was an older man, with graying temples beneath his hat, and a sour expression at having been sent to the McAllister House in the wee hours of the morning. He didn't look the least bit compassionate. What would he say if she told him that the problem concerned a ghost? She wished Sergeant Baeth had been sent out to handle the call. At least he had been congenial.

Brett put a hand on his hip. "There's been a rape. An assault and a rape."

The policeman scribbled away. He raised his uninterested eyes to look at Brett and then at Jamie. She pulled
her robe more tightly around her. The officer continued.
"Who was raped?"

"An actress named Tiffany Denae. She's the one downstairs."

"Miss Denae has been taken to the hospital," the policeman remarked. "Now who was assaulted?"

"Me." Brett craned his neck to see if the officer was
recording all the information. "Brett Johansen."

"Do you know who attacked Miss Denae?"

"Sure." Brett indicated Hazard with a sideways tip of
his head. "Him."

The policeman looked over Brett's shoulder. His gaze
wandered around the room and then fixed upon Brett
once more. His eyes were cold. "You trying to be funny,
Mr. Johansen?"

Jamie turned, wondering why the policeman didn't see
Hazard lying on the floor. Brett turned as well, and his
face paled around his black eye. Hazard was gone.

"But he was there on the floor just a minute ago!" Brett
blubbered. "Right there on the floor."

"He couldn't have just up and walked away," the officer
replied testily. "You better tell the truth and tell it now."

"The truth?" Brett shouted. "I am telling the truth!
This guy named Hastings McDougall—or I should say
Hazard McAllister—raped Tiffany and beat me up."

The policeman crossed his arms. "You're a wise guy,
aren't you?"

"I'm serious." Brett motioned to his face. "How do you
think I got this black eye?"

"The housekeeper says you had quite a party this evening. Got wild, did it?"

"You don't seem to understand, officer! A crime was committed here!"

"That I don't doubt." For the first time, the policeman smiled, but his smile made Jamie even more nervous.

Brett glared at him, realizing his story sounded far-fetched, but was frustrated because he was telling the truth and the policeman didn't believe him.

"Mr. Johansen, do you want us to investigate? That means I'll have to go through every room. Do you want that, Mr. Johansen?"

Jamie hugged her torso. If the police searched the house, they would likely find controlled substances that would land somebody in jail. Brett couldn't risk that.

"Or," the officer continued, "do you want to tell me what really went on here?"

"And what do you think really went on here?" Brett's voice was cold and clipped.

"I think someone overstepped their bounds with Miss Denae. From what I've seen she looked pretty darned scared. You stand there with your face all beat in, making up some cock-and-bull story about another person assaulting Miss Denae, when I think you did it."

"Me?" bellowed Brett. "Me! Goddammit!"

"Yes. You mentioned a Hazard McAllister. Where'd you come up with that name? Just made it up? Well, everybody knows old Hazard McAllister is dead and gone, and not about to rape some poor little actress."

"But—"

The policeman held up his hand. "We'll just have to wait until Miss Denae is able to tell the story before we can go any further on this."

"But—"

"Or, I can have Frank Baeth come to the house and we'll start the search right now."

Brett sighed in exasperation. He scowled and crossed his arms. "I'm going to write a letter to your superior officer and make sure you're reprimanded for this. I'm a goddamn tax-paying citizen, for Chrissake! I don't have to take this shit!"

"Brett—" Jamie took his arm. "Take it easy." From the look in the policeman's eye, Jamie could tell that an investigation would ensue immediately if Brett said anything more. She smiled at the officer.

"Thank you for coming by, officer." She extended her hand and he shook it.

"What do you know of all this?" the policeman asked.

"Not much. I was asleep when it all happened. I guess we'll all just have to wait for Tiffany to tell us what went on."

As soon as the policeman was out of sight, Brett grabbed Jamie's wrist and dragged her down the hall to Mark's room. Without even knocking he burst into Mark's chamber and shouted for Mark to get up. Mark raised up on both elbows and blinked. He had been so exhausted by the party that he had slept through all the noise.

"Wake up, Kent!" Brett demanded, pulling Jamie to the bed with him.

Mark inspected Brett's face. "What happened to you?"

"I got in a fight with McDougall—or should I say McAllister?"

Mark shot a glance at Jamie. "You didn't tell Brett—"

"No!" Jamie shook her head emphatically. "I didn't. But something happened, Mark, something awful!"

"I want to know what's going on," Brett shouted. "That thing isn't McAllister, not really, is it?"

Mark sat up, wincing. "What happened, Jamie?"

"Brett and Hazard got in a fight over Tiffany. And

when the fight was over, Hazard collapsed. He started to glow. He seemed to be made up of blue light, nothing else."

Mark stared at her and sank back to his pillows.

"What's going on?" Brett stormed. "I want to know what's going on!"

"Shut up, Brett!" Mark retorted impatiently. "Let me think."

Jamie leaned over the bed. "And now Hazard's gone. He just disappeared." "Oh, Mark! Where is he? What's happened to him?"

"Sounds like energy depletion." Mark sighed. "You've heard the saying 'energy flows downhill,' haven't you?"

Jamie nodded. Mark patted her hand. "Well, in Hazard's case, his energy is winding down. He is returning to his natural state. His batteries are getting old, you might say."

Brett listened and his expression grew more and more incredulous. "You mean to tell me that McDougall *is* McAllister?"

Mark nodded grimly.

"My God, he's one of your holograms, isn't he? He's one of those newfangled holograms!" When Brett saw his words confirmed in Mark's eyes, he whipped around and strode to the window. Then he whirled.

"But how could a hologram do this to my face?"

"McAllister possessed mass. He could affect his physical surroundings. Including people."

"But why McAllister?" Brett touched his swelled upper lip. "I can't believe I'm saying this, but isn't he the ghost that Jamie saw when she was little?"

Jamie raised her head. "Yes." Her gaze met Brett's, condemning him for the years of his lack of trust in her. Brett quickly looked away.

"But how?" he sputtered. "How did it happen?"

Mark released Jamie as she dragged to her feet. "It was an accident," Mark explained. "His spirit somehow managed to get into the computer."

"Christ! Now what?"

Mark shrugged. "Your guess is as good as mine. We're in unexplored territory here, Brett."

"But what about our plans?" Jamie asked. "Now that Hazard has disappeared?"

Mark raked a hand through his hair. "I think we should leave as planned, Jamie."

"We can't," Brett put in, unaware that his plans differed from Jamie's and Mark's. "Tiffany's in the hospital. We'll have to postpone our flight back to L.A. until she's discharged."

Jamie looked at Brett and stuffed her hands in her robe pockets. What should she do? Wait for Hazard? Wait for Tiffany? Or get her brother out of town? She decided to wait until the end of the day at least. Perhaps then Hazard would reappear and they'd have news of Tiffany's condition. Surely, a few extra hours wouldn't matter.

Jamie, Brett, and Bob spent the rest of the morning cleaning the house after the party. Jamie found dirty dishes, food, and trash in every room on the first floor, as well as in the bathroom upstairs and on the steps leading to the third story. Cigarette butts and ashtrays were everywhere. She moved like a robot, her mind far away from her hands. Where was Hazard? Had he vanished forever? What would she and Mark do if he didn't show up in a day or two? And what if Dr. Hamilton got so desperate that he tried another kidnapping, taking Mark the next time?

By the end of the afternoon Jamie was beat. On her

way to a shower and a change of clothes, she found Brett staring at his face in a mirror above the small side table where Mrs. Gipson placed the mail.

"God," he commented as she walked by. "I won't be able to show my face in public for two weeks."

"It doesn't look that bad," Jamie replied. "Did you put some ice on it last night?"

"There wasn't a cube of ice to be found." He rubbed his neck and closed his eyes. "I feel like hell."

Just then the phone rang. Wincing, Brett reached over for the receiver and picked it up. Jamie watched him, wondering who was calling. Brett scowled and then winced again from the effort.

"No, she hasn't," he finally said into the phone. "Of course. We will. Thanks."

He hung up the phone and glanced at Jamie.

"Tiffany's left the hospital."

"Oh?" Jamie put her hands in her pockets and strolled to the fire. "So she's all right then."

"No. She just walked out. She didn't even take her clothes."

"What?" Jamie turned in surprise. "When?"

"About two o'clock this afternoon." He looked at his watch. "About two hours ago. She should have turned up here by now."

"Where could she be?"

"How the hell do I know?"

"Do you think we should call the police?"

"That was the police. They've been looking for her."

"I think we'd better hop in the car and see if we can find her."

"Are you crazy?" Brett glared at her. "I'm not going anywhere looking like this!"

"Yes, you are. Now get a coat, Brett. I'm going to find Bob. He can drive while we look."

THE SEARCH FOR TIFFANY PROVED FRUITLESS. After two hours of driving through Port Townsend and the surrounding area, Brett, Jamie, and Bob returned to the McAllister mansion. Jamie knew the moment she walked through the door that something was amiss. The house was too quiet, and an unfamiliar cologne lingered in the air.

She stopped in her tracks, causing Bob to nearly trip over her.

"What's wrong, Jamie?" Brett asked.

"I don't know." She sniffed and tilted her head, listening intently for any telltale sound. "Something's wrong."

"Excellent deduction, Miss Kent."

Jamie whirled in the direction of the familiar condescending voice. Dr. Hamilton stood in the doorway of the parlor, holding a gun on them. She could see one of his men behind him, clutching Mrs. Gipson around the throat. A wide piece of adhesive tape kept her mouth shut, but her eyes were wide with terror, sending a message of alarm to the three unsuspecting people who had just entered the house.

"Dr. Hamilton!" Jamie gasped.

"Is this the guy who kidnapped you?" Brett asked.

"Yes."

"I'll ask the questions, Mr. Johansen!" Dr. Hamilton snapped, stepping forward. "You two men," he pointed the gun in the direction of the bathroom under the staircase, "get over there."

"What is this?" Brett exclaimed. "Who do you think you are?"

"Tie them up, Reeves." Hamilton nodded his head toward Brett, ignoring his questions. "And lock them in the bathroom." He turned to Jamie. "You, my dear, are going to tell me where your brother is."

Jamie glanced at Mrs. Gipson, who was roughly pulled into the parlor again.

"Now, Miss Kent." Dr. Hamilton leveled the gun on her.

Jamie could see Brett kicking and squirming as Reeves held him to the floor and tied his hands behind his back. Bob Fittro, unaware of the reasons for the situation, stood quietly while his hands were bound, knowing there was nothing else he could do.

Jamie turned back to the doctor. "Mark isn't here?"

"No, Mark isn't here." He mimicked her. "Don't play games with me, Miss Kent. I've had quite enough of your shenanigans."

"We don't know where the hell he is," Brett retorted as Reeves yanked him to his feet. "We've been out all afternoon!"

"Silence!" Dr. Hamilton roared.

Reeves shoved Brett into the bathroom. Bob Fittro followed and the door slammed behind them. One of them kicked the door, pounding violently until Reeves fired his gun at the molding. The pounding ceased instantly, and Jamie stared in horror at the door, hoping Brett or Bob hadn't been hit.

"Please," Jamie implored. "Please don't hurt anyone! I don't know where Mark is."

"I'm losing my temper," Dr. Hamilton warned, shaking the gun at her. "You don't want to see me get really angry, do you, Miss Kent?"

Before Jamie could respond, she saw Reeves suddenly lean to one side to look out the window which bordered the front door. "Hey, boss, somebody's coming."

Jamie whipped around. She could see out the window, too, just enough to glimpse her brother climbing out of a small U-Haul truck. He paused, looked at the house, and then walked toward the door.

Reeves scrambled out of sight and Dr. Hamilton lunged for Jamie, intending to pull her out of sight, too. But just as he grabbed her, Jamie looked up to see Mark glancing through the window. She shook her head violently, trying to warn him before she was thrown to the ground. Had he seen her? She wasn't certain.

"Fool!" Dr. Hamilton swore and kicked her. Jamie curled up in pain, hugging her abdomen, while Dr. Hamilton rushed to the window, holding his gun in front of him. Jamie waited for an eternity for Mark to come through the door and step into the trap. But the door never opened. She heard a car door slam and an engine rev up. Tires screeched as Mark pulled away in the truck.

"Come on," Dr. Hamilton shouted. He burst out the front door. Reeves dragged Jamie to her feet and another guard pulled Mrs. Gipson to the front door. They scrambled down the steps, and Jamie was half carried, half pushed toward an awaiting sedan. The driver must have been sitting in the car down the block, waiting for any sign of trouble from the house. Jamie dug in her heels and dragged her feet, doing her best to give Mark more of a head start.

Once again Jamie was forced into the blue sedan. Mrs. Gipson scooted in next to her, grunting and making muted high-pitched noises in protest of the rough treatment.

"Kent'll never get away in that truck," the driver declared, roaring into the street. Jamie's neck snapped back as the car fishtailed in the gravel alongside the road. Mrs. Gipson clutched the seat in front of her, hanging on for dear life as the car whipped around the corner and barreled toward the bluff. Once or twice she nearly fell into Jamie's lap.

The guard sitting on the other side of the car looked at Jamie and smiled. "I've got plans for you," he snarled.

Jamie blanched at the viciousness in his voice. She noticed that his head was bandaged under the ball cap he wore. He was the guard she had walloped with the toilet tank lid. Obviously, he planned to seek revenge. Jamie wondered what he had in mind, and by the gleam in his eye she could tell he was looking forward to spending time alone with her. Jamie looked away, refusing to consider his threat.

The car careened down the hill and out to the highway, flying through a red light in pursuit of the orange and white U-Haul truck ahead of them. At first Jamie worried that Mark would never make it. There was a long incline outside of town which would slow up a big vehicle like a truck. Would Dr. Hamilton drive up alongside and hold a gun to her head, forcing Mark to pull over? Was there something she could do?

Jamie looked at the door handle beside her. She could

take her chances by jumping out of the car as it went up the hill. But that wouldn't serve any real purpose. Mrs. Gipson would still be left behind as a hostage. There was no way on earth that two people could jump out of the car. Jamie abandoned that plan and was trying to come up with something else when the light turned red at the base of the hill. A whole troop of kids walking hand in hand with two adults supervising them trailed across the highway, filling the crosswalk from one side of the street to the other.

"Christ!" the driver said, impatiently tapping his fingers on the steering wheel while the children filed by.

Jamie watched the U-Haul truck crawl up the highway ahead of them and shudder as Mark downshifted near the top of the hill. Go, Mark, go! Please, God, let him get away. Jamie closed her eyes in a silent prayer of desperation, knowing in her heart that Mark didn't have a chance in hell.

"Come on! Come on!" Dr. Hamilton said, as he watched the children step onto the curb on the other side. "We're going to lose him."

"No we won't, boss. He won't get far."

As soon as the light turned green, the driver floored the gas pedal and the car squealed through the intersection. Jamie's stomach lurched sickeningly and Mrs. Gipson moaned, her head rolling back on her neck.

Mark's truck disappeared over the crest of the hill. By the time the sedan raced to the top, the U-Haul was nowhere in sight.

"We've lost him," Dr. Hamilton shouted. "Goddammit."

"He's just around the bend, doc." The guard beside Jamie interjected. "This highway curves for miles. We'll find him."

Jamie looked behind them. Where were the police? Why weren't they around when you needed them? Why didn't someone call in and report the speeding blue sedan going seventy-five miles per hour in a thirty-five-miles-per-hour zone? She looked to the front once more and saw the U-Haul just ahead, rolling around a curve into a glen dark with cedar trees and blackberry brambles.

"There he is!" the driver said and hunched forward.

Dr. Hamilton rolled down his window and extended his arm along the sill. He fired two shots without causing any noticeable damage before the truck dipped into the glen and disappeared.

"If you kill him," Jamie warned, "you'll never have the hologram project."

"Shut up," said the guard near Mrs. Gipson.

"You don't know everything, Dr. Hamilton," she continued, undaunted. "The hologram project is not finished."

"Quiet," Hamilton ordered.

"If you kill Mark, you'll never know the secret."

Dr. Hamilton ignored her. The truck appeared again on the other side of the glen. Blue water sparkled between the branches of the trees to the left where the road curved along a cliff overlooking the bay. Hamilton fired another shot and hit a rear tire. Instantly the truck swerved, wobbling madly across the center line as the tire blew.

"No!" Jamie screamed.

The truck bumped through the shallow ditch on the left side of the road, moving with jerky speed that reminded Jamie of old Buster Keaton films. She watched in horror as the truck veered off the road and plowed through the brambles.

"No!" she screamed as the driver of her vehicle screeched to a halt.

She saw the U-Haul crash through a grove of saplings, shearing them off at ground level, and then the truck disappeared.

Dr. Hamilton and Reeves jumped from the front seat of the sedan and loped across the road, their guns drawn. Jamie watched them pick their way through the berry bushes. Where was the truck? She held her breath, hoping for the best, fearing for the worst.

Hamilton and Reeves disappeared for a few minutes and then ran back to the car. Jamie inspected the doctor's face as he hung in the frame of the car beside the open door. The gun hung in his limp right hand resting on the top of the door.

"He's gone," Dr. Hamilton's voice was curt with exasperation.

"What do you mean?" the driver retorted.

"The damn truck went over the cliff. He's at the bottom of the bay."

"No!" Something snapped in Jamie. Something white hot snapped in her head, blinding her. "No!" She flung herself out of the car, screaming for her brother, tearing across the highway to the raw path of broken trees blazed by the U-Haul. She raced through the brambles. The canes tore at her shirt and jeans, leaving trails of blood, but she ran unmindful of the pain to the edge of the cliff. There the land dropped away in a tumble of boulders and snags to the ocean hundreds of feet below.

"No!" Jamie wailed, dropping to her knees. Two sea gulls soared in a graceful arc above the cliff, keening with her.

Hours later, Jamie returned in a squad car to the McAllister mansion. Dr. Hamilton had left Mrs. Gipson bound and gagged in a motel on the edge of town while he and his men sped away to their ship. Even if the U-Haul could be located off shore, any equipment recovered would be ruined and worthless. Mark could not have survived the accident, so there was no point in Dr. Hamilton remaining in the area. Murdering Jamie and Mrs. Gipson without getting the hologram project in return was too much trouble, even for him. So he bought time for his escape by leaving them at the Breakwater Inn, room 6, roped to chairs.

Jamie and Mrs. Gipson managed to catch the attention of a maid by moaning in unison through their gags until the noise became annoying enough to investigate. After the police were informed of Mark's accident, they raced to the scene with Jamie to show the way. Divers combed the area for hours, but found nothing, and finally gave up when darkness and a severe wind storm made further searching impossible. Sergeant Baeth explained that the bay was unusually deep at the base of the cliff, much deeper than the surrounding waters. Dangerous undercurrents made diving extremely hazardous as well, especially during a storm. He doubted that the U-Haul would ever be found, but promised to resume the search in the morning.

Brett met Jamie and Sergeant Baeth at the door. It took all of Jamie's strength to drag across the threshold. When Brett held out his arms, she fell into them with a sob, collapsing out of sheer exhaustion and grief.

"Is she going to be all right?" the police officer inquired, looping his thumbs in his belt and inclining his head so he could see her face.

Brett patted Jamie's back. "Sure. We'll just get her into bed. She's been through quite a shock today."

"You think she needs to see a doctor?"

Brett shook his head. "She'll be fine. I'll give her a stiff drink and put her to bed."

"Well," Sergeant Baeth stepped backward. "I'll come back tomorrow then, after we do a more thorough investigation."

"Thank you, sergeant," Brett replied, holding Jamie close.

She raised her head. Her eyes were red and puffy. "Thanks," she murmured.

Officer Baeth nodded stiffly and clumped off the porch into the black November wind.

Jamie fell into bed and closed her eyes. She was dead with weariness but did not know how she would ever sleep. Her Dalmane capsules were in the bathroom, but she was too exhausted to get up and take one. Besides, Brett had insisted that she belt down some brandy to settle her nerves, and she knew it wasn't a good idea to take medication and alcohol together.

A pressing weight sat upon her chest, making it difficult to breathe. She wanted to cry but couldn't. Mark was dead. Just like that. Hazard was gone. Just like that. No good-byes, no farewells, just like her parents had been wrenched from her so long ago. Jamie sucked in a ragged breath. How could she go on? Why did she want to? Without Mark and Hazard, what was left? And why had she never told Hazard that she loved him? Maybe she should take that Dalmane capsule, maybe three or four, perhaps the entire bottle, and check out altogether.

"Jamie."

Jamie stiffened. That was Hazard's voice. How real it sounded in her thoughts!

"Jamie lass."

This time the voice sounded closer. Jamie jerked to a sitting position. At the foot of her bed she saw a blue sparkling shape, not quite in human form. Her heart thumped wildly.

"Hazard?" she whispered.

The form sparkled and glowed and suddenly Hazard appeared in human form. No trace of the fight with Brett was evident on his cleanshaven face.

"Oh, Hazard!" she cried, scrambling out of bed. She longed to run up and hug him, feel his warm solid body pressed into hers. She forgot that he had given himself to another woman. She ignored the fact that he might have been dallying with her all along, and that a hot-blooded Scot might take as many women as he could to his bed. All Jamie could think of was the incredible comfort she would find in his arms. She flung herself against his chest.

"Ah, lass."

She couldn't speak. She could only clutch him in a desperate grip, finding her solace in his quiet strength. He stroked her back and hair, murmuring endearments while she wept unashamed. She felt as if she had cracked in two and tears were pouring out like water from a warm hose on a driveway, draining her. Her heart floated away on the flood of tears, rolling over and over and over, far away from the awful black shell that remained of Jamie Kent. She was empty, void, a broken vase.

Hazard, seeing her distress, swept her into his arms and carried her to the bed. Jamie clung to his neck and would not release him, even when he tried to stand up. He bent down to kiss her, to seek release from her grip, but she could not let him go. Her lips sought his, frantic with hope that he could stave off her grief. Without saying a word to him, she pulled away from his mouth and tore off her clothes. Hazard watched her fall back on the pillows—

naked—her alabaster skin glowing in the dark, her hazel eyes glinting with deep tormented lights.

Hazard peeled off his sweater and shirt. Jamie watched him bend over to take off his shoes and socks while a feeling of utter finality passed through her, as if someone had thrown a heavy quilt over her. She closed her eyes and let Hazard's weight anchor her to earth, let his lips seal her screams, let his body take her far, far away.

Afterward, Jamie fell into a jagged slumber, curled against Hazard's chest. But a few hours later, she woke up, crying.

He squeezed her gently. "Jamie, what's wrong?"

"Oh, Hazard!" she exclaimed, anguished. "Where were you?"

"I was caught between here and there. I'm fadin', lass. I'm losin' th' ability t' come back."

"Oh, God!" she cried. "Hazard!" She spread her fingers over his chest. "If you had only been there to help."

"Do what?"

"Save Mark."

"Save him? Where is Mark, anyway?"

"He's dead. Mark's dead."

Hazard stiffened. "What?"

"He was trying to get away in a truck. Dr. Hamilton shot his tire and his truck went out of control. He drove over a cliff."

"Ah, Jamie!" Hazard exclaimed. "Ah, lass!" He engulfed her in his arms and cradled her head against his chest, pinning her grief to his heart. "Jamie, I'm sae sorry!"

Jamie pressed her face into the tendons of his neck. "Don't leave me, Hazard. Please—you can't leave me again."

He looked down at her, amazed at how powerfully she gripped him, as if her hard embrace would root him to the physical world. His eyes searched her tearful ones as a sad expression stole across his features. "I canna help leavin', Jamie girl. I'm tirin'. An' I just go."

"But it isn't fair! It just isn't fair."

"Life isna fair. We both know tha', lass." He squeezed the tops of her shoulders and smiled sadly at her.

"But you're fading just when I—" She broke off and sighed.

Hazard looked at her expectantly. "When ye what, lass?"

"Just when I was discovering that"—Jamie swallowed—"that I love you."

"Ye do love me." He crushed her against him. "Ah, lass. Ye do love me! I've been dyin' t' hear ye say it."

Hazard bent to her lips and she released herself to his mouth, telling him with a kiss all the things she couldn't tell him in words.

"Jamie," he murmured. "I love ye, too. I love ye with all my heart and soul!" He closed his eyes. "My little sparrow, my sweet flutterin' little sparrow."

Their lips clung together until Hazard drew back and smoothed Jamie's hair. "What I'd give t' have another week wi' ye, Jamie. Another month. A year!"

"Oh, Hazard." She hugged him, knowing the time would come soon when she could no longer touch him like this.

"And what I'd give t' have last night back t' live over again."

Jamie's hands stopped stroking him. "What did happen last night, Hazard?"

"After ye left me, I lay abed, fightin' a strange feelin' o' lassitude. In my day I could drink any man under th' table. But as a hologram, or whatever th' hell I am now, I shouldna have drunk a drop. I felt strange, lass. Discon-

nected. I couldna see straight, think straight. Then someone came t' me in th' darkness, a vision in a white and
green gown, the gown ye wore t' th' party. Jamie, I
thought it was ye comin' back t' me, too lonely t' spend
th' night by yourself. I couldna believe my eyes. But I
wanted t' believe my eyes. I wanted t' make love t' ye,
Jamie, no matter how blind drunk I was."

Jamie shut her eyes, trying not to imagine Hazard with
Tiffany. He continued to speak.

"She came t' me, wearin' your scent, and never said
a word. She just stood by th' bed and held out her arms
t' me. I was like a man possessed, thinkin' it was ye, Jamie.
But as soon as I touched her skin, I knew it wasna you,
lass. 'Twas tha' witch, Tiffany. I threw her off and she
laughed like a banshee. My disgust only made her more
determined t' seduce me. She came at me and I tried to
resist her. She thought I was playin'. But I'm tellin' ye,
Jamie girl, I had no more strength than a wee bairn. I
willed mysel' t' fade, t' disappear. Th' act drained me as
if somethin' came pourin' out, all my strength, all my energy, worse than what happened with ye on th' ship. I
couldna move or speak, even when Tiffany screamed and
ran out o' th' room. I lay abed, paralyzed. Not until Brett
came up t' my room did I recover, an' then only temporarily." He sighed heavily. "An' now I'm losin' my steam minute by minute, Jamie. Even now I can feel it comin' on,
tha' strange enervation—"

Blue light flared on his extremities. Jamie clung to him,
as if she could hold him back. But all she did was clutch
at light, grasping at air, until her arms suddenly collapsed
onto her torso.

"Hazard, come back."

"Fare thee well, lass." She heard his voice rumble.

"Hazard!"

20

THE NEXT MORNING, Jamie went downstairs to contact the police to see if they had found the U-Haul truck yet. Unfortunately, they had nothing new to report. Divers were on the scene, but they hadn't found anything. Jamie hung up the phone and stared dully at the kitchen table, wondering if she could force herself to eat. She wasn't the least bit hungry but knew she should eat something. She compromised by fixing a cup of tea and a slice of dry toast.

The house was quiet. Mrs. Gipson had the rest of the week off, since Mark was no longer around, and Jamie had told her not to return until she felt up to it. Bob Fittro and the rest of the crew had flown back to L.A. the previous afternoon. The only person in the house was Brett. He had left the radio on in the kitchen.

Jamie sipped her tea and listened to the music for a few minutes. At nine, the news came on. She paused when she heard mention of her brother.

"Mark Kent, internationally known physicist, died in an automobile accident yesterday outside Port Townsend,

Washington. Dr. Kent had been living in Port Townsend where he was being treated for a serious illness. He is survived by one sister, Ellen J. Kent, from Los Angeles, California. Dr. Kent received worldwide recognition for his—"

Jamie snapped off the radio, unable to hear any more. The news story validated Mark's death, which was something she could not face so soon. She took a sip of tea. Her hand trembled so much that she spilled some tea down the front of her blouse. But she made no attempt to get up. Instead, she collapsed onto the table, cradling her head in the crook of her elbow, weeping.

Jamie spent the rest of the day listening to Mark's music and sitting in his bedroom, too distraught to do anything productive. Brett left her alone for most of the day, for which she was grateful.

Late in the afternoon, the police brought Tiffany to the door.

"We found her walking along Highway 20, out by the old bunkers," Sergeant Baeth explained, guiding Tiffany into the hall. Jamie surveyed the woman, whose smirking expression had been replaced by a wild vacant look and darting eyes. "She must have slept there overnight," the policeman continued, tipping back his hat. "It's a wonder she didn't die from exposure."

Tiffany's hair, matted and tangled, hung down her back in a greasy mass. Her face was smudged and she still wore a hospital gown under a trench coat that someone had thrown over her shoulders. Her feet were bare and black.

Brett came up behind Jamie. "You found her!" he exclaimed. "God, she's a mess!"

"I don't think she knows or cares," Sergeant Baeth put in. "I think you ought to have her see someone. She seems to be in a state of shock."

"We'll do that," Brett agreed. "But let's get her cleaned up first."

"I'll help her take a shower," Jamie volunteered.

"What about the hospital report. Did they find anything? Any proof that she had been attacked?"

Baeth shook his head. "Not a thing. No sign of rape. No hairs, no abrasions, not even any body fluids."

"I can't believe it." Brett threw up his hands, disgusted.

Baeth shrugged. "That's what the report said."

"But look at her. Something happened to her."

"Well, whatever it was, it wasn't physical."

Brett glowered, angry that he could not legally blame Hazard for raping her.

"You know what I think?" Baeth said. "Off the record?"

"What?"

"I think she got hold of some bad stuff that put her in her own private Idaho for awhile. That's my theory."

"No way." Brett shook his head vehemently. "It was that Hastings McDougall character."

"And he has disappeared," Baeth put in.

"Yeah. Conveniently." Brett draped his arm around Tiffany. "Well, whatever—I'm taking Tiffany upstairs to the bathroom if you want to come on up and help, Jamie."

"Okay, I'll be there in a minute." She waved Brett off and turned to the sergeant. "What about my brother?" Jamie asked. "Any news?"

"I'm sorry, Miss Kent, but we've decided to call off the search. There's a real nasty squall brewing. We can't jeopardize our men. And even if we did find that truck, it wouldn't do your brother much good."

Jamie nodded mutely.

"I'm real sorry, Miss Kent." He backed toward the door. "If you need help with Miss Denae, give us a call."

"Thank you."

She opened the door for the policeman and watched him stride to his car parked at the end of the walk. Even though it was only five o'clock, the sky was already dark, a boiling purple mass of storm clouds. The trees across the street waved madly, obliterating the old street light and flinging dead leaves into the air. Jamie pushed the door shut and shivered from the cold.

She found Brett upstairs in the bathroom. Tiffany sat on the edge of the tub while Brett drew a hot bath. Jamie took over, helping Tiffany disrobe and step into the water. Tiffany moved as if she were in a trance, as if she had no direction of her own. Jamie realized after a few minutes that Tiffany might sit unmoving in the bathtub all night if left to her own devices. Jamie felt awkward about washing another adult, but saw no other recourse. Jamie knelt on the bathmat and doused the washcloth in the water.

"All right, Tiffany," she said. "Let's get you cleaned up."

When she was done she called for Brett to help get Tiffany out of the bathroom. Brett carried Tiffany to her bedroom and put her on the bed. Tiffany sank onto the pillow without a sound. Never once had she looked either of them in the eye.

"She'll be better after she gets some sleep," Brett ventured.

Jamie doubted it, but she nodded. Brett sat down on the mattress beside Tiffany and adjusted a blanket around her.

"Did you notice her hair?" Jamie asked.

Brett glanced down. "Her hair? What about it?"

Jamie sidled closer. "I noticed when I washed her hair that part of it had turned white."

"Strange." Brett leaned over Tiffany and lightly spread her damp hair over the pillow."

"See there?" Jamie pointed to the hair at the nape of her neck.

"Weird. I've heard that people's hair turned white after being terrified. But I never believed it. McAllister must have scared the shit out of her."

Jamie watched Tiffany's face. Tiffany appeared relaxed and peaceful as she slept, but her eyes belied the outward calm. Her eyes rolled and jerked under her lids, betraying Tiffany's inner turmoil. Was she having nightmares now, too? Jamie was angry at Tiffany for lying about Hazard, but she was not angry enough to wish her terrifying dreams on the red-haired actress.

"I'll sit here and watch her for awhile," Jamie said, sinking into the chair near the bed. "Just to make sure she doesn't go anywhere."

"Do you think that McAllister hologram is going to reappear?" Brett asked.

"I don't know."

"When he does, I'm going to make him pay for raping poor Tiffany."

"He didn't rape Tiffany," Jamie retorted tiredly.

Brett's head shot up. "What?"

"No one dragged Tiffany up to Hazard's room. She went there on her own accord to seduce him."

"What?"

"She went up there dressed in my costume. She went up there to seduce him and got more than she bargained for."

"You mean to tell me that a woman who probably weighs one hundred and fifteen pounds raped a guy who could tip the scale at two hundred? Give me a break!"

"There was no rape. Hazard says he didn't touch her."

"You're serious! You can sit there and defend that

McAllister character while poor Tiffany lies here traumatized? I can't believe it!"

Jamie shrugged. "I find it easier to believe Hazard than Tiffany."

"I'll bet you do. You've been taken in, Jamie. Taken in good this time."

"What's that supposed to mean?"

He surveyed her, his lip curled. "You know damn well what I mean! You're ready to throw your life away on some goddamn ghost, on somebody that doesn't even exist. And you know what?" When she didn't answer, Brett leaned forward as he hurled his insults at her. "I say good riddance. Hazard McAllister has been the great stumbling block of your life, the monkey on your back for years. So why change a good thing? Why not throw your entire life away on him! I just hope you're goddamn happy!"

Slowly Jamie rose. She was so angry she felt cold inside, like an iron heated so thoroughly that it felt cool to the touch. She leveled her eyes on Brett.

"Get out," she said, deadly calm.

"What do you mean, get out?"

"I mean leave. Leave the house."

"You can't be serious! What about Tiffany?" Brett dropped his hands.

"I can handle her."

"What about your brother's funeral arrangements?"

"You never cared about Mark," Jamie replied, turning away. "Just get out of here. I don't want to see you again, Brett. Ever."

"You can't mean this! It's seven o'clock at night for Chrissake!"

"I don't care what time it is, Brett."

"What about us?" He grabbed her arm.

Revulsed, Jamie shook him off. "If you aren't out of here in the next five minutes, I'm calling the police."

For a moment Brett gaped at her, startled by the new decisive Jamie Kent. Her blazing stare did not falter, however. She meant every word she said. And it was obvious she was not going to back down. He turned on his heel and stomped out of the parlor.

Tiffany moaned and Jamie glanced at her as she sat down. "Welcome to my nightmare, Tiffany, old girl," she muttered bitterly. She heard Brett slamming doors down the hall and throwing things around his room.

Go ahead and throw things, Brett, she thought. I don't give a damn.

Tiffany slept soundly for hours. At midnight, Jamie got out of the chair and stretched. She put down the book she had found near Tiffany's alarm clock. The glitzy novel about diamond thieves had barely kept her interest, but she wondered if any book would be capable of keeping her mind off Mark and Hazard.

Jamie made certain Tiffany was covered and then walked to her own bedroom down the hall. She closed the door and stripped off her shirt. In the bathroom, she looked at her bottles of medication on the shelf below the mirror. How long had it been since she had taken a Valium? How long since she had suffered a crippling headache? Could days have actually gone by without her taking any medication? Jamie looked at her reflection in surprise.

She fell asleep to the sound of wind whipping through the gingerbread trim above her window, screaming through the railings of the captain's walk on the roof, and a shutter banging somewhere on the third floor.

Tree of Heaven.

Jamie rose up on her elbow. Was that Nelle's voice she heard?

Tree of Heaven.

Jamie struggled to sit up while her eyes adjusted to the darkness. She could see Nelle standing in the middle of the bedroom, beckoning for Jamie to follow her. Jamie draped her legs over the side of the bed and pushed her feet into her slippers.

Nelle turned her faceless head toward the chamber door and floated away. Jamie, fumbling with her robe, followed her through the dark hallway, down the stairs, out of the house, and into the storm. Wind whipped her robe back and blew her hair into her face. But she didn't feel the cold, bitter wind or the biting rain. She was in a dream, following the lady in the blue dress to the edge of the bluff.

This time, however, Jamie did not see any carriages parked along the road. And this time, the trip to the edge of the bluff was more difficult, longer than usual, and she was panting heavily by the time she and Nelle arrived at their destination.

Tree of Heaven.

Nelle pointed to the empty lot below. This time Jamie knew where the Tree of Heaven was planted. She held her robe between her breasts and peeled back the wet clump of hair that slapped her face. She peered through the sheets of rain to the empty lot. The Tree of Heaven stood like a black sentinel in the rain. Jamie could hear a sound above the din of the storm, a mechanical sound— the clanking and screeching of a bulldozer.

"No!" Jamie shrieked into the wind. She could see the bulldozer pulling away from the Tree of Heaven. One end of a chain was wrapped around the trunk of the tree, and the other end was connected to the bulldozer. Jamie knew in an instant what was happening below her. Someone was trying to pull down the tree during the storm, to make it look as if the wind were responsible for the tree being uprooted. Frank Veith would get his video store and no one could be blamed for killing the tree.

Tree of Heaven.

Jamie threw a wild glance at Nelle and then tore down the wooden stairway to the bottom of the bluff. This was no dream. This was real. She had to do something to stop the bulldozer.

Jamie leapt off the last step and scrambled through the empty lot, slipping in the mud. One of her slippers flew off. Her foot slopped through a puddle and landed on a patch of sharp gravel. Jamie winced in pain, but didn't slow down. She could see the tree shivering ahead of her as the dozer pulled on its ancient trunk. The machine strained, tugging against roots and earth that bound the tree to the ground. Jamie ran across the lot unseen by the bulldozer operator, who was intent on his job.

She reached the tree just as the ground around it gave way, erupting beneath her feet as if an earthquake parted the soil. The tree groaned and Jamie scrambled to a stop as the dirt fell away beneath her frozen feet. She screamed, watching in horror as the tree fell over, tipping up a root base of snags and boulders and a strange metallic chest. But Jamie caught only a glimpse before she plunged into the root hole, falling into the dank earth on her hands and knees. Dirt and gravel rained down on her hair.

She heard the dozer shut down as she struggled to stand up. She shook her head, trying to get the dirt out of her hair. Her palms were red and scratched, her robe and nightshirt were sodden and covered with dirt. She was so cold that her limbs felt stiff as she clawed her way out of the hole.

Tree of Heaven.

Jamie scowled, stubbing her toe on a rock. Tree of Heaven—so what? What could she do about it now? The tree had been pulled down. There was no hope for it. Why didn't Nelle just leave her alone! Jamie climbed out of the hole.

Tree of Heaven! Tree of Heaven! Tree of Heaven!

Nelle screamed at her, chanted at her, as if Jamie were ignoring something by leaving the hole. Couldn't Nelle say anything else, for God's sake? Jamie stood up, her knees throbbing, just as Frank Veith appeared at the base of the tree.

"What are you doing here?" he demanded, regarding her soaked nightclothes with derision.

Jamie ignored his question. "How could you do this to the tree!" She wiped the rain off her forehead with an impatient swipe.

"Do what?" Veith sneered. "I just saw the wind blow down the tree."

"Liar!" Jamie shouted.

"And I thought I'd better get it out of the road."

"Liar! You just pulled it down with that dozer."

Veith stepped closer. "You're that Kent woman, aren't you?" He tilted his head and stared at her. "The one with that ass McDougall."

"You were told to leave the tree alone."

"And I did. Can't help an act of God, now can I, Miss Kent?"

She whirled. "I'm calling the police."

"No you aren't!" He caught her arm.

Jamie tried to wrench away, but he held her, painfully squeezing her arm to convey his intent to stop her.

"You just had to meddle, didn't you?" he snarled. "Just had to stick your nose where it doesn't belong."

"Let go of me!" she cried, lunging backward as far as she could get without pulling her arm out of the socket.

"You've got no business here. And you aren't going to call the police!"

Jamie stared at him in alarm as he raised his hand to strike her. She flinched, anticipating the blow, but it never came. Surprised, she opened her eyes and beheld a glittering blue light dancing next to Frank Veith. He gaped at the light, his fist still raised, as he was mesmerized by the sight of Hazard McAllister materializing out of the rain.

"Bastard!" Hazard bellowed. Lightning streaked across the sky, lighting up Hazard's face with an unearthly glow. He reached for Veith and spun him around as thunder crashed above their heads.

Veith let Jamie go free. She stumbled backward and nearly toppled into the hole again before she regained her balance. Rain fell in torrents after the lightning flash, pummeling her face and shoulders with drops the size of peas. Water streamed down the roots of the tree. Jamie flung an arm over her forehead to shelter her eyes and watched as Hazard fought Frank Veith.

Jamie skittered sideways, heading for the storefronts and the sidewalk on the other side of the street. While Hazard kept Veith busy, she had to find a phone. She had to call the police so they could catch Veith with the tree still chained to the dozer. She ran down the sidewalk, her numb feet splashing across the cement, her robe twisting around her legs, tripping her. She careened around the corner and saw the Laundromat in the old McAllister building. She scanned the sign as she ran across the street: Open Twenty-four Hours. The lights were still on. Please, God, let there be a phone!

Jamie burst through the door and skidded across the floor. There was a gray pay phone on the far wall. She tore past the empty laundry carts, past the folding table and the soap vending machine, and slid to a halt in front of the phone. She picked up the receiver and poked O with a shaking white finger.

"Operator," a calm voice said on the other end.

Jamie tried to form a word with her frozen lips, but her mouth would not cooperate.

"Hello? Is anyone there? This is the operator."

"Police!" Jamie rasped. "Send the police!"

Jamie tore out of the Laundromat a few minutes later and ran back around the corner. She could see Hazard and Veith still fighting in the rain, two dark shapes struggling against each other. She ran to the tree and lurched to a stop as Hazard bashed Veith in the face with his left fist and sent him sailing into the root hole. Frank Veith landed with a splash, for the hole had quickly filled with water running down the bluff and over the street.

Hazard straightened up to his full height, his chest heaving, his face wild and pale in the storm. Lightning rent the sky, flashing across his white teeth and through his indigo eyes as he stood with his hands still raised, daring Veith to climb out of the hole. Jamie stared at him, awed and a little frightened by his formidable appearance. She heard the wail of a siren. In seconds a squad car raced around the corner and up the street, blinding Jamie with its bright headlights. She squinted, looking toward the car, and saw Sergeant Baeth hop out, his gun in one hand and a huge flashlight in the other. His partner ran up beside him.

Jamie turned to Hazard, but he was nowhere to be seen.

"What's going on?" Sergeant Baeth demanded, running up to the tree. He trained the flashlight on the man in the root hole. Veith sank against the side of the hole, cradling his cheek in his hand, his eyes crazy with pain. Hazard had broken his jaw.

"Frank!" Sergeant Baeth cried. "What's happened? You all right?"

"He pulled down the Tree of Heaven," Jamie put in.

Baeth glanced at her. "Is that you, Miss Kent. Lord Almighty!" He flashed the light in her eyes and blinded her all over again. "What're you doing out here in your pajamas?"

"Frank Veith pulled down the tree!" she repeated. "He wanted everyone to believe it came down in the wind storm."

"Frank," Baeth called down. "Is that right?"

Frank didn't answer.

Baeth turned to his partner. "Radio for an ambulance. Looks like Frank is hurt. Must have hit his head on that chest sticking out there."

Frank shook his head in denial, but the effort was too painful. Jamie did not correct the policeman. How could she explain that a hologram had appeared out of nowhere, fought Veith, and then disappeared again. Hazard had probably saved her life.

Lightning flared, illuminating the tree and the chest trapped in its roots. Jamie looked at the chest. Rain had swept away the surrounding soil, leaving the box jutting out. It was a large trunk, probably five feet long, with rusty metal corners and a huge metal clasp along one side.

Tree of Heaven.

Jamie wondered if Nelle's voice would ever leave her thoughts. The voice no longer scared her. In fact, the more she heard the phrase, Tree of Heaven, the more it aggravated her. She'd had enough of that tree and enough of that voice. Jamie ignored Nelle and watched Baeth lean over to help Veith clamber out of the hole. Veith huddled in the rain, glaring at Jamie with malevolent eyes. She was relieved when Baeth's partner guided him to the squad car to get him out of the rain.

"You come on, too, Miss Kent. You're soaked to the skin."

Sergeant Baeth reached for her elbow, but she drew back. "Wait a minute, officer. Can we look at that chest?"

"What—now?"

Jamie nodded. "It looks like it would just fall out of that clump of roots if we pushed on it."

"I'll tell you what, Miss Kent." He put his gun in its holster. "You sit in the patrol car and I'll see what I can do."

"But—"

"No buts. You're in no shape to stand out here in this god-awful storm any longer." He clutched her elbow and walked to the awaiting. Jamie sank into the front seat. The heater blower hummed, filling the car with warmth. When the door closed after her, she leaned back, gratefully soaking up the heat.

Moments later the ambulance arrived and Veith was taken to the hospital. Baeth's partner came back from the ambulance and walked to the felled tree. He helped Baeth manhandle the trunk from the roots in which it was tangled. Jamie watched them through the windshield. Her nose started to run as her feet thawed.

Once the two men had freed the chest from the roots, they placed it on the ground by the tree. Jamie watched the police try to open it but it seemed to be rusted shut. Baeth drew out his revolver. He shot the clasp once, twice, blasting it apart. Then they bent to open it, and this time the lid swung upward. Baeth shined the flashlight into the chest. He said something to his partner and then looked over his shoulder at the squad car. The hairs on the back of Jamie's neck raised. What was in that chest?

She didn't wait for the police to give her an explanation. She yanked open the door and burst back into the rain.

21

"**W**HAT IS IT?" Jamie asked, reaching the base of the tree. "What's in there?"

Sergeant Baeth grabbed her shoulders and pulled her away before she could peer over the side of the chest. "Nothing you should see, Miss Kent. You've had enough excitement in the last few days."

Jamie struggled against him, trying to look around him to see into the chest. "Please. I have a right to know!"

"Miss Kent! Get hold of yourself!" He shook her. "Now come on back to the car. We'll take the chest down to the station and get you home. We're going to be hit by lightning if we stand around out here."

"I don't want to go home!" Jamie screamed. "I want to look in that chest!" She yanked backward, jerking away from him. He lunged forward, but she dove sideways, evading him. His partner shone the flashlight on her, blinding her again. She held up her hands to ward off the light as she stumbled toward the chest, but Baeth caught her.

He dragged her sobbing to the car and guided her into the back seat where she could not get out. Then he drove up to the tree, and he and his partner hoisted the chest into the trunk of the car.

The car splashed through the black streets. Jamie glared at the back of Baeth's head.

"What were you doing out in the storm, anyway, Miss Kent?" he asked.

"You wouldn't believe me if I told you," she muttered and turned to look out the rain-spattered window.

"Try me."

Jamie considered for a moment. "If I tell you, would you let me see the contents of that chest?"

Baeth turned in his seat and looked at her. "Maybe."

Jamie stared at his face. "It's a long story, officer."

"Well, how about if you tell us anyway?"

The car pulled up in front of the McAllister House.

"I'll tell you what, Miss Kent." Baeth opened his door. "You take a warm shower and get into some dry clothes. Jim and I'll drag this chest into the house. We'll hear your story, and then have a look at the chest. Deal?"

Jamie nodded. "It's a deal."

When Jamie had showered and dressed in a dry pair of slacks and a sweater, and walked downstairs, she heard the grandfather clock strike two. She should have been exhausted, but she was far from tired. A peculiar sense of anticipation tightened her chest. She had decided to tell Baeth everything. Now that Mark was dead and the hologram project destroyed, there was no reason to hide anything.

She stepped off the last stair. The rusted chest had been left just inside the front door. Jamie stared at it, wondering why she felt compelled to see inside the box. But she had made a promise with Baeth to tell her side of the story first. Jamie turned her back on the chest and walked down the hall. She could smell coffee brewing in the kitchen.

Sergeant Beath and his partner Jim Olson sat at the kitchen table, but both of them got to their feet when she strode through the doorway.

"Feeling any better?" Baeth asked.

"Much better, thank you."

"Coffee?" Jim asked. He was a plump man with curly brown hair, not much older than a high school student. Jamie smiled wanly at him.

"Thanks."

"Black?"

"Yes."

She took the mug of coffee and sat down. Baeth watched her expectantly.

"I'll start at the beginning," Jamie stated. "When I first saw Hazard McAllister."

She told them everything—about her visions, her brother's illness, his project, the creation of Hazard McAllister in hologram form, her dreams of Nelle McMurray, her belief in Hazard's innocence, Tiffany's trauma, and the part played by Dr. Hamilton in Mark's death.

By the time she had finished, the coffee pot was empty and the two police officers were leaning forward, enthralled by her tale.

"Jesus!" Baeth exclaimed. "What a story!"

"So where is this hologram of McAllister?" Jim asked, putting his cup on the sinkboard.

"I don't know. He fades in and out now. I never know when or where he'll show up."

"It's a good thing he showed up at the tree," Baeth commented. "Frank Veith is unpredictable sometimes."

"It's just too incredible not to believe." Olson came back to the table.

Jamie nodded. Then she rose. "What about your part of the deal?"

"The chest?"

"Yes."

Baeth got to his feet and hiked up his pants. He looked Jamie up and down and then pursed his lips. "Well, I guess after all you've been through, you can stand a little more. You must be a lot stronger than you look."

He turned on his heel and led the way to the hall. Jamie followed, her heart pounding. Baeth leaned over the chest and lifted the huge clasp. He glanced at Jamie, as if considering once more whether he should reveal the contents to her or not. Then, with a sigh, he raised the lid and held it up, stepping aside to let her get a closer look.

Jamie looked in the chest. Her hand flew to her mouth and her eyes widened in horrified surprise as she stared down. There, jammed into the box were the remains of a human being, a very tall human being whose knees had been folded to his chest so the body could fit within the confines of the chest.

"Oh!" Jamie gasped. A feeling of overwhelming sadness tore her breath away. In one crushing moment, she recognized the dark-gray suit, the once-white shirt, the stickpin and watch fob that still shrouded the bones of the skeleton. Jamie sank to her knees. She could not tear her gaze from the gaping skull crowned by faded tufts of burnished hair. Her hands clutched the rim of the chest as she struggled against a scream that threatened to tear her heart out of her chest.

"No!" She forced the scream back down. "No!"

"What is it?" Baeth asked.

She reached out her hand. She could see her fingers

quaking, and she watched as if the hand did not belong to her as she touched the hair, smoothing it down on the skull.

"No!" she whispered. "Not like this, not like this!"

"What is it?" Baeth demanded, leaning closer. "Miss Kent!"

She swallowed and glanced up at the police officer. Her body had turned to stone, her senses were completely dead. She could feel herself slipping into shock, but she had no energy or will left to fight it. "This is Hazard McAllister's body," she stated tonelessly.

Jim Olson bent closer. "What?" he barked.

"This is Hazard."

"Look at the watch," Baeth interjected. "See if there's some inscription."

Jim Olson fumbled with the old gold watch until he had unfastened it. He snapped open the lid. "To H.M.," he read. "With all my love, N."

"H.M.," Baeth said. "Hazard McAllister. This *is* him!"

"Who's N.?" Olson asked, rising to his feet.

"Nelle McMurray," Jamie replied flatly. "She must have known that he was here, that he was here all along, buried beneath the Tree of Heaven."

"And what's this?" Olson bent over again, picking up a moldering volume that had been tossed in behind Hazard's feet. He carefully opened the cover.

Baeth stepped closer, still holding the lid of the chest. "Looks like a ledger. Somebody's books. You supposed he was murdered?"

"Kind of looks that way," Olson agreed.

Jamie laid her head on her hands and closed her eyes. "You were telling the truth, Hazard. You were telling the truth," she murmured. "All along, you were here in this horrible place, and nobody knew but Nelle."

*   *   *

Jamie went to bed after the police left. She didn't even remember saying good-bye or dragging up the stairs to her bedroom. But later, she found herself under her covers, trying to get warm after her ordeal in the storm. Her nose was a block of ice, her hands and feet chilled to the bone. She hunched under the covers, closing her eyes, blocking out the memories of the last few days.

The clock ticked downstairs. The wind died down. Jamie slept.

Sometime later, she felt a wonderful warmth surrounding her, a warmth that wrapped around her from her head to her toes. She sighed and turned on her side when she felt a hand run over her breasts. She nestled against the wall of heat behind her and reveled in the sensation of the hand fondling her breasts. Jamie slowly opened her eyes as warm lips kissed the tender skin between her shoulder and her neck, and silken hair tickled her ear.

"Hazard!" She sighed, turning in his arms.

He lay beside her, naked, blazing with heat. Then he smiled at her, and Jamie felt her chill melt away.

She kissed him, her happiness and sorrow mingling with tears that welled up in her eyes and trickled down her cheeks. Hazard held her and stroked her and pressed her to his heart.

"Sweet sparrow, ye found me," he murmured.

Jamie nodded, her cheek against his chest. She embraced him, tracing his body with her hands as if to memorize every line, every sinew. She felt him harden against her and her body responded with a flush of heat. Hazard's flat hands ran down her back and he pulled her onto his solid frame. Jamie's hair tumbled onto his chest as she lowered to him, her lips clinging to his as she sank upon his hips. Hazard sighed and closed his eyes. Jamie raised up and kissed his lips and then each of his eyelids. She brushed back his unruly golden hair and kissed his forehead, his temple, and his ear. Hazard's lips parted. She left a trail of kisses along his jawline until she reached the generous fullness of his lower lip. She nipped the edge of his mouth and he sighed.

"Hazard," she whispered. "My love, my dearest love." She kissed the tendons of his neck, his Adam's apple, his collarbone and then ran her tongue down his chest until she reached his nipple. She took the hard tip between her teeth and Hazard stiffened immediately, causing her own breasts to swell and tighten in response. His breath came hard and fast as Jamie released his nipple and leaned over for the other one.

"Jamie, ye drive me t' distraction," he murmured in a husky voice. His hands caressed her waist, spreading across the slender roundness of her hips. Then he pulled her down, impaling her on his straining shaft. Jamie sank down, down, down until he was deep inside her.

Both of them sighed, ecstasy washing over them.

Jamie leaned forward and her rigid nipples brushed the soft hair of Hazard's chest as she pressed a kiss to his mouth. His tongue slipped between her lips, echoing the movement they both felt as his hands guided her hips up and away from him. Jamie gasped at the sensation when she came back down and rubbed against him. She moved over him again, raising up, her breasts thrusting forward as she arched her back. She closed her eyes and lost herself to the unbelievable feeling that burgeoned inside her.

Hazard suckled her, sending her closer and closer to the brink, driving her crazy with his teeth and tongue. She could feel him swelling inside her. She rubbed against him, gasping and desperate, as he moaned and writhed beneath her. Then with a cry, Hazard grabbed her, rising, lifting her knees off the bed. For an instant he knelt on the bed, clutching her to him as if to meld her flesh to his. Jamie hugged his neck to keep from falling as he imprisoned her buttocks with his hands. He thrust inside her, still holding her in midair, grinding into her until his skin was her skin. Then he forced her to the bed, collapsing on top of her, plowing into her with urgent, unbridled strokes that flung Jamie into a realm of white-hot ecstasy. She grabbed his arms, then his rump, and met each shattering thrust with one of her own. Hazard strained above her, his head tipped back, the veins on his neck bulging. With a cry, he exploded inside her as she reached a blood-rushing climax. Light bursts lit up the room and exploded beneath her eyelids. She clung to him, wrapping her legs around him, pinning him to her as she felt her body squeezing him, draining him. Yet at the same moment her climax faded, she burst into tears.

Hazard cradled her face in his palms and wiped away her tears with his thumbs while Jamie gazed at him, her eyes heavy with misery.

"That's the last time for us, isn't it, Hazard?" she whispered.

"Aye." His eyes glistened with sadness.

"You—you're going to leave me, aren't you?"

"Aye. Ye've cleared my name, Jamie Kent. Whatever bound me t' this earth for a hundred years is now lettin' me go."

"If I would have known this would happen, I never would have looked in the chest." Huge sobs shook her shoulders as her heart broke. "I never would have gone to that tree."

"Ah, lass, ye would have looked. 'Twas ye're fate, Jamie, t' find tha' chest."

"I don't want fate. I want you, Hazard. You."

He sighed and brushed back her hair. "Ye do have me, Jamie. I love ye. Ye know I always will love ye. No matter where I am."

"But where will you be? You won't be here with me."

"I'll be with ye. I'll find a way t' come t' ye, Jamie. Nothin' can snap th' tie between us. Not death, not life."

His eyes bore into hers, branding her with his conviction. "Not even time can come between us, Jamie girl."

"But how will you do it? How will I know?" She clutched his head between her hands, plunging her fingers into his shining hair. "You can't leave me here by myself, Hazard. Hazard."

"I have no choice, lass. God knows, I'd stay wi' ye if I could." He gathered her into his arms and kissed her fervently, embracing her until her weeping tapered off. Then he drew back and smoothed her hair away from her face, his eyes full of love and tenderness.

"Farewell," he said, "my bonny, bonny lass."

"Please, Hazard—" She reached out for him as he began to sparkle and fade.

"I'll come t' ye, love. Somehow I will."

Jamie lunged out of bed as the blue light sparkled in the center of the room. She trailed after it, pleading for Hazard to come back. But the light grew fainter and fainter until nothing remained. Jamie sank to her knees, sobbing. A flash of blue in the mirror on the closet caught her attention, and Jamie stared with bleary eyes as she saw Nelle appear in the glass. Then Nelle turned away and Jamie heard her cry, "*Hazard!*" in a voice full of incredulous hope and happiness. Jamie collapsed on the floor.

She was dreaming. She was at college in a calculus class. She hadn't gone to class for the entire quarter, and yet there she was, faced with a final exam. Jamie tossed and turned, wondering why she had failed to attend class, why she hadn't known about the test. Suddenly, something broke the window above her desk. Jamie jerked awake at the sound.

She looked around her. Why was she asleep on the floor? And what was that silver stuff all over the floor by the closet? She rose up on her hands and knees. The mirror on the closet door had shattered, spilling shimmering shards of glass all around her. Then Jamie smelled smoke. She snapped her head around. Billows of smoke rolled under her bedroom door. Jamie coughed. Her eyes stung. The floor beneath her palms felt warm, and she was suddenly aware of a rumbling noise all around her. The house was on fire!

Jamie scrambled to her feet and stumbled to the window. She yanked on the casement, but the sash wouldn't budge. Then she remembered the board that Hazard had put in the window to keep Dr. Hamilton's men from gaining entrance to the house. She tugged at the board, but it was wedged firmly in place.

She whirled around, coughing, trying to locate something with which to break the window. She groped blindly through the smoke until she found the history book on her desk. She grabbed one end and swung it through the window, shattering the pane. Behind her she could feel the heat of the fire, and a scorching wind lifted her hair and hurt her lungs as she pounded the book against the glass, knocking out a space big enough to crawl through.

She scrambled through the window, slicing her right hand as she dropped to the porch roof below. Someone yelled at her to jump. She couldn't see anymore. Smoke was everywhere. Her clothes burned her back.

"Jump!" a man yelled.

Jamie jumped, landing in a wet clump of dahlias.

"Roll her!" someone shouted. "Her clothes are on fire!"

Epilogue

"——AND SO SAYING, we rededicate this library to the memory of Captain Hazard McAllister." The mayor of Port Townsend turned to a shrouded object behind him and pulled off the canvas sheeting. Jamie watched from her seat of honor near the podium as the bronze statue of Hazard McAllister was unveiled. She had provided the photographs used by the artist, had described Hazard as thoroughly as she could, and had approved the wax model for the statue. But she broke down at the sight of the life-size bronze glinting in the December sunshine. The artist had done a magnificent job of capturing Hazard's fearless, jaunty expression, an expression that made Jamie's heart ache with longing.

"Speech! Speech!"

The crowd around her burst into applause as Jamie rose to her feet. Sergeant Baeth, who stood next to her, patted her back gently, realizing how much the sight of Hazard had affected her. She smiled bravely at him.

Jamie looked over the townspeople in front of her.

Many of their faces were familiar to her now. There were the doctors and nurses from the hospital, Jim Olson the policeman, Mrs. Gipson and her friend from the café, the activists who had protested the destruction of the Tree of Heaven, the artist who had sculpted the statue, and the library staff, not to mention many of the shopkeepers with whom Jamie had become familiar. All of them were her friends, more friends than she had ever had in her life. She was proud to count these people as friends, proud to call Port Townsend home.

Jamie stepped to the podium and braced her hands on either side. She winced. Her right hand was still a little tender where the scar from the window glass cut across her palm. She knew she was lucky to have escaped from the fire with only minor burns and scrapes. Sergeant Baeth had told her that if she had waited a mere moment to leap from the porch roof, she would have been totally engulfed by flames. The McAllister House had burned completely to the ground that night. Tiffany had not fared very well either. She had been sent to a mental institution, where doctors would try to discover the cause of her madness and her reasons for setting the McAllister House on fire. Jamie knew their job would be difficult, a fight which they were not equipped to win.

Jamie looked up. She refused to dwell on the tragedy any longer.

"Hey, Jamie, when's the book coming out?" someone yelled from the crowd.

She brightened at the question. She had written the true story of Hazard McAllister during the month she had spent in the hospital, recuperating from her burns. A publisher had immediately jumped at the opportunity to print the tale. "It should be out this summer," she replied. "Late August."

The crowd clapped at the news. When the noise leveled off, Jamie swept a glance around her audience.

"Hazard would have been delighted to see you all here today. He loved this city. He loved it as only a Highlander can love—with all his heart and soul." She glanced at the statue looking over the bluff and out to the bay. "He was an honorable man, a truly honorable man. And I am sure that he rests easy now, knowing his good name has been cleared, his good works restored. Thank you all for your generous contributions and your valuable time. You have made this dedication an event we shall all remember! Thank you." She bowed her head and backed away from the podium as everyone clapped and cheered. Baeth pumped her hand, as did the mayor. Jamie smiled and looked up at the face of the statue as the first flakes of winter drifted out of the sky.

Mrs. Gipson bustled up, waving her handkerchief. "Jamie, Jamie!" she called. Jamie turned to her.

"Hi, Edna. Isn't this a fine likeness?"

"It is. It is, Jamie. But here—" She thrust out a post-it. "I got this call about an hour ago from the Taft Gallery in New York. You'd already left for the dedication ceremony preparations."

Jamie took the post-it and looked at the phone number. "What did they want?" she asked, wiping a snowflake off her nose.

"They want to show your work. I guess the new owner is just raving over your stuff."

"He is?" Jamie gasped, incredulous.

Mrs. Gipson nodded, beaming in delight.

Jamie grasped Mrs. Gipson's gloved hand and shook it. "Oh, thank you, Edna. Thank you."

"You should call them right away, Jamie."

"I will."

*   *   *

A month later, Jamie waited in the conference room of the Taft Gallery. The entire gallery was done in a geological motif. The walls and floor were covered in a granite material, the fixtures were fashioned from metal sprayed with flecks of black, gray, and white. The desk in front of her was a slab of marble supported by two chunks of rough-textured stone. Even the chair she sat in was made of rough-hewn stone. Jamie glanced around in approval. The spareness of the decor and the lack of color was a spectacular backdrop to her photographs.

She crossed and uncrossed her legs, wondering how she looked in her new dress. She had found the jade-green suit at Saks Fifth Avenue yesterday, and instantly fell in love with it, even though she rarely wore such an intense color. She smiled ruefully. She might not look as good as she felt, but she was sure the color was a knockout against the blacks and grays around her.

Jamie bit her lip nervously. Where was Mr. Hastings anyway? He had arranged to meet her before her show, anxious to greet his new star before the onslaught of admirers descended upon the gallery that evening. She had never seen the new owner of the Taft Gallery, had never even talked to him on the phone. If she had spoken to him, maybe she wouldn't have been so blasted nervous now. Jamie shook her head and smiled sadly as the thought of Hazard crossed her mind. He was with her constantly, even yet.

"Jamie Kent!"

Jamie jumped at the sound, startled. She could have sworn Hazard had called her name. She hadn't heard voices or seen visions since the fire. She had assumed the nightmares and voices were behind her now that Hazard had faded from her life. But maybe she was mistaken.

"Where is the lass?" a voice thundered.

Jamie stared at the doorway of the office. That voice wasn't in her head. That voice was coming from the hallway. And that voice was Hazard's! She heard a step-tap, step-tap, step-tap as someone approached the room. Slowly, Jamie rose from her chair, swimming in a cloud of disbelief.

"Ach! There ye are."

Jamie's glance landed on a pair of shoes, two brown loafers standing next to the tip of a cane. She lifted her glance and followed a pair of jeans up and up and up a long set of well-muscled legs until she spied a deep-blue corduroy shirt. Then she forced herself to look at the face of the man, and there the fantasy ended. Jamie's heart plunged to the floor.

The man was not Hazard. He was tall and broad shouldered, and he had a deep Scottish burr, but he was not Hazard. Jamie inspected the man's craggy face, with the prominent black eyebrows and the deep brown, nearly black eyes which regarded her as closely as she surveyed him. He ran a hand through his hair, and Jamie followed the movement. His hair was jet black, as black as the marble desk at her side. He had the hair of a pirate—glossy, rich, blue-black.

"Mr. Hastings?" she ventured.

He stared at her, his hand still poised in his hair, as if he were caught in his own fantasy. Perhaps the green suit had captured his attention.

"Mr. Hastings?" Jamie repeated, holding out her hand.

He glanced at her hand, a scowl wrinkling his forehead, and then his gaze returned to her face.

"Jamie Kent?"

"Yes."

He grasped her hand then, and the warmth of his skin

sent a jolt of fire up her arm. Startled, she looked at him, wondering why she wasn't pulling her hand away, why he wasn't saying anything, why he was staring at her with such a peculiar expression in his eyes.

"Jamie Kent," he finally declared. "Ye startled me. Ye look like someone I know."

"Oh?"

He narrowed his eyes. "Can't place ye, though." He sighed. "Since the accident I've had trouble remembering things."

"You were in an accident?" Jamie asked, her hand still draped in his.

"Aye." He finally released her and hobbled away. "That's why I have this bloody cane. The accident made me a cripple. But only temporarily." He shook the cane in the air. "Aye, only temporarily. A few more weeks with this bloody thing and I'll be as good as new."

He turned and grinned. "I'm not used t' bein' laid up, ye know."

Jamie didn't doubt his words. He was a large man, as large and vigorous as Hazard had been. She smiled, enjoying the sound of a rich Scottish voice again, and the charisma of a strong Scottish man. What *was* it about a Highlander that she found so fascinating?

"Auto accident?" she inquired, to draw him out.

"Nay. My ship broke her back off the Hebrides last October. 'Twas in a coma I was, for nearly two weeks. Everyone thought I was halfway t' th' grave."

"It looks like you've made a marvelous recovery, Mr. Hastings."

"Aye." He beamed. "I've been in great shape most o' my life. Gave me th' power t' come back, it did."

"The power to come back?" Jamie repeated, her voice cracking.

"Aye." His voice trailed off as he studied her. He limped around her, regarding her intently while Jamie slowly turned, puzzled by his odd behavior.

"Are you sure I've never met ye before?" he asked. "I don't look familiar t' ye, lass?"

"No." Jamie shook her head. But even as the reply passed her lips, she realized she was wrong. She did know this man. Somehow she was certain that she knew him. It was a gut-level feeling that she couldn't deny.

Mr. Hastings scratched his cheek. He was not an ugly man. In fact, once she got past his craggy features, she discovered a rugged handsomeness in his swarthy face.

"Well, I want t' tell ye, Miss Kent—"

"Please, call me Jamie."

"Aye. Jamie it 'tis, a bonny name for a lass."

"And yours?"

"My Christian name is Douglas."

I should have known. Douglas Hastings. Hastings McDougall. Ellen and Nelle. We're all intertwined. Across time, beyond the grave!

"But my friends call me Hasty," he added, "a nickname I acquired on the soccer field and not in the kip, I'll have ye know!" He winked.

"Then I shall call you Hasty," she smiled, blushing.

"Ye plan t' be my friend, do ye, Jamie Kent?"

"I think we shall be great friends," she replied. "It's a gut feeling I have."

He looked at her askance, measuring her words, and then he broke out in laughter—rich, happy laughter that rippled its way into her heart. Jamie felt her grief falling from her shoulders like wet snow off a warm tin roof.

"What I wanted t' tell ye, Jamie, before ye sidetracked me," he continued, chuckling, "was that I admire your work. I would like t' buy th' whole series."

"You want to buy the entire set of Real People?"

"Aye." He nodded. "You've a rare talent. And I have a grand house in Edinburgh with a lot o' bare walls."

Jamie stepped back, stunned.

"But if ye want t' see how well your work is received by the others, ye can consider my offer for your next series instead, in case ye get buyers this evenin'."

"Mr. Hastings—Hasty—what a generous offer!"

He waved her off. "I've confidence in ye, lass. You'll be famous after tonight, mark my words."

She laughed and shook her head. But she glowed inside and out at his praise. For a moment Hastings gazed at her and she gazed at him, lost in the obsidian blackness of his sparkling eyes. She felt drawn to him, as if she should run to him and embrace him and crush his lips with hers.

Abruptly, however, Hastings reached into his shirt pocket and broke the spell. "Oh, I forgot somethin', lass. Here."

He gave her a folded envelope.

Jamie reached for it, thankful for an excuse to break eye contact. She unfolded the envelope and glanced at the front. The letter was addressed to her, in care of the gallery. The envelope bore a three-day-old postmark. Who could have sent this? Jamie opened the letter, unfolding a single sheet of paper that she found inside.

Dear Brat.

Jamie's heart slammed against her chest. Only one person ever called her "brat." She glanced at the signature at the bottom of the page. The letter was from Mark! How could this be?

"Where did you get this?" she whispered, sinking into the chair.

"It came in the mail."

Jamie scanned the letter, prohibiting herself from be-

lieving anything she read. Mark hadn't died in the accident. He had fooled everyone into thinking he had gone
over the cliff in the U-Haul truck. He hadn't been dying.
He had coerced a friend of his to tamper with his medical
records. His bout with pneumonia had just been a freak
occurrence. He was still alive and in hiding. His death
had been staged to get Dr. Hamilton and all Dr. Hamil-
tons off his back, once and for all. Jamie's vision blurred.
This had to be a trick, somebody's sick idea of a joke.

Hastings allowed her to finish and then hobbled closer.

"Bad news is it?" he asked.

Jamie gaped at him, her throat tight and dry all of a
sudden.

"This is—this is from my—my brother."

"Your brother Mark?"

"Yes. But he's dead." Jamie let her hands fall into her
lap. "At least I thought he was dead. Everyone thought
he was dead."

Hastings leaned against the desk and tapped his cane
on the toes of his shoes. Jamie looked up at his face. He
was smiling at her.

A shiver coursed down her back. "How do you know
my brother's name?" she asked suspiciously.

"I know your brother."

Jamie jumped to her feet. Mr. Hastings had been dallying with her all along, playing with her in another elabo-
rate game of industrial espionage, just like Dr. Hamilton.
Enraged, she flung herself at him. She landed with a thud
against his chest, knocking him to his back on the desk-
top. She pummeled him with her fists.

Hastings grabbed her wrists.

"Bastard!" she cried. "You bastard!"

Her gut instinct had been totally wrong about this man.
He wasn't Hazard in another time and place. He was just

another greedy bastard wanting to cash in on Mark's genius.

Hastings rolled onto his side, throwing his weight across Jamie to trap her thrashing legs. He pinned her hands beside her head and raised above her, imprisoning her beneath him on the desk.

"Bastard!" she said. She glared at him. His eyes smoldered at her as his face lowered to hers. She couldn't believe he was going to kiss her. She twisted and jerked, but he held her fast, and soon his mouth closed upon her, silencing her protests. Jamie paused as his lips opened on hers, and stiffened when she felt his tongue plunge into her. She tried to turn her head, tried to deny the power of his lips. But his kiss was a heady drug that quickly obliterated her rage, her grief, and her memory. She was swept away until she forgot everything but her hunger for this dark-haired man. She melted beneath him, surrendering to him, closing her eyes to tears of loneliness and desire as her body sang to the glorious press of his weight. She reached up and caressed his head, sinking her fingers into his coal-black hair.

After a long moment, Hastings drew away. He looked at her, his eyes full of heat. His hand slid up her thigh and slipped under the sheath of her skirt. Jamie sucked in her breath.

"Where's my brother, you bloody Scot?" she said, pushing his hand down.

"He should be here any moment now."

Jamie glowered, ashamed that she had let him kiss her, embarrassed that she had put herself in such a compromising position, amazed at her own wantonness in succumbing to him so easily. "What do you mean, any moment now?"

"I asked him t' accompany us to dinner."

"Dinner?"

"Aye. But if ye would like t' stay here on th' desk, Jamie lass, I'd be happy t' cancel th' reservation."

"Mark is alive? Truly alive?"

"Well now, kissin' ye, Jamie, brings a whole new meanin' t' the word *alive*. But, aye, Mark is safe and sound." He rolled off her and sat up, lending her a hand to do the same.

Jamie stood up and brushed the creases from her new suit. He watched her, his eyes twinkling. " 'Tis a bonny outfit, lass. It suits ye."

"Thank you," she replied softly.

"Have ye ever been t' Scotland?"

"No."

"Would ye like t' go?"

Jamie glanced at him, wondering if he was serious. "I never thought much about it."

"We can leave at th' end o' th' week."

"But I hardly know you—"

He crossed his arms. "Well, I know you. And it'll come t' me where I've seen ye."

"Will it?" she teased.

"Aye. But in the meantime," he stood up and held out his hand to her. "I'm not letting ye out o' my sight."

PATRICIA SIMPSON received a B.A. degree from the University of Washington where she works as a graphic designer. She lives near Seattle with her husband and two daughters.